Jack Kramer's Journey

By Frank Adkins

Higher Ground Books & Media
Springfield, Ohio.
http://highergroundbooksandmedia.com

Printed in the United States of America 2018

Jack Kramer's Journey

By Frank Adkins

For Kristan,

Who believes in me

Even when I don't

Introduction

The road was dark and slick, and it had begun raining again.

In the swath of Jack Kramer's headlights thousands of droplets fell.

They pelted the hood and roof of his truck in a collective roar. Jack

turned on his wipers. Moments later the rain stopped. "Mother

Nature, make up your mind!"

Jack checked the clock, pausing just long enough to make

sense of the numbers. Eleven forty-three. *Marsha's going to be*

pissed. Again. At least he had remembered to call. *I did call, didn't*

I? It didn't matter. If Marsha was up, the next hour would be hell.

Jack was sure the boys had been asleep for quite a while. He hoped

Marsha was, too.

Up ahead the road made a sharp right. Jack braked, closed

one eye to clear his vision, and steered into the curve. He was sure

he had rounded the turn perfectly until he heard the thud of his

fender grazing a mailbox. *Just a pothole,* he told himself. *Couldn't*

avoid it. Road's full of 'em.

After the curve Jack centered the truck in his lane. "Dad, I

know you're out there. I won't talk your ear off about Marsha and the boys tonight. I know things were tough for you, too. But can you keep an eye out for me and help me make it home in one piece? Thanks."

When Jack reached his home, he extinguished the headlights and drove up the driveway in darkness. The living room lights were off. That was good. Marsha was probably in bed.

Jack parked near the top of the driveway next to Marsha's car and entered the house through the garage, located at the end of the house opposite the bedrooms. Once inside, Jack stopped to observe his nineteen seventy Plymouth Road Runner. The once gleaming yellow paint looked dull under a heavy layer of dust. The car leaned to the right, for both tires on that side had gone flat years earlier. A blanket covered the hood, protecting it from the boxes that rested on it. "Someday," he said.

As he entered the kitchen Jack was surprised to find the light on. Marsha sat at the table poring over a stack of bills. She didn't look up. "Hi," Jack said. He leaned in the doorway to keep from swaying.

Marsha did not respond.

"What are you doing?" Immediately Jack regretted asking a

question with such an obvious answer.

"Trying to decide who's going to get paid and who won't."
She kept her eyes on the papers before her.

"Oh." Jack closed the door behind him and went to the
refrigerator. He took out a Coke, then leaned against the counter for
support as he took the first sip. Normally Marsha would have
greeted him with, "Where have you been?" or, "Do you know what
time it is?" But she said nothing. *Maybe she's not mad after all,*
Jack thought. But he knew better. He wanted to leave the room. He
was uncomfortable in her presence, and he needed to use the
bathroom. Still, something in her demeanor compelled him to stay.

Finally, Marsha said, "I don't suppose you remember what
tonight was."

Jack thought for a moment. "Uh-uh."

"The Cub Scout initiation ceremony!" Now Marsha glared at
him. "The boys talked about it all summer, Jack."

"Oh, no! Tonight? I forgot all about it!" Jack took the chair
across from Marsha. "Oh, I'm so sorry!"

"Jack, save it. It wasn't my heart that you broke."

"I'll explain it to the boys in the morning. You know, I

stopped in for a beer on my way home...."

"...from work, and one beer turned into another, and the next thing you knew, it was late," Marsha finished for him. "Come on, Jack, after ten years do you really think I don't know the ritual? I know your habits and your excuses better than you do. Unfortunately, so do Johnny and James!"

"Look, this isn't about them!"

"Oh, so you're saying it's about you? Isn't it always, Jack?"

"No, that's not what I'm saying! Don't put words in my mouth! I owe them an apology and I told you I'd explain to them tomorrow."

"You owe them much more than an apology. You know, we waited as long as we could for you to show up, but of course you didn't. James asked where you were, but before I could say anything Johnny said, 'He doesn't care about the ceremony. He's out getting drunk.' I wish you could have seen the hurt on their faces."

"Look, I admit it. I screwed up!" He slapped the table for emphasis. "What more can I say?"

Marsha met Jack's eyes with a level gaze. "Jack, that's not going to work this time. A hollow apology isn't going to cut it. I won't have you doing this to our sons any longer."

Jack leaned back in his chair. "So, what are you telling me?"

Marsha looked back at the pile of statements before her. In the silence Jack heard the first faint tap of a teardrop landing on the top sheet. "Jack, we can't live like this anymore."

"You're right. I'll do better. I promise."

"No." Marsha looked up at Jack. Tears spilled down her cheeks. "That's what you always say, but it doesn't happen. This can't go on any longer. I'm putting a stop to it now. I have to!"

"What are you saying?" Jack was afraid he already knew the answer.

"The boys and I are leaving. We're going to live with my parents."

"What? No! They're across the country! That's too far! Find someplace closer. Hell, there's no reason to go anywhere. We can work through this!"

"No, Jack, we can't. I've tried, but you haven't."

"But I will."

"No. It's too late now."

"Please, Marsha, don't do this to me! Don't do it to the

boys!"

"I'm not the one who's done this. You are. And that's all there is to it."

"Look, if you want to go, I can't stop you. But for God's sake, don't take the boys. Please!"

Marsha started to speak, then stopped. She stood and cinched her robe tighter. "I'm going to bed."

Jack watched her go. "Fine! If that's what you want, that's just fine with me! Go ahead and leave. If I'm so impossible to live with, go on!" He went to the sink and poured out his cola, then opened the refrigerator and took three cans of Coors. Sinking into his chair, he popped open the first can. He took several gulps, then leaned back. "So, I forgot about tonight," he muttered. "Wasn't like I skipped it on purpose. It was an honest mistake. I forgot! What's more honest than that?"

But as he sat staring at the pile of bills Marsha had left on the table, he knew it wasn't the first time. He'd let her and the boys down more times than he cared to remember. It didn't matter that he had never meant to. "I can't believe it's come to this. She's really giving up." Jack squeezed the tears from his eyes with his palms, then finished the first can. "I can do better. I *know* I can. God, tell me it's not too late!"

Chapter One

One Year Later...

It's been too long since life was simple and good.

With this thought, Jack popped the plastic cap from a fresh can of starting fluid, then sprayed a mist into the center carburetor of his Road Runner. He set the can on the corner of his workbench and dashed to the cockpit to twist the ignition key. The mighty four-hundred-forty cubic-inch engine fired almost immediately, only to sputter and stall. Jack picked up the can and shot another blast into the carburetor, then started the engine once more. Just as the engine was about to stall, it picked up speed and began to run smoothly. The deep rumble of exhaust echoed within the garage, filling Jack with exhilaration. He grinned as his ears drank in the engine's music for the first time in more than ten years. Jack monitored the gauges as he rapped the accelerator a few times. Each time, the engine barked through its dual pipes and the car rocked sharply.

Jack held the engine speed above idle. With the throbbing of the engine ringing beautifully in his ears, he scanned the interior.

Although he had rolled up tens of thousands of miles on the odometer many years earlier, he studied his surroundings as if he was sitting in the car for the first time. The simulated woodgrain rimmed steering wheel with the cartoon Road Runner in the center of the horn button, the 150 MPH speedometer, the tall, curved Hurst four-speed shifter with its woodgrain Pistol Grip handle, and the texture of the vinyl-covered bench seat all made him feel as comfortable as he would be in his threadbare avocado green recliner. To Jack it seemed as if his car was welcoming him home. As the throaty pipes sang their robust tune, Jack thought of his high school days, long before he'd met Marsha. Back then he had driven this car every day.

While working at the Sinclair station one day during the summer between his junior and senior years, he had met Kim Hurley. Kim was a bright girl who liked to laugh. She was endowed with a curvy figure, a sexy smile, and long blonde hair which bobbed about her shoulders as she walked. The moment he first saw her, Jack felt his heart bulge within his chest, icy and torrid at once. But more than a year of non-stop dating ended with a teary kiss at the airport in Denver one August evening three months after they graduated high school. At the last moment Kim had dashed to catch the jet that would whisk her away to Philadelphia, where she would attend art school, leaving Jack and Colorado Springs far behind. Now Jack slowly shook his head. "God damn it! The things that should have been!" he muttered.

Jack found himself staring at the vacant seat Kim had occupied daily more than twenty years earlier. Next his eyes fell on the ashtray. Thinking of the necklace inside, he resisted the urge to open it. *Now is not the time,* he thought. Instead, he turned his attention to the gauges in the dash. The oil pressure was holding steady and the temperature gauge had begun to rise. He allowed the engine to idle, then he returned to the front of the car to check for fuel and fluid leaks. Satisfied that there were none, he glanced at the clock. It was time to get ready for his AA meeting. He reached through the driver's window, shut off the ignition, then patted the fender as he rounded the corner of the car and headed into the house.

Chapter Two

As Jack neared the Presbyterian church where his meetings were held, he braked and signaled. He had arrived a few minutes later than usual, for nobody was outside. He parked his faded blue Dodge Ram four-wheel drive truck and hurried to the door. People were still milling about the lobby. As Jack stepped toward the coffee pot, Donald, a grizzled man easily twenty years Jack's senior, stood with his back toward Jack. He was quietly counting sugar cubes as he plopped them into his steaming cup of coffee. "Good evening, Donald," Jack said abruptly in an ornery attempt to distract him. "How are you today?"

Donald whirled about. "Well, I haven't drank yet today," he answered with a grin. "How about you?"

"No, me neither," Jack replied. "And I hope I don't." Jack poured a Styrofoam cupful of coffee, added a plastic teaspoonful of powdered creamer, then dropped four sugar cubes through the floating mound. He stirred the mixture with a flimsy plastic stir stick.

"Get that car of yours running yet?" Donald asked.

"Yes, as a matter of fact. I got it fired up late this afternoon. Sounds pretty good, but I still have a few things to do to it before I take it out onto the road."

"That's good. I'm anxious to see it."

"Shouldn't be long."

Several people in the Alcoholics Anonymous group exchanged pleasantries, and a few were engaged in light conversation. Gradually the members trickled from the lobby into the meeting room. Most took seats around a large wooden table while a few others sat in chairs that lined the walls of the room. Jack took his usual place near the far end of the table.

"Okay, it's seven o'clock. Let's get started," Molly said. She was a jovial woman, short and plump, who had been attending meetings for two decades. Although she had never been officially appointed the director, it was she who usually got the meetings underway and kept them on track. She then read the preamble and the Twelve Steps. "Does anybody have any announcements, anniversaries, or crises?" Molly scanned the room for raised hands. "Does anybody else have anything to share at this point?" Nobody spoke. "Okay, do we have newcomers here for whom this is their first meeting?" A thin woman in her early thirties with wavy brunette hair raised her hand. "What is your first name, dear?" Molly asked. "Just your first name. We don't need your last. After all, this is called Alcoholics *Anonymous.*"

"Carla." The woman's voice was jittery, and she fidgeted with the straps of her purse.

"Hi, Carla," the group said.

"Welcome to our group, Carla," Molly smiled. "Are you at all familiar with AA?"

"Not really, but I have done a little reading."

"Well, Carla, by virtue of the fact that you're here I can assume there is something going on in your life. If at any time this evening you decide you wish to share it with the group, please feel free to do so.

"In the meantime, some of us will share our stories of how we came to AA. We like to do this whenever there is a newcomer. You may be able to identify with some of the things you will hear. Don't worry about trying to remember it all. In fact, you may find that you remember very little of your first meeting. That's okay. The important thing is that you are here."

Molly then addressed the group. "Who would like to go first?"

Donald raised his hand. "My name is Donald, and I'm an alcoholic."

"Hi, Donald," the group said in unison.

Donald addressed Carla. He then told with great detail the story of a young Navy man with a penchant for getting drunk. As the years passed, his escalating drinking took a heavy toll on both his marriage and his military career, eventually claiming both. "Those were some dark days," Donald declared in a quaking voice. "But thanks to my family right here in this room I've been sober for sixteen years now. Thanks for listening."

"Thanks for sharing," the group chimed.

Next, Jack raised his hand. "My name is Jack and I'm an alcoholic."

"Hi, Jack."

Jack faced Carla, but his gaze fell to a tiny knot in the wood tabletop. "I come from an alcoholic family, but I didn't realize it growing up. I was an only child. My mother died in a car accident when I was two years old, so it was just my father and me. He was a mechanic in a Dodge dealership when I was really small, then went to a Chrysler-Plymouth dealership when I was about eight. He loved cars, but he despised the dealership environment. Dad turned to alcohol as a means of numbing his loneliness and taking the edge off the stress of his job. As the years passed, he drank more and more, but he wasn't a binge drinker. He'd work all day, then come home and drink beer at night until he fell asleep, then get up the next day and do it again. It was just something he did, and I never thought there was anything wrong with it since it didn't seem to interfere with our lives.

"In 1970, when I was nine, he bought a brand new Plymouth Road Runner. This car became my first car, and I still have it today. During my teenage years we would work on the car together, and I would help him with the occasional side job he took. As far as fathers and teenage sons go, we had a good relationship.

"Because there was always beer in the house, it was available to me. Once I was sixteen or so Dad never really cared if I had a beer or two at home, and more than once we enjoyed a beer together while watching a movie on television. I drank regularly through high school, but it was usually just a beer or two. Only a few times did I get really plastered. No problem, right?"

Jack sighed, glanced at Carla, then stared at the table once more. He rubbed his sweaty palms together, then continued.

"I had a girlfriend in high school, and things were pretty serious between us. But a few months after graduation she left to go to school in Philadelphia. I never saw her again.

"I started drinking more heavily that fall, perhaps due to boredom, but also as a means of getting away. Soon I noticed Dad was starting to look sickly. I remember trying to talk to him about it. I said, 'Dad, you really need to see a doctor,' but he just laughed it off saying he was getting old. It turned out he had liver cancer. He didn't make it through the winter.

"After Dad died, I began working long hours to fill the emptiness of my days, but I still found plenty of time to drink. I wasn't much of a wild man, but lived a simple, quiet life alone. I wasn't particularly happy, but I got by. I got into fishing more and more, and finally, in the late 1980s I restored the Road Runner Dad had bought new.

"In time I met a woman named Marsha. We were married eleven years ago. It wasn't long before she saw my drinking problem for what it was. As the years passed, we began to argue over money, how to raise our boys, you name it. Of course, the arguments always came back to my drinking, but I wouldn't hear of it. I simply drank more and more."

Jack looked around the room. A few members nodded as if to say, *I've been there. Hell, we've all been there.*

"Marriage counseling was a last-ditch effort, but by then it was too late. My wife left me about a year ago. She and my sons now live with her folks in Charlotte, North Carolina.

"When I found myself alone again, I really fell apart. At work I landed in serious hot water over a couple of costly mistakes. Finally, my supervisor sat me down for a talk one night. I thought he was going to fire me, but he didn't. Turns out he's a recovering alcoholic, too. He told me that here I'd find the people who would love me until I could love myself. Molly said the same thing at my first meeting. And do you know what? They were right.

"I've been sober for nine months now. It hasn't been easy, but my life has definitely gotten better. I still cannot control alcohol, but as long as I keep alcohol out of my life it cannot control me, either. As for my boys..." Jack paused and blinked away the dampness from his eyes. "Let me just say I still have a lot of work

to do. Thanks for listening."

Chapter Three

Early the next morning Jack backed the Road Runner out of the driveway, shifted the tall Pistol Grip shifter into first gear, then eased the clutch out. Gently he accelerated through each of the gears while listening and feeling for any strange noises or vibrations. He flipped the Air Grabber switch under the dash. The front edge of a square panel in the center of the hood popped open a few inches, forming an air scoop above the engine. Although the Air Grabber scoop had been an option for the car, it was one that Jack's father had not ordered. Jack had found the hood and related pieces on a Plymouth GTX during a junkyard excursion while he was in high school.

Without a current registration, Jack headed away from town. The further he drove, the more comfortable the Road Runner felt. The curves of the hood, fenders, and dash were all familiar, though he hadn't observed them in motion for many years. The Spartan feel of the bench seat, the hearty sound of the large displacement V-8 engine and the lack of power steering and power brakes served as constant reminders that this car was from a bygone era. The layout of the gauges and the speedometer needle that wavered slightly

below 35 miles per hour, the vibration in the steering wheel and

shifter handle, and the rumble of the exhaust were all departures

from newer cars, but all these subtle characteristics of the Road

Runner welcomed Jack back to his childhood and teenage years.

How could I have gone without my Road Runner for so long?

Jack thought. It was as if a part of him had been debilitated years

earlier. He had learned to get by without it, and in time he had even

grown to where he didn't really miss that part of himself. But

suddenly that almost forgotten part was alive, strong, and well. Now

he couldn't remember how he had managed to let go so long ago.

Later that day Jack treated himself to dinner at the truck stop

on Interstate 25 just south of town. Jack was no great lover of the

big rigs. Unlike the men who drove them, he could not tell the

difference between a Mack and a Peterbilt, or any other make for

that matter, without reading the emblem affixed to the grille. Nor

did he care to. To him, the cacophony created by a parking lot full

of diesel engines clattering away at idle was anything but a

harmonious blend of sounds, and sometimes a heavy whiff of diesel

exhaust would trigger his gag reflex. What Jack liked about the truck stop was the atmosphere inside.

The dining room of the truck stop was not fancy, but it was warm and inviting. The black and white checkered linoleum floor had been recently replaced, but the worn Formica countertop told the story of thousands of truckers who had stopped there seeking refuge from the monotonous thumping of tires over expansion joints on the interstate. Permanently anchored swivel top stools formed a neat row in front of the counter while cozy booths lined the walls. Behind the counter stood several coffee brewing machines and a short, wide window through which the cooks passed completed orders to the waitresses.

Jack went to the truck stop once or twice a month, usually on Sunday mornings, but occasionally for dinner. Most of the people he knew had never set foot in the place, but Jack felt comfortable there. The waitresses were friendly and quick-witted, always joking and poking fun. The truckers were hard working bunch doing their best to earn a living, and Jack felt comfortable among them. Occasionally there was a loud-mouthed egotist in the group, but for the most part they were simple men making the most of life on the road.

On this Sunday afternoon Jack took a stool near the end of the counter. A slender waitress named Rachel approached him. "Hon, can I get you some coffee?" she asked.

"Sure," Jack said.

Rachel returned a moment later with a cup of steaming coffee. She placed it before him, then dropped three creamers with it. "Would you like to see a menu?"

"No, that's okay. I know what I want." Jack ordered a cheeseburger with pickles and French fries.

While he waited for his food, he began to read the copy of the Auto Buyer he had picked up the evening before. Until recently he hadn't planned to purchase another car, but he always felt compelled to read the ads just the same. There was, after all, the possibility that one day a deal too good to pass up would come along.

Lately, however, he had begun to think more seriously about purchasing another project car. Getting the Road Runner back on the road had benefited him in a number of ways. In so doing, he had presented himself with a goal. During those months he had worked to achieve that goal, whenever he had completed a step, he felt satisfaction, and those small doses of satisfaction helped him to keep a positive attitude in the other areas of his life.

The revitalization of the Road Runner had consumed many hours of Jack's idle time, to him it was time well spent. The hour or two he worked each week night after his meeting and the full Saturdays and Sundays had been enjoyable. Besides, when he was engrossed in his work on the car he rarely thought about drinking.

But with the Road Runner nearly completed, Jack wondered, *now what?* Buying another project car seemed to be the best answer. He could simply shift his attention to it while keeping the momentum he had built up over the last few months.

Jack had already done much of the planning. Another car in the garage meant that the Road Runner would have to go outside. That simply wouldn't do. He had managed to save a few thousand dollars, but with the child support he was paying there was no way he could afford an addition to his existing garage. A custom-built shed, ten by twenty-five feet, with an overhead door would run a tad over two thousand dollars. With nearly four thousand dollars in the bank, Jack felt he could afford to spend fifteen hundred dollars on a project car.

When Jack's meal arrived, he looked up from the ads just long enough to thank Rachel. As he took the first bite of his cheeseburger, he circled an ad for a nineteen sixty-five Dodge Coronet. The ad didn't give many details about the condition of the car, except that it didn't run. But the six-hundred-dollar price sounded reasonable enough. As he finished his burger, another ad caught his eye. It was for a nineteen sixty-eight Dodge Dart GT. The ad stated that the body and interior were in very good condition, but it needed engine work. It was powered by a modified six-cylinder engine and had a four-speed manual transmission. *If this car is anywhere near as nice as the ad says, it won't last long for twelve hundred bucks.* Jack hurried through the remainder of his meal, then rushed back to his house, for there was barely time to inquire about the car before leaving for his meeting.

Jack looked at the Dart the following evening. With an excellent body, deep blue paint, a black vinyl top, and glistening chrome accents it was striking. The engine, however, was another story. Upon starting, it knocked and clattered so loudly that Jack expected it to explode on the spot. Even so, the owner had gone to considerable trouble and expense, installing numerous high-performance parts in order to maximize the output of the minuscule six-cylinder engine. Jack purchased the car and had it towed to his house later in the week. He then began searching for a replacement engine.

Chapter Four

Early the following Saturday morning Jack opened the garage and backed the Road Runner outside. With a current emission inspection and registration, it would be his first legal ride in the car since its lengthy hibernation. He smiled as the sparkling rays of sunlight played across the bright yellow surfaces of the hood and fenders. The needle of the gas gauge was leaning precariously close to "E." Jack knew his first stop must be for gas. Almost instinctively he drove to the Sinclair station where he had worked many years earlier.

The original building with its service bays and the gas pumps and islands had been demolished years earlier. In their place had been erected a modern mini-mart and several islands with self-service pumps. These new computerized pumps were faster than the old mechanically metered pumps, and they accepted credit cards. Even so, Jack felt these expressionless robots lacked the character of their mechanical forefathers. Their stark LCD display screens were cold and sterile in contrast with the softly lit painted metal faces and rolling numbered wheels of the former pumps. Furthermore, these new pumps spoke a language of annoying ear-piercing beeps--hardly

a worthwhile progression from the soft, delicious metallic clicks of

the pumps of yore.

Jack guided the Road Runner to the left side of one of the

islands and stopped with the rear bumper nearly even with the pump.

As swiped his Visa in the credit card slot, a youthful voice called

from the other side of the island.

"Wow! Cool car!" Jack hadn't noticed the green Dodge

Caravan on the opposite side of the island, but now he peered around

the pump to see its occupant. A young boy stood in the opening of

the driver's side sliding door. He had dark brown hair, a round face,

and black framed glasses with thick lenses. Jack guessed him to be

around seven or eight years old.

"Thanks!" he called back.

"What kind of car is it?" the boy asked.

"It's a Plymouth Road Runner," Jack said.

"A Road Runner?" the boy asked in disbelief.

"Yup. A Road Runner," Jack said as he walked to the front

of the car. "Look here," he said, pointing to the decal near the front

of the fender.

"Cool!" the boy exclaimed. "It's the Road Runner from TV!" A long dust trail decal stretched from the bird's whirling feet down the side of the car and disappeared into the fake side scoop behind the door, suggesting that the Road Runner had just zoomed out of the scoop.

"What size engine does it have?" the boy asked.

"440 cubic inches."

"Is that a big engine?"

"Yeah, it's pretty good sized." Jack figured it was pointless to explain that it was the largest V-8 engine that Chrysler Corporation had ever produced.

"Is it fast?"

"It goes pretty well," Jack smiled.

"My uncle has a Monte Carlo SS and it's fast. Can a Road Runner beat his car?" the boy asked as he shoved his glasses up the bridge of his nose.

"I don't know. I think it would be a pretty close race," Jack said. In truth, Jack knew the Road Runner would devastate a Monte Carlo SS. But if the boy believed that his uncle's car was fast, there was nothing to be gained by challenging that belief.

Just then the pump clicked off. Jack removed the nozzle, reinstalled the gas cap, and placed the nozzle in its holder. The pump beeped as it printed out his receipt. "I've got to go now. See you later," he said with a wave.

He got into the car and started the engine. The boy grinned in delight as the exhaust pipes snarled. Jack watched the boy's expression as he flipped the Air Grabber switch under the dash. When the Air Grabber scoop rose from the center of the hood, he heard an excited, "Wow! That's cool!" from the opposite side of the island.

Jack shifted into first gear, eased out the clutch, and steered the car toward the exit. The boy's eyes were locked on the car. Jack smiled and waved. As he left the gas station, he gave the horn button two quick jabs, and the special "Voice of the Road Runner" horn produced the familiar "Beep-Beep!" He accelerated a little harder than usual, allowing a broad range of exhaust resonance to fill the boy's ears.

Inside the convenience store of the Sinclair station a recent hire struggled to gain mastery over the electronic cash register. A more experienced co-worker watched over his shoulder and coached him patiently. The pair voided transaction after erroneous transaction, both seemingly oblivious to the long line of shoppers that had formed. This line now stretched across the check-out counter, past the coffee island, and part way down one of the aisles.

Near the middle of the line stood the boy's mother, a woman of about forty. Her straight blonde hair hung about the shoulders of her shapely frame. Her natural good looks didn't need mascara and make-up, but the droop of her eyelids suggested exhaustion, and her forehead was streaked with lines of worry. In her left hand she clutched a toothbrush and a dozen eggs, while a gallon of milk hung heavily from the fingers of her right hand and laid against her thigh. She shifted her weight from one hip to the other and sighed as her patience waned.

A much older man with a stocky build, thin gray hair, and a ruddy complexion entered the store. He removed his sunglasses and tucked them into his shirt pocket, which clung tightly to his barrel shaped chest. As he moved toward the coffee island, he noticed the long line of shoppers snaking from the check-out counter toward the rear of the store and stopped abruptly. "Aw, bullshit!" he boomed as he turned and left the store. Several shoppers chuckled, but this woman laughed aloud. The deep wrinkles of her forehead grew shallower as the solemn expression on her face broke in humor. As the moment passed, her eyes fixed on the newspaper rack, and she slipped back into a brooding trance.

It had been a scant twenty-four hours since she had received the telephone call about her father, but at this point it seemed like a week had passed.

Suddenly her thoughts were shattered by the snarling rumble of a powerful engine. She turned toward the window at the front of the store and glimpsed a bright yellow flash. There was something vaguely familiar about the tone of the exhaust, but as the car accelerated from the parking lot, she dismissed the thought.

Finally, her turn at the cash register came. She placed the sweating jug of milk, eggs, and toothbrush on the counter, then wrung her hands to stimulate the circulation in her cramped fingers. She paid the cashier, then she was on her way at last.

"Mom! Mom! Did you see that car?" Stephen shouted as she opened the driver's door of the van.

"What car?" she asked.

"The Road Runner!" Stephen said.

She froze. She recalled the brilliant yellow flash she had seen through the store window and once more the distinctive exhaust note rang in her ears. For a moment she forgot all about the circumstances that had brought her back to Colorado Springs. "What kind of car did you say it was?"

"A Road Runner, Mom! It was a yellow Road Runner, and it was cool!"

Could it be? she thought. *After all these years, could it be?* Her overstressed brain began to whirl. "Hold on, a minute," she said, raising two fingers and pressing them against her temple. "Stephen, how do you know it was a Road Runner?"

"Because the guy who was driving the car said it was. Besides, there was a Road Runner sticker on it."

"Wait a minute. You *talked* to the man who was driving the car?" Stephen didn't answer. "Stephen! You said you talked with the man in the car?"

"Well, yeah," Stephen said. "I know he's a stranger, but I didn't get out of the van, Mom. I stayed in the van!"

"What did he look like? Was he tall? Was he short? What color was his hair?"

"I don't know, Mom. He just looked like a regular old ordinary man."

"Think, Stephen. Was he tall?"

"I don't know, Mom. He wasn't too tall, but he wasn't too short, either."

"So, you are saying he was of average height." Stephen nodded. "What color was his hair?"

"I don't know, Mom."

"Did he have any hair?"

"I guess so."

"Please think, Stephen. What did his hair look like?" Was it long? Short? Blonde? Brown? Green and purple polka dots? Did he wear it in a braided ponytail?"

Stephen giggled. "I don't know, Mom. I think it was brown. It wasn't long, but it wasn't real short, either."

Yellow Road Runner. Average height and brown hair. It could be Jack! It really could be Jack! Kim took a deep breath.

Whoa, hold on a minute, a voice in her head warned. *It's been over twenty years since you knew Jack. He probably sold or junked the Road Runner long ago. Oh yeah, he is of average height and probably still has brown hair, but that description must fit half of the men in this town. Who's to say Jack is still in the area? Even if it was Jack, he is probably married.*

You have to come to your senses. You have more important things to worry about right now than some guy who you knew when you were a school girl. You've had a rough night as a guest of the Friendly Skies and you've got a rough day in store for you. Don't start thinking crazy shit.

Kim began fumbling through her purse for the key to the rented van. "I don't believe this! What did I do with that key?"

"Mom, it's in the ignition," Stephen said.

Sure enough, there it was. The key was still fully inserted in the ignition, its plastic fob gently swinging to and fro as it dangled from the key. Kim laughed. She tussled Stephen's hair. "Let's go. Grandmom and Grandpop's house is only a few blocks away." Immediately she realized her mistake, for it was now just Grandmom's house. Stephen was an unusually intelligent child, but he didn't catch her slip-up. She chose not to bring it to his attention. He would deal with his grandfather's death in his own time.

As the sun settled behind the mountains Jack went for another ride in the Road Runner. He headed north on Interstate Twenty-Five, driving for more than an hour before turning around and heading for home. There was something in the evening air that called out to him. It could have been the hum of his tires as they gobbled mile after mile of smooth roadway while he sat in solitude. Perhaps it was the way the stars were beginning to pop one by one through the darkening sapphire sky, seemingly just out of fingers' reach. Or maybe it was the dim glow on the horizon ahead that in just a few minutes would become a city. Whatever brought it on, Jack soon realized he was experiencing a rare moment of closeness with his inner self. It was an occasion of stark honesty, a time during which he could hide nothing from himself.

For much of his life Jack dreaded these times, for during these times a bookkeeper deep within his mind would take a personal inventory, and Jack would have no choice but to answer for all of the things in his life that were missing, as well as those things that were present but didn't belong there. For many years it had seemed to Jack that as long as he kept the bookkeeper drunk, he didn't have to be accountable to him. That had been easy. As long as Jack was drunk, so was the bookkeeper. But the day had come when alcohol could no longer silence this voice. Only then did Jack discover that his alcohol dependency had been largely to blame for his botched personal inventories.

Within the last year Jack had come to cherish these times of closeness with himself. He had discovered that his bookkeeper was not only intuitive, but usually right on the mark. Jack had also learned that if he heeded his advice, the related aspects of his life would improve. This usually meant doing things that were not particularly pleasant or easy, but Jack had come to trust his bookkeeper and put faith in his revelations.

On this night Jack experienced powerful feelings of longing and guilt as he thought of his sons. Johnny was now nine, and James was seven. Jack had memories of various high and low points during his sons' early years. These recollections were stored as still photos in the back of his mind, and at once his mind began to replay them in slide show fashion.

First was the beginning of fatherhood for Jack. He thought of the ride to the hospital with Marsha in labor with Johnny. Nine months of waiting and anticipation were about to reach a pinnacle, and within a few hours their lives would be changed forever. It was a time filled with questions and uncertainty, but it was a time of exhilaration, as well. The next six hours had seemed to drag on forever, but in retrospect the duration of Marsha's labor seemed like a few short minutes, at least to Jack. He had been in the delivery room coaching her, keeping a close watch in the mirror mounted atop the opposite wall as Johnny's head became visible, and studying the doctor's eyes for any sign of complication. Jack wasn't sure if it was still customary to swat a newborn on the rump to induce breathing, but in Johnny's case it wouldn't have been necessary anyway. He began gasping for air and crying immediately upon leaving Marsha's womb. At that instant Jack felt a change take place deep within himself. He watched with awe as the doctor placed the newborn at Marsha's breast. As the tiny, fragile-looking infant wiggled and writhed Jack was taken by his beauty and innocence. He sensed much of himself in the movements of the child. He felt an intangible, inexplicable, yet veritable connection with his newborn son. For the first time the reality that this child was an extension of Jack's own being struck him. This was his son.

His *son!* As tears streamed down his cheeks, he hugged and kissed Marsha, then gently kissed his son's head. Jack had stepped over the threshold into fatherhood.

A chain of "firsts" was soon to follow. There was the first diaper change, first sampling of table food, first tooth, first step, and first word. Each of these events had served as a mile marker in his young son's life. When James was born Jack and Marsha had included Johnny as a vital part of the preparation to help him establish his role as the Big Brother.

Marsha's pregnancy with James had included nearly all of the same steps and small events as her first pregnancy, but this time both she and Jack knew what to expect. Their experience in matters of child bearing had lessened the significance of these events. Even the birth of James had seemed like a somewhat less monumental occasion than the birth of Johnny.

Jack had begun drinking more and more. He now realized that his memory of the events following James' birth was cloudy and contained large gaps. He remembered coming home late one night and Marsha chattering about how he had suddenly begun walking. Unlike most kids who take a few steps at a time, once James discovered how to walk, that child *walked*. Within hours of his first step he was walking with confidence. Only in the sobriety of the following morning did Jack witness this for himself.

Jack could vaguely remember working with Marsha to potty-train the boys. He knew there had been slip-ups and relapses, but he had no vivid recollections of them. Despite being more than a little tipsy at the time, the one event he could recall clearly was the day he led Johnny to the bathroom in order to teach him to urinate while standing. "This is what is so neat about being a boy," Jack had told him. "Girls can't do this!"

"Can Mommy pee like this?" Johnny had asked.

"No, because Mommy is a girl."

"Mommy *was* a girl when she was little. She's a lady now."

"Well, ladies can't pee like this, either. Only big boys and men can pee while standing up." It was a special moment of bonding, a moment that could be shared only by fathers and sons. By anatomical design, mothers missed out on this one. Sadly, Jack now realized he hadn't shared this experience with James. In all likelihood, Johnny had let James in on this unique male ability at the appropriate time while Jack sat in some dark barroom pickling his brain.

Jack knew that his and Marsha's marriage had been over for quite some time before she had decided to make it official, and he had come to terms with that. When she announced that she and the boys were moving to North Carolina, Jack had objected for fear that his relationship with his sons would be ruined. But the truth was his relationship with his sons could not have been damaged, for he and his sons had no real relationship to speak of.

At that moment Jack tightened his sweaty grip on the steering wheel and swore to himself that he would do whatever he could to establish a relationship with his boys. It was certainly too late to make up for lost time, but they each had more than a few years of childhood left. Instead of trying to rebuild something that had barely existed in the first place, Jack wondered if it would be possible to start anew. Would his sons give him a chance? There was but one way to find out. "I'm going to call my boys tomorrow!" Jack said to the darkness.

Chapter Five

Jack awoke the next morning feeling groggy and out of sorts. As he rose from his bed, he heard raindrops pelting the window. He hadn't slept well, and as he glanced in the mirror above the sink in the bathroom, his pasty white color and the puffiness below his eyes served as testament to the way he felt. "God, I look like hell," he muttered.

He stumbled to the kitchen, filled the coffee maker with water and fresh coffee grinds, then made his way to the living room and flicked on the television. He cycled through all of the channels in hopes of finding something to occupy his mind while the coffee brewed, but his choices seemed to be limited to television ministers, cooking shows, and the Rugrats. Discouraged, he settled for the Rugrats.

While the coffee brewed Jack tried to gather his thoughts. He had awakened several times throughout the night from disturbing dreams. He tried to concentrate now in hopes of recalling some of them, but all that remained in the light of a new day was an air of gloom and uneasiness. Growing annoyed with the television, Jack clicked the remote control and silenced it, then sank deeper into his tattered green recliner and closed his eyes.

At length, he gave up. He could recall nothing of the dreams. Jack stood and walked back to the kitchen, prepared a cup of coffee, then returned to his chair in the living room. He took a sip of coffee and winced as the hot liquid nearly scalded his lip. Instinctively he swallowed, then shook his head in agony as the fervid coffee burned the back of his throat. "Dumbass," he mumbled to himself as he placed the cup on the coffee table, then leaned back into the chair and closed his eyes.

The next thing Jack knew he was standing at the entrance of a shopping mall. A steady flow of shoppers filed in and out of the building, some carrying bags, others empty handed. There were people of all ages; many traveled in clusters, while others straggled alone. Parents and grandparents escorted the youngest shoppers, while teenagers, a group far disproportionate in number, often traveled in packs of five or more.

Jack stood quietly and observed the crowd for some time when two boys, perhaps ages twelve and fourteen, caught his attention. He tracked them as they shuffled toward the doors, joking and clowning with each other. As they reached the doors, the older boy turned toward the younger one, and Jack caught a glimpse of his face. It was Johnny! But something about his appearance didn't seem right. Johnny was much older than Jack remembered him, but there was no mistaking Johnny's eyes or his smile. He then realized that the other boy was James, but he, too, was much older. Jack quickly followed them into the mall and down the main corridor past a hair salon, a nutrition store, and a Radio Shack. Unaware that they were being followed, they turned and entered a novelty gift store. Jack walked into the same crowded store moments later and spied the boys laughing their way through the birthday card selection.

"Oh my God, look at this one!" Johnny exclaimed as he handed a card to James. On the front was a fisherman pointing from the dock where he stood. The caption read, *Thar she blows!* On the inside of the card was a photo of the naked posterior of a grossly overweight woman jutting upward from the surface of the water in a calm lake. A blinding spray of water had been airbrushed shooting from her "blow hole." Beneath the photo was the statement, *Hope your birthday doesn't blow.* Both boys were nearly hysterical over the card. "Aw, Jim, this one looks like you," Johnny said as he handed him a card with a monkey on the front.

"Screw you, John! Even if that is me, I'm still better looking than you!"

John and Jim, Jack thought. *They aren't Johnny and James anymore! I wonder when that happened.*

"Ha, ha, here you go," Jim said as he handed a card to John. On the front was a drawing of a men's room door and the words, *Another birthday...* On the inside was a drawing of a urinal and the words, *Piss on it.*

John then picked a card and began reciting the ten reasons why beer is better than women. It was obvious that over half of the reasons given were out of Jim's grasp, and Jack suspected that a few were beyond John's comprehension. But even if that was the case, John's poker face kept his secret safe.

Jack was thrilled to see his sons. They were growing up healthy and seemed happy. He wanted to approach them, talk with them, tell them how much he missed them, and that he was proud of them. Even so, he was overwhelmed by how much they had changed. Sure, a couple of years had gone by, but they seemed so different--so *grown up*. Sadly, Jack realized that John would be driving soon, and that Jim wouldn't be far behind. He wanted to call out to them, but what would he say? What could he say after all this time? Jack wasn't sure that there were any words that could ease the pain and bridge the gap of time. And where had all the time gone, anyway?

Suddenly the boys began moving toward him. *Oh shit!* he thought. He took a breath as if to speak, reconsidered, then quickly looked down and fumbled with a palm held electric shock handshake buzzer. As the boys passed him, Jack hoped to go unnoticed. John glanced directly at him, then did a double-take and studied his features for a moment. When they reached the poster display rack at the far wall, John nonchalantly turned and looked in Jack's direction once more, careful to avoid eye contact. He looked away uncomfortably. Jim was rapidly flipping through the posters, pausing only to take in the details of a scantily clad Britney Spears in a suggestive pose. As Jim neared the last of the posters, John spoke to him, but Jack was out of earshot. Suddenly they hurried out of the store, turned right into the wide corridor that ran down the middle of the mall, and were quickly gobbled up by the crowd.

Jack darted after them, but he had no more than left the store when he realized he had lost them. He hurried through the mob for the first fifty feet or so, then slowed to the excruciatingly slow pace of the horde of shoppers. As he shuffled along Jack studied every inch of the mall in an effort to find his sons. After several minutes he neared the far end of the mall. Just when he was sure that he wouldn't find them, he spotted the boys moving away from the ice cream counter, each with a chocolate and vanilla swirl cone. As Jack approached, the boys stopped walking and turned to face each other, each eerily watching the other lick and slurp his ice cream. "Hey, Johnny! Hey, James!" Jack called as he neared them. "It's me, your dad. How are you guys?"

"No pain," John replied in an icy tone without looking away from his brother.

"Well, good. I'm glad there is no pain. But how have you guys been? How is school? Are you playing sports?" Jack leaned a little closer. "Are you treating the girls well?"

"I told you. There is no pain." John's words were slow and deliberate. He continued to stare at Jim's ice cream cone as he began to smirk.

Jack felt a chill shoot up his spine as an uneasy feeling came over him. Still, he persisted. "Guys, it's been a long time. You have no idea how difficult it's been for me not having you around. I've missed you both so much. I still haven't gotten used to how quiet the house is now. I know I haven't been in touch, but that says nothing about the way I've missed you. So come on, talk to your old man. How has it been for you two?"

A look of agitation came over John's features. "I said, there is no pain." This time he spoke more slowly. "We are beyond that now. We don't hurt in your absence anymore." The boys turned to face Jack. They grinned as their eyes burned deep into his, as if looking into his soul. "The question," John continued, "is how in the hell are you ever going to live with the guilt?" He took a step toward Jack, then another, and another. With each step he seemed to grow taller. Jack couldn't feel his feet move, but he was aware that he was moving backward. At the same time, he seemed to be sinking into the floor. "For years you didn't take the time to visit us. You didn't bother to call us. You didn't even go to the trouble to write to us. Some father we had!" John thundered. "You didn't give a shit about us! Your sons! Your own flesh and blood!"

"But I did care," Jack said.

John glared at him, then spoke in a more quiet tone. "Your actions told us otherwise. It hurt. And we cried. We suffered because we knew you didn't care about us, and because you wanted nothing to do with us. We kept asking ourselves what we had done wrong. What did we do to make you stop loving us?" John paused for a moment. "But that's over now. Our pain and suffering ended when we finally learned to give up on you.

"Ah, but here is where your pain and suffering begin! You have driven away your sons for good! Your golden years will be lonely and perhaps not so golden after all. Pain, suffering, and guilt. Have a nice time of it, Daddy!" Both boys turned from Jack and broke into a dead run through the crowd. Jack tried to call after them, but his throat tightened, and he was unable to utter a sound. His strength was drained, and he collapsed to the floor in a sobbing heap.

Jack's head snapped back suddenly as he awoke from the dream. He had an acute pain in his chest, and he was unable to catch his breath. At first, he thought he might be having a heart attack, but within a minute or two his breath came more easily, and the pain subsided to a dull ache. There was no question about what he must do. He rose to his feet and moved to the kitchen. Jack was sure that Marsha, her parents, and the boys would be up by now. He leafed through his address book to find Marsha's phone number then looked toward the phone with trepidation. After staring at it for several seconds, he muttered, "Fuck it. Here goes." He punched the digits into the phone and waited.

On the third ring a tired young man's voice answered, "Hello."

"Hello, Johnny?"

"No, this is James," the youth said cautiously. "Who is this?"

"This is your dad. How are you doing?"

"Fine." James answered with uncertainty.

After an uncomfortable moment Jack queried, "Well, aren't you going to ask me how I am?"

"How are you?" James complied.

"I'm okay. How is school?"

"Fine."

There was another short awkward pause as James offered nothing to their chat. Jack scrambled to think of something to say to stimulate the conversation, but nothing interesting came to mind. "How do you like your teachers? Are you learning a lot?" Jack knew they were lame questions, but they were the best he could come up with.

"They're okay." Jack could now hear a voice in the background speaking to James. "It's Dad," James responded to this voice. "I don't know what he wants."

"Is that Mom?" Jack asked.

"No, she's at work," James said.

"Is it Grandmom or Grandpop?"

"Nope. They're at church."

"Well, then, it must be Johnny!"

"Yep. Want to talk to him? He's right here." James sounded relieved by the thought of escaping the conversation by simply passing the phone to Johnny. A muffled exchange of unpleasant words ensued between the brothers. "But he wants to talk to you," Jack heard James said to Johnny.

"Well I don't want to talk to him," Jack could barely hear Johnny reply. There were more hushed words, then Johnny groaned, "Aw, man!" A moment later he spoke into the phone with a grumpy, "Hello!"

"Johnny! How are you doing?" Jack asked, doing his best to sound cheerful.

"I'm okay," Johnny said in a flat tone.

"Are things going well in school?"

"Yeah, they're fine." There was more than a hint of resentment in Johnny's voice.

Jack struggled to think of something to say. "So how is life on the Atlantic Coast?"

"Dad, I really don't have time to talk right now. Grandmom and Grandpop will be home soon, and we have to clean up our mess in the kitchen, then clean our room. If we don't, we'll be in trouble." It was a poor excuse to end the conversation, but it was clear to Jack that neither boy was keen on talking to him, and he couldn't blame them.

"Okay, I won't hold you up. I don't want you guys to be in trouble with your mom or your grandparents. Will you be around later in the week?"

"Yeah, we're here almost every night. Why, are you going to call again?" Jack recognized this as more a challenge than a question.

"If you two will be there, I'll call," Jack said. "Will that be okay?"

"We'll be here," Johnny said.

"Fine. I'll talk to you then." They exchanged good-byes, then hung up.

Jack moved to the living room and sank into his chair once more. He began to feel a great sense of relief having made the phone call, but in its wake came sadness. His sons had given him anything but a warm reception, and Jack knew that he was fully to blame for any ill feelings they harbored toward him. Still, the reality of it came as a shock.

Jack yearned to be with his sons. He wished more than ever to build a healthy father-son relationship with them. But after all this time, how normal could it be? Johnny and James had never had a real father, a stable male role model committed to family obligations and the happiness of his family.

Jack knew he could not focus on the various milestones and special times of his sons' lives that he had missed. Those times had passed, and there was no way to recapture them. He knew the only way to build any close ties with his sons was to look ahead and be committed to doing right from now on. With a lot of luck and perseverance, perhaps one day they would be able to look up to him, accept him as their father and forgive him for the past.

If Johnny and James were to grant him a second chance, he would have to earn it. Earning that chance meant proving to his sons that he genuinely cared for them and giving them a reason to believe in him. He had to prove to them that he was worthwhile as a human being as well as a parent.

But doing so would be difficult. In all likelihood it was too late. He buried his face in his open palms. "How did I let things get to this point?" he moaned. "I've got to do better. I <u>will</u> do better!"

Jack had missed his meeting the night before, and that didn't help the way he felt. Right now, he wished he could go to a meeting, for the company of the others in his group almost always raised his spirits and soothed his troubles. He told himself that despite his sons' reaction to his telephone call, he had finally found the courage to make that call. It was the all important first step, and it occurred to him that he should recognize this as progress and congratulate himself. He would treat himself to breakfast at the truck stop.

While he dressed Jack enjoyed the last of his coffee. He slipped into his sneakers and jacket. When he opened the front door, he spied a green Dodge Caravan slowing as it approached his house. Jack figured that its driver might be lost, so he waited for a moment to see if the driver would spot him and turn into his driveway to ask directions. Instead, just when it seemed that the van was about to turn, it suddenly sped off. *Oh well,* he thought. *I would have helped you if you'd asked.* He thought nothing more of the incident as he drove through the icy rain toward the truck stop.

After a leisurely meal of creamed chipped beef on toast Jack sought a convenience store for a cup of coffee, a Sunday newspaper, and the latest *Auto Buyer.* Once he was home, he flipped through the *Auto Buyer's* tiny parts section, which made up the last few pages of the publication. Although his first thought had been to replace the Slant Six engine in the Dart with a more powerful V-8, it seemed like a shame to waste the performance parts the previous owner had installed on the existing engine. Jack perused the ads in search of a Slant Six engine, but there was no such ad. He then thumbed through the car ads for a suitable donor car. The only listing he spotted was for a nineteen seventy-six Plymouth Volare, a car which was said to be in rough, but running condition. Jack recognized the first three digits of the phone number as a local exchange. He dialed the number, then spoke with a young female who identified herself as the owner's daughter. "He and my mom went to the store. They'll be back in a little while," she said. Jack decided to wait an hour or so, then try back.

He nestled into his green recliner and sipped his coffee while scanning the automotive classified ads in the Sunday paper. After coming up empty, he began browsing through the other sections of the paper. Last, Jack scoured the obituaries. There was a force which drew him to this section whenever he read the paper. It was not a morbid curiosity or attraction, but still it was a compulsion that he found difficult to resist. He froze as one name nearly leapt at him from the paper.

Robert E. "Bob" Hurley

Age 66, died Friday, September 24, 2001

at his **Colorado Springs** home.

Mass: 10 AM Tues. Sept. 28 at St. Johns Church,

Oak Lane and South Street, Colorado Springs.

Friends may call Mon 7-8 PM at

Chadwick Funeral Home,

147 Commerce St., Colorado Springs.

Jack was stunned. Although not a day passed that he didn't think of Kim, it had been over twenty years since he had seen her or her parents. He felt the need to express his sorrow to Mrs. Hurley and to Kim, wherever she might be. He knew nothing of her whereabouts, but he was certain she would be coming back to town at least for her father's funeral.

Jack knew that sending flowers was the most common way of expressing sorrow to a bereaved family, but after all of these years, he wondered if flowers would be appropriate coming from him. It had been two decades since he'd had contact with any of the Hurleys. Was this an appropriate time to make contact?

And what of Kim's husband and kids? Although Jack had no way of knowing for sure, he envisioned Kim happily married with three or four kids, for she had always spoken of children.

Suddenly Jack realized it was time to call the owner of the Volare listed in the classified ads. He read the ad again, lifted the telephone receiver, and punched in the telephone number. "Hello!" a gravelly voice barked after the fourth ring.

"Hi," Jack said. "I was calling about the Plymouth Volare you have for sale in the paper."

"It's sold," the man growled. "A kid's supposed to come back and get it tonight."

"I see," Jack said. "Well, thanks for your time. You have a good day."

"Whoa, hold on a minute," the man said. "If you want to give me your name and number, I'll call you if this kid don't show up."

Jack gave the man his phone number, then he had another idea. "I understand the car has been sold, and I'm not going to try to get you to change your mind. But I have plenty of time this afternoon to look at it. If you would be okay with it, I'd like to see the car today. If the deal with the kid who is supposed to take the car goes through, that's fine. If it doesn't, then I will have already seen the car. It will save us the hassle of trying to get together later in order for me to look at it. Would that be okay with you?" Jack asked.

The man agreed, and Jack scribbled directions to the man's house, then grabbed his coat. He started for the door, then stopped suddenly and turned toward the kitchen. Hanging next to the telephone was a meeting list with days, times, and locations of all of the Alcoholics Anonymous meetings in his area. Jack took the list, tucked it into his pocket, then strode toward the door.

Minutes later he rolled to a stop in front of the house where the Volare sat. The rain had nearly stopped. Although he hadn't thought to ask what body style the car was, he had pictured a four-door. Instead, a dilapidated brown two-door with large splotches of gray primer sat in the driveway near the house. A gray Ford Taurus was parked behind it. As Jack slid from behind the wheel of his truck and started up the driveway, he noticed the hood of the Volare was not fully closed. Litter was strewn about the interior, and jagged scraps of sheet metal had been pop-riveted over gaping rust holes. This was definitely no more than a two-hundred-dollar car, assuming that it ran.

Jack continued to the front door of the red brick ranch house. A broken storm window sat propped against the front wall, and Jack stepped around the shards of glass that were strewn about the flimsy aluminum frame. From a half-inch round hole in the brick molding adjacent to the front door dangled two wires that had apparently been connected to a doorbell button at one time. Jack rapped on the door. He could hear sounds from within as somebody scurried to answer. "Hold on, hold on," said the gravelly voiced man. Moments later the door knob turned and on the third hard tug the door swung open to reveal a short, heavy set, bald-headed man in his early fifties. "You the guy who just called about the car?" he asked.

"Yeah, that's me," Jack said. "My name is Jack."

"I'm Harvey," the man said as he slapped his front pockets. "Key must be in it. Let me grab my coat." He disappeared for a moment, then returned. Jack followed him as he moved toward the car. "The battery ain't in the best of shape. I put a trickle charger on it last night. It started this morning when the kid came to look at it, but I don't know what it's gonna do now."

"How many miles does it have?" Jack inquired.

"Oh, the odometer shows forty-three thousand, but that's actually a hundred forty-three thousand. Damn thing's been broke for the last two years, so I figure it's got somewhere between a hundred fifty and a hundred sixty thousand."

"Wow!" Jack said.

"Hey, it's a Slant Six! You can't kill the damned things. If you take care of 'em, they'll go well past two hundred thousand."

"Yeah, that's true," Jack said.

"Now, I've changed the oil every three thousand miles," Harvey continued while raising the hood. "Look at this," he indicated as he removed the oil filler cap. "Look in there at the rocker arms. See any sludge? It's clean in there because of the way I took care of it. I know the car don't look like much but believe me when I say it is well maintained."

Jack nodded. As his trained eye scanned the engine compartment, he noticed a new fuel filter and belts, and fairly new spark plug wires and coolant hoses, all indications of regular maintenance.

"Now, let's see if this old bitch will start," Harvey mumbled as he yanked on the door handle. As the door popped open it sagged on its worn hinges. It creaked and groaned as Harvey swung it outward. He cursed as he struggled to wedge himself between the seat and the steering wheel. Once in position, he pumped the accelerator several times, then turned the key. The starter responded with a lazy *ruh-ruuh-ruuuh* as the battery quickly lost its charge.

"Damn it! Let's give it a minute," Harvey said. He seemed hopeful

that the engine would start, despite the weak battery. Jack was not at

all optimistic. Seeing the look of skepticism on Jack's face, Harvey

waited mere moments before pumping the accelerator and turning

the key again. *Ruh-ruuh-ruuuh-vroom!* "Ha! I knew she'd start!"

Harvey shouted above the clatter of the cold engine on fast idle.

"Valves need to be adjusted," he added, justifying the raucous

engine noise.

Jack nodded. He listened to the engine as it warmed up.

Satisfied that it was suitable to rebuild for the Dart, he stepped back

and peered over the hood at Harvey, who was still in the driver's

seat. "You can shut it down," he yelled.

Harvey flicked the key off, then writhed from behind the

wheel. "So, whadda ya think?"

"If the kid doesn't come back for the car, I'll take it," Jack

said.

"Don't ya want to drive it first?"

"No, I don't need to drive it. Actually, the only thing I need

is the engine. I just bought a Dodge Dart with a blown-up Slant Six, and I need a motor that I can rebuild for it," Jack said.

Harvey gave Jack a wry smile. "Even if the kid comes back for the car, I think I can help you. See, a few years ago my brother-in-law had a Valiant. I think it was a seventy-three or seventy-four. It was a really clean, low mileage car. Typical little old lady car. Anyway, he was on his way home from work one day when some young kid in a Mustang blew a stop sign and broadsided him. Demolished the car. It was a real shame. He told me I could have anything I wanted off the car, so I pulled the motor and transmission and stuck them in the shed out back. I was going to use them in this car if I ever needed to, but I never did."

"What do you want for the motor?" Jack asked.

"Tell you what," Harvey said. "I'll let you have the spare motor for fifty bucks, and I'll throw in the transmission for free. Sound fair?"

"Yeah, that sounds more than fair!" Jack said. "Mind if I see the spare engine?"

"Not at all. Just watch your step," Harvey cautioned as he led the way to the back yard. Jack soon discovered the reason for Harvey's warning, for once they passed through the wide gate in the chain link fence the men began stepping over and around mound after mound of dog droppings. As they rounded the corner of the house a large dog sensed their presence from within the house and began growling menacingly. "Missy, shaddup!" Harvey shouted. When they reached the ramshackle plywood shed Harvey swung both doors open in order to let as much light into the structure as possible. He moved a few cardboard boxes and a couple of lawn chairs out of the way to reveal an engine and transmission still bolted together as an assembly. The engine was complete, including the air cleaner and all of the accessories.

Jack stepped into the shed, pausing for a few moments as his eyes grew accustomed to the dim light. At length he squatted before the engine, grasped the fan, then slowly applied just enough pressure to rotate the engine. "I just wanted to make sure that moisture hadn't gotten to it and made the rings stick," he explained. "It turns fine. Yeah, I'll take it," he said as he stood. "By the way, how did you get it in here?"

Harvey laughed. "That wasn't easy. It took three of us, a case of beer, and a whole lot of cussing. Speaking of which, do you want a beer?"

"Uh, no! No thanks," Jack said. Jack was not sure why, but Harvey's offer took him completely by surprise.

Harvey stroked his chin as he surveyed the engine, the shed, and the yard. At length he said, "I have an engine hoist up there by the house." He pointed toward a piece of equipment that had been cloaked with a canvas tarpaulin. "If I throw a piece of plywood on the ground here in front of the shed, you could hook onto the motor with your truck and drag it out of the shed onto the plywood. Then we can lift it with the hoist and put it into the bed of your truck. Shouldn't take too long. Do ya want to take it now?"

Jack thought for a moment. There were still a few hours of daylight remaining. During the week there would be no daylight by the time he left work and arrived at Harvey's house. "Sure, I suppose we can do it now," Jack said.

"Okay! Back your truck through the gate. I'll round up a sheet of plywood and a rope."

Jack plodded through the dung-riddled yard. *To anyone who's watching, it must look like I'm playing a slow-motion game of hop-scotch!* he thought. When he reached the gate, he turned back in time to see Harvey procure a sheet of well-weathered plywood from a stack behind the shed. Jack opened the gate fully, then continued toward his truck. He then backed across the front yard and through the gate toward the shed. Harvey guided him toward the shed opening and indicated when to stop. Jack jumped from the driver's seat and joined Harvey behind the truck. Together they loaded the engine in short order.

Jack toted his engine home. The dense cloud cover had disintegrated further by the time Jack pulled into his driveway and a gusty wind had begun to blow. He moved the Road Runner from the garage to the driveway, then backed his truck into the garage. Using the chain hoist which dangled from a heavy beam in the ceiling Jack unloaded the engine and transmission, then moved his truck outside. He pulled the Road Runner into the garage, then closed the garage door and headed inside to wash up and prepare for his meeting.

Chapter Six

The next day was Monday. As Jack drove to his job at the United Express Shipping depot, he thought of the two telephone calls he needed to make that day. The first was to order the shed where the Road Runner would spend the winter. He had decided the only extra cost options he really needed were the overhead door and double thickness plywood floor. He could run his own wiring for lights and electrical outlets later if he decided to, and he could even add vinyl siding at a later date.

The second telephone call would be to order flowers to send to the Hurley family, but he was still undecided about what message he should ask to be put on the card. As he drove Jack jotted down notes and phrases, but the right words wouldn't come. He wanted to express his sorrow but did not want to feign closeness with a family to whom he had not spoken in two decades.

Jack's first job of the day was to replace the clutch in one of the large gray United Express delivery trucks. There was nothing unusual about this particular job, for the clutches in these trucks required frequent replacement due to the constant stop-and-start driving they saw. Jack decided to place his telephone calls after he completed the clutch job. By then he hoped to have the wording for the message on the flowers sorted out.

Ordering the shed proved to be no problem. Mike, the man who took Jack's order, simply asked Jack the pertinent questions as he filled out the blanks and checked the appropriate boxes on the order form. When he asked how long he would have to wait before taking delivery, Mike said it might be ready by the end of the week, but most likely it would probably be sometime the following week.

Next Jack browsed the Yellow Page ads for a florist. At random he chose Flowers by Rita. It occurred to him that florists must be approached constantly by people who need help finding the words to best convey their feelings. He dialed the number and moments later a chipper woman who identified herself as Bonnie answered. Jack explained his dilemma while she listened. "Sounds like you want the family to know you still care and that you feel badly for them, but after all this time you don't want to get too mushy."

"Yeah, that's pretty much it," Jack said.

"What did you say his last name was?" Bonnie asked.

"Hurley," Jack said.

"Okay, so how about this:

> *In remembrance of Mr. Hurley,*
> *And thinking of you in your time of sorrow.*

"Your name would then go at the bottom, of course. How would something like that sound?" Bonnie asked.

"That's perfect. Send it just like that." Jack then specified a modest arrangement and gave Bonnie name of the funeral home.

The week passed slowly. Jack attended his meetings as usual, and during a couple of evenings he worked late into the night to separate the engine he had bought for the Dart from the transmission that had come with it. In the corner of the garage sat an engine stand that had been Jack's father's. It was a stout piece of equipment constructed of thick round pipe with full welds and caster wheels that would have been at home on a safe. Jack and his father had last used the stand to rebuild the 440 now in the Road Runner after the original 383 had begun burning oil. Late Wednesday night Jack mounted the six-cylinder engine to the stand.

Jack thought of his sons frequently as he worked in the garage. He had promised them he would call later that week, and he promised himself that Thursday would be the night. He would call as soon as he arrived home from work, for five-thirty his time would be seven-thirty Eastern time.

For days he had tried to think of something to talk about with the boys, some topic they could talk about with shared interest. Perhaps this would help to relieve some of the uneasiness and allow the conversation to flow more freely. But he could think of nothing. As he dialed the number, his stomach ached. His palms grew damp and slippery. Once again, he had no idea what to say.

"Hello," a man answered. There was a hoarseness in his voice and more than a slight drawl. Jack recognized it as Marsha's father.

"Hello, Ralph? It's Jack. How are you doing?"

"Oh, hi there, Jack." He emphasized Jack's name. Jack was sure he had done so to inform another person or persons in the room who was calling. "What can I do for you?"

"I was wondering if Johnny or James was around. I'd like to talk to them."

There was a tense silence before Ralph responded. "Well, I'm sorry Jack, but the boys are at their karate lesson right now.

They won't be back for a while."

"Karate? I didn't know they were taking karate lessons," Jack said.

"No, I don't suppose you did. They've been taking lessons for some time now. I expect it's been at least six or maybe eight months."

"Sounds like they must really like it if they are sticking with it," Jack said.

"Yeah, they do. Doin' real well at it, too. They had a competition a few months back. All of the parents were there, and wouldn't you know, both of those boys took home awards. Shoulda been here. Could've seen it for yourself."

Jack could feel the impact of Ralph's verbal jabs. He squirmed in his chair as he felt his face flush. "I wish I could have been there."

"I'll bet you do."

"Well, Ralph, when would be a good time to talk to the boys?"

"Oh, I don't know. You know how kids are these days. Always on the go. But I'd suggest that you just call when the mood strikes. If you make the effort, I'm sure you'll catch them here."

"Thanks, Ralph."

"Good-bye, Jack." With that, both men hung up their phones.

Jack attended his meeting as planned. When he returned home two hours later, he spotted the red light on his answering machine blinking. "Probably those damned telemarketers," he mumbled as he pressed the play button. In none of the messages did the caller speak. There was the barely audible sound of breathing as the person waited for several seconds for Jack to answer, followed by a click. Just then the telephone rang. "Hello," Jack answered.

"Jack, it's me, Marsha," said a soft female voice.

"Marsha, how are you doing?"

"Fine. I need to talk to you about something," Marsha began, shooting past Jack's pleasantry. "I understand that you called Johnny and James the other day, and that you tried to call them again tonight."

"Yes, that's true," Jack said. He instantly recognized the familiar cool tone of Marsha's voice as a thin veil concealing fiery anger.

"Jack, what the hell are you doing?"

Oh, boy! Jack thought. *This, from the woman who never used foul language and gave me hell whenever I did.* "What do you mean?" he asked.

"I think you know what I mean. We've been gone for a year now and I can count on one hand the number of times that you've called them, and those calls were right after we left. They haven't heard from you in almost a year, but now you suddenly call twice in the same week."

Jack sighed.

"You can't keep taking these kids on a roller coaster ride."

"Roller coaster ride? What the hell are you talking about?"

"Jack, you have no idea how confused these kids are. They really miss you. Every time you used to call, they got excited, and they stayed that way for days. Then, when they didn't hear from you again, they got depressed and irritable. They thought you didn't care. Slowly they came around, and they got back to normal. Then you went a year without calling them at all. Now, out of the blue you call, and the whole thing starts again. You have no idea what you're putting them through."

"Look, I know that I haven't exactly been the world's greatest father, and I am sorry for that. Things haven't been easy for me here alone. But now that I am getting myself back on track, I know I need to turn my attention to the boys. I know I haven't been there for them. I want to do better as a father. I need to do better, and I am *going* to do better, Marsha."

"Oh, Jack, stop with the self-pity. And quit making empty promises. We've heard it all before. 'I'm going to stop drinking. I'm going to spend more time with the boys. I'm going to be a better husband and a better father,'" she sneered. "Go ahead. What were you going to say next? That you've finally learned to control your drinking?"

"Marsha, I don't want your pity. I know it's over between us, and looking back, I'm pretty sure it was over long before you left. I know how badly I fucked up while we were together and during the time, we've been apart. I wouldn't blame you if you hated me for the rest of your life, but I want you to know that I know I screwed up. I need for you to know that.

"The same thing goes for the boys. I know I've hurt them and sent them some crossed signals. I never meant for it to be that way, but I accept full responsibility. It's my fault. I don't want their sympathy, but I do want them to know that I am sorry and that I really do love them. Marsha, please don't deny me the chance to bond with my sons," Jack pleaded. "I know that I can't make up for the past, but I need to feel there is hope for the future. If they are willing to give me a chance, then I'm willing to work to earn it."

"Oh, so it's about you, huh? That's right. Everything is always about you! Well, that's where you are wrong, Jack. This isn't about you at all. It is about Johnny and James. I'm looking out for their well-being because, quite frankly, one of us needs to. I'm not going to stand by and see them hurt any more by a man who fills their heads with hope and promises, only to disappoint them later. I won't stand for it."

"I know you probably won't believe this, and I can't say I blame you. I don't want to continue what I've done in the past. I want to start fresh. When I called them last weekend, I promised them I'd call back later in the week. That was why I made sure to call again tonight. I made them a promise, and I stuck to it. It is a small step, but at least it is a step in the right direction. From now on I intend to call them at least once a week, and I hope to visit with them. I want my sons to be a part of my life, and I'd really like to be a part of their lives, too."

"And why should I believe you? What makes this time different?"

Jack drew a deep breath, then exhaled slowly. "Marsha, in the past I was an alcoholic who was in denial. I can see now that I had a shaky grip on my life. But at the time I believed I had everything under control. Although I was weak, I thought I was strong. I believed whatever problems I faced could not have been my fault, so I blamed everyone around me, including you and the boys.

"But that was then. Since then I have been slapped in the face by reality, not once, but twice. The first slap came when you and the boys left. And, as I'm sure you expected, I crawled deeper into my bottle. The second slap was when I nearly lost my job. Since then I've been forced to look inward, and I've come to realize my mistakes. I've accepted responsibility for them. You have no idea how hard it is to swallow your pride and admit that you alone are to blame for your life turning to shit. Let me tell you, it is a humbling experience. But that's what it takes if you are going to rebuild your life. Marsha, I have been sober for almost a year now. I go to AA meetings almost every day.

"The empty promises of the past were made by a guy who thought he was on top of things, but who was barely holding on. The promises I make now come from a guy who has fallen hard but is working to climb back up. That's the difference."

"Sober for almost a year?" Marsha's voice rang with doubt.

"Sober for almost a year," Jack said. "I'm trying for real this time."

"Okay," Marsha said hesitantly. "It's late here now, but if you call back tomorrow night, I'll let you talk to the boys. But so help me, Jack, you had better stick to your word. Don't let them down!"

Moments after he hung up the telephone it rang again. "What now?" Jack mumbled as he reached for the receiver. "Hello," he answered, expecting to speak with Marsha once more.

"Hello. Is this Jack Kramer?" the female caller asked. She spoke quickly and breathed in short breaths. Jack was relieved that it was not Marsha. Something about the caller's voice was familiar, but Jack could not identify her.

"That depends. Does he owe you money?" Startled by his own response, even Jack was not sure why he had answered this way. The words had tumbled from his mouth.

"No, not that I can remember," the woman at the other end of the phone line chuckled. "Of course, it has been a very long time."

Jack's thoughts began to whirl inside his head. *Jesus Christ! Is this Kim!* "Well, if Jack Kramer doesn't owe you money, then I'm him."

The woman continued to laugh. "Jack, it's Kim Mann. Oops! I mean Kim Hurley. And it sounds like you haven't changed a bit!"

It's Kim! Holy shit! It's Kim! "My God, what has it been, like fifty or sixty years since I've talked to you?" Jack asked.

"Yeah, it sure seems like it. In another lifetime, in a land far, far away. So how have you been over the last fifty or sixty years?"

"Oh, you know, about the same. Same house, same phone number, same hair style, same wardrobe, same old sneakers," he joked.

"Same old Jack," Kim said.

"And you?" Jack asked.

"I live in Maine where I run a bed and breakfast during the summer months and write children's books during the long winter months."

"No kidding! You're an author, huh? I'm impressed. I'm not surprised, but I am impressed."

Kim scoffed. "Ah, it's just a job. Tell me more about you. Are you married? And if so, is your wife giving you dirty looks because you're talking to some strange woman on the phone?"

"I *was* married, but that's a long story," Jack said.

"Yeah, I've got my own long story. Any kids?"

"Two. Both boys. Johnny is nine, and James is seven. They live in Charlotte, North Carolina with their mother and grandparents. And you?"

"One. His name is Stephen. He's eight years old, and let me tell you, he thinks he's a man of the world. We've been on our own for two years now, so since he was six, he's been the man of the house."

There was a lull in the conversation as each scrambled to think of something to say. It was Jack who spoke first. "I don't suppose you ever talk to anybody from high school, do you?"

"No. In fact, you were the last classmate I was in contact with, and as we've established, that's been fifty or sixty years ago. How about you? I'm sure you run into some of our old school friends from time to time."

"No, not really. I probably wouldn't recognize any of them today anyway. You remember my old Road Runner, don't you?"

"Yes, of course. I was going to ask you if you still had the car."

"Oh yeah, I still have it. It hadn't been run in over ten years, but over the summer I decided to break it out of the moth balls."

"Does it still look the same?"

"Pretty much. I did a full restoration in the late 'eighties and made a couple of minor changes. Then, a couple of years later, I parked the car in the garage and didn't drive it again until just recently."

"Does it still have the Air Grabber hood?"

Jack paused in amazement before answering. "You still remember that hood and what it was called?"

"Of course, I remember! I remember how excited you were when we found it in that junkyard, and I remember borrowing your father's truck to go get it. Once you put it on the car, I thought that

little door that pops open like a scoop was just the coolest thing I'd

ever seen! Tell me you still have the same hood!"

"Oh, don't worry. The yellow bird still has the same hood."

At once Jack's mind froze and he could think of nothing more to say.

His stomach was tingling and his palms and armpits were drenched

with nervous perspiration. Beads of sweat had formed on his

forehead, and he wiped them away with the back of his wrist. The

telephone had fallen silent.

This time it was Kim who spoke first. "This is terrible," she

stated. "Here we are, two grown adults, and we're acting like young

teenagers. I wasn't this nervous the day we met!"

"Nervous? Speak for yourself. I'm not nervous," Jack joked

in as calm a tone as he could muster.

"Oh, bullshit, Jack!" Kim laughed. "I can hear a quiver in

your voice every time you speak. Don't tell me you're not nervous."

"Okay. Guilty as charged," Jack laughed.

When their laughter faded Kim spoke again. "Jack, I called

to thank you for the flowers you sent. You really didn't have to do

that, but my mother and I really appreciate it. Thinking of you gave us both something to smile about in the midst of this rough time.

I'm sure you know Mom and Dad both thought an awful lot of you."

"Hey, I always thought an awful lot of them, too. It was really a shock to read about your father in the paper. But as long as it has been, I didn't know whether to send the flowers or not. I didn't know if it would be the right thing to do. But I wanted you and your mother to know that my heart went out to you."

"Well, I'm glad you sent them. It meant a lot coming from an old friend. Speaking of my mother, I'm sure she would love to see you. So would I, for that matter. Do you think we could get together over a cup of coffee sometime soon?"

"Absolutely!" Jack said, unable to contain his excitement. "Uh, I mean, sure. I suppose that would be okay."

Kim laughed. "Try to control yourself!"

Jack chuckled. "Are you going to be in town for a while?"

"Probably for a week or two. I don't want Stephen to miss too much school. Mom is handling this whole thing pretty well, but I want to be sure she will be okay before we head back to Maine."

"How about sometime Saturday afternoon?" Jack asked.

"That sounds fine. What time?"

"I'll pick you up around two o'clock. Would that be okay?"

"Sure!" Kim said. "Under one condition."

"What's that?"

"You have to pick me up in the Road Runner."

"Lady, you drive a hard bargain, but you've got a deal!"

After they said their good-byes Jack noticed that his cheeks ached. He realized he had been grinning the entire time he had spoken with Kim.

The next day, Friday, dragged by. Jack was exhausted, for in his excitement he had hardly slept the night before. Still, his exuberance shone through the grogginess, and he wore a dreamy smile for much of the day.

He reminded himself repeatedly that he and Kim were only going to go out for a cup of coffee. This was to be a reunion of friends, not a date. What they once shared had been left in the past. Many years had gone by, and they had both grown and changed. Besides, their homes were two thousand miles apart. Even if there was a remote possibility that they would want to date, it was geographically impossible. Although Jack kept telling himself these things, he was on an unshakable high.

When Jack arrived at home that evening he dialed Marsha's number. "Hello," Ralph answered.

"Hi, Ralph. It's Jack. How are you doing tonight?"

"Oh, hi Jack. Marsha said something about you might start calling some for the boys. Better late than never, I suppose. All I ask is that you do it regular. Don't call once or twice, then stop. That's hard on them. Gets their heads all mixed up. If you're going to call, then call once or twice a week. If you're not going to call, then don't call. Do you understand what I'm saying?"

"Yes, Ralph, I understand. I don't know if Marsha told you anything about our conversation, but..."

Ralph cut him short. "You don't have to make excuses or explain anything to me. I'm just tellin' you the way it's got to be. Understand?"

"Yes, Ralph, I understand." Jack had learned it was useless to try to talk to Ralph when he wasn't in a listening mood.

"Fine. I'll get the boys."

James was the first to come to the phone. "Hi, Dad."

"Hi, James. How are you doing tonight?"

"I'm not doing too good. Mom won't let me watch TV She

made me go to my room."

"Well, why did she do that?"

"It was Johnny's fault," James whispered. "He kept pushing me and making me mad, and so I called him a dick. Grandpop heard me, and then he told Mom, and then I got in trouble."

Jack covered the phone with his palm as he burst into laughter. Moments later he said, "Well, James, you know that words like that shouldn't be used. I'm not saying that Johnny was right for picking on you, but you can't go calling him names like that."

"But, Dad, he was making me real mad. I told him to stop, but he wouldn't do it. He just kept on pushing me and poking me and calling me a retard. I got so mad, it just slipped out. I didn't mean to say it. I should still be able to watch TV"

"James, I think your mom might have had a good reason to send you to your room. See, we are responsible for what we say. Now sometimes we might slip and say things that we shouldn't, but we are responsible for those things, too. Maybe you didn't mean to call Johnny that word, but you did. I think your mom sent you to your room to give you some time to think. Hopefully, next time you can remember to think about what you are going to say before you say it."

"I still hate him," James said.

"Hold on a minute," Jack said. "Hate is a pretty strong word."

"I know, and I hate his slimy guts."

Jack sighed. "Is your brother there?"

"Yes," James said. He did not move.

"Well can you go get him?" Jack prodded after several moments.

"Sure. Dad, are you going to call us again?" James asked.

"Yes, I will call again."

"Soon?"

"Yes, I will call again soon. How about one night next week?"

"Yeah! That's good! I'll go get Johnny now. Bye, Dad!" Surprised by the excitement in James' voice, Jack grinned.

Johnny came to the phone moments later. "Hullo."

"Johnny, it's Dad. How are you doing tonight?"

"I'm okay."

"What's new? How did school go this week?"

"Fine".

"Your grandfather tells me that you and James are taking karate lessons. He says you both seem to like it. That's great."

"Yeah, it's okay."

Jack had considered mentioning the incident that had taken place between Johnny and James earlier but decided against it. Their sibling rivalry had often infuriated him when the boys were younger and he was drunk. He had usually responded with punishments, ones which in retrospect seemed too harsh. But now it was not his place to referee from afar the spats between brothers.

"Do you have any plans to do anything fun with your buddies this weekend?" Jack was quickly exhausting his ideas of topics for discussion.

"No." The telephone line fell silent as neither Jack nor Johnny spoke.

"What do you want to talk about?" Jack asked.

"Nothing. I'm not in the mood to talk."

"I see. Well, I told James that I would call back one night next week. If you think of anything you want to say or anything you want to talk about, we'll talk then. Okay?"

"Yeah, I guess so."

After Jack and Johnny exchanged good-byes, Jack hung up the phone. He glanced at the clock. It was now six-ten. He had just enough time to microwave a slab of frozen pizza and to shower before his meeting.

Chapter Seven

Jack's shed arrived at nine-fifteen the next morning. Once the two delivery men unloaded it from the flatbed truck, Jack took a couple of two-by-ten planks from the garage to use as ramps. He eased the Road Runner into its new home, satisfied by how well it fit. The interior of the shed smelled of fresh pine, reminding him of Christmas trees. All the while he thought of Kim.

Later, as Jack showered, a numb feeling spread through his gut. Soon it was accompanied by a dull ache. It was as if his stomach was a kettle filled with popcorn kernels that had just grown hot enough to initialize their staccato explosions. *It's not a date. We're just two old friends getting together to talk,* he told himself. But as he drove his Road Runner toward the Hurley residence to pick Kim up for the first time in more than twenty years, he realized that nothing could have felt more right.

When the Hurley house came into view Jack slowed, then guided the Road Runner toward the curb into the same space it had occupied regularly years earlier. In the driveway sat a blue Ford Crown Victoria. Behind it was a green Dodge Caravan. As he walked past the Caravan, he sensed that there was something familiar about it, but he dismissed this thought. There were thousands on the road just like it.

When Jack reached the front door, he rapped on it five times. A moment later he heard rustling as somebody approached the door, then it swung open. "I thought I recognized that knock," a spry Mrs. Hurley said as she eyed Jack from head to foot. Her silvery gray hair glistened in the sunlight, and Jack was quick to notice that her thin five-foot-four-inch frame had retained its shape remarkably well for a woman of her age. "Jack Kramer, you come inside and give me a hug right this instant!" Jack grinned as he stepped into the foyer and hugged Kim's mother.

As Jack released his embrace, he glanced down the hallway and spied a young boy peering around the corner at him. Jack was sure he had seen the boy before but could not recall where. He figured that he had to be Stephen, Kim's son, but where could he have seen him before this moment? Slowly the boy made his way down the hallway, his bespectacled eyes open wide.

Mrs. Hurley leaned into the doorway and looked toward the road. "Oh my! Kim told me that you still had that car. Boy, seeing it parked there sure brings back memories! The boy brushed past Jack as he went to his grandmother's side and peered outside. He turned to face Jack once more, his eyes still wide. "You're the guy with the Road Runner!" he said in disbelief.

Jack realized this was the boy he'd met at the Sinclair station a week earlier. "Yeah, that's me. I'm the guy with the Road Runner," he said with a smile.

"Wait a minute," Mrs. Hurley said. She faced her grandson while pointing at Jack. "You mean this is the guy with the Road Runner you've been chattering about since you got here?"

"Yes, Grandmom, that's him."

Mrs. Hurley now turned toward Jack. Her face bore a puzzled expression.

"Last Saturday I pulled into the Sinclair station to gas up the car," Jack said. "As luck would have it, across the island from me was a green minivan with a friendly young man who took an interest in my car." He nodded toward the boy. "We talked while I pumped my gas. I had no idea we would run into each other again. Small world, huh?"

"I'll say!" Mrs. Hurley turned toward her grandson once

more. "Stephen, why don't you go tell your mom that Mr. Kramer is here?"

"Mom, guess what? The guy with the Road Runner is here, and he knows Grandmom!" Stephen shouted as he ran toward Kim's room.

After Stephen left, Jack spoke to Mrs. Hurley. "I was terribly sorry to read about Mr. Hurley. I know it's been a long time since I've seen either of you, but it still came as a shock. You might not believe this, but I still thought of the two of you often."

"Jack, I don't doubt that you did. You were quite a fine young man, and you always treated Kim well. Mr. Hurley and I still talked about you from time to time. It's so hard to believe that it has been over twenty years."

"Yes, it's hard to believe so much time has passed." Jack was quickly running out of things to say. "Well, I just wanted you to know how sorry I am about Mr. Hurley."

Mrs. Hurley smiled and patted Jack's hand. "Thank you. That means an awful lot."

Jack turned to face the sound of soft footsteps coming down the hallway. Kim's eyes locked on his as she approached. She wore lightly faded jeans which clung to her hips. Her gray sweater caressed the copious curves of her upper body, conforming to her figure. The soft, smooth skin of her cheeks belied her age, and even at forty her face had not lost the simple beauty of a pretty tomboy. Her straight blonde hair swished about her shoulders with each step and she gave Jack a coy smile as she moved toward him.

Oh my God, she's still gorgeous! Jack strained to take in all of her beauty at once and dampness accumulated along the lower rims of his eyes, threatening to spill down his cheeks. *Oh, this is just great! I feel like I'm going to melt into a big puddle of piss right here where I stand!*

"Jack Kramer, it seems like only yesterday that you stood in that very spot waiting for me while I got ready." She raised her arms, encircled Jack's neck, and placed her head on his shoulder as she squeezed him. Jack welcomed her with open arms; he held her with his palms clasped tightly against her back. His head began to spin. He thought of the airport where they had last embraced in nineteen seventy-nine before Kim caught the plane bound for Philadelphia. Her body felt just as good against him now as it had then.

Moments later as they stepped back from each other Jack felt a tear trickle down his cheek. *Damn! I feel like a fool!* He scratched his nose, then flicked away the tear with his thumb, hoping Kim wouldn't notice.

It was then that Kim began to wipe away the tears that streamed down her cheeks. "I'm sorry," she said. "I feel like a fool."

At that moment Stephen appeared. "Mommy, are you all right?"

"Yes, I'm fine. Stephen, I want you to meet a friend of mine. His name is Mr. Kramer."

Jack bent down to shake Stephen's hand. "Pleased to meet you," he said.

"Mr. Kramer and I were friends when we were in high school," Kim said.

"That was a long, long, looong time ago, wasn't it, Mom?" Stephen asked with a devilish gleam in his eye.

"Yes, Stephen, that was a really long time ago. Not quite as far back as the dinosaurs, but shortly after they became extinct." Kim looked toward Jack and rolled her eyes. Stephen giggled.

Mrs. Hurley stepped toward Stephen and took his hand. "Stephen, you come along with me. I'm sure I can find something for you to do." She then turned toward Jack and Kim. "You two kids go and have a good time. Jack, please have my daughter home early. And no excuses!"

"Yes, Mrs. Hurley," he grinned.

As Jack and Kim walked toward the car Jack could hardly contain his excitement. He opened the door for Kim, closed it once she was seated, then bounded around the front of the car to his door. He took his seat, only to discover that he had forgotten to remove his keys from his pocket first. He stood and dug for his keys, then resumed his position behind the wheel. He fumbled with the keys, then dropped them on the floor.

"A little nervous, are we?" Kim teased.

"No, no. Not at all. Why?" Jack's words were jerky. They both began to laugh. Jack retrieved his keys from the floor, then inserted the ignition key and started the engine.

"Wow!" Kim said as she looked about the interior of the car. "This car is a time machine. Suddenly it feels like the old days are back!"

"I know what you mean," Jack said as he pressed the clutch pedal and slipped the tall Pistol Grip shifter into first gear. He revved the engine slightly as he eased out the clutch and pulled away from the curb. Accelerating a little harder than usual through first gear, from the corner of his eye, he could see Kim smiling in approval as her body was pressed into the seat.

"Jeez, I remember all those nights we used to hang out at El's. We'd talk and BS for a while, then go cruise around or pick a drag race. Is this car still as fast as it used to be?" Kim asked, needling Jack for a demonstration of the Road Runner's performance ability.

Jack knew exactly what she was driving at. In fact, he'd anticipated it. "I can't show you anything here in town, but maybe we can go a little way outside of town and I can take you for a white-knuckle hell ride."

"Well, you used to think nothing of doing burn-outs in town," Kim taunted playfully.

"Yeah, but that was a long time ago. Things were different then. I was just a teenage punk with a healthy disregard for traffic laws," Jack said. Kim laughed. "So, where are we going?" Jack asked, changing the subject.

"I don't know. I'm not from around here."

"Oh. I just assumed that when you suggested going for a cup of coffee you probably had a place in mind."

"No, not really. I don't know any of the places around here anymore. Besides, I only mentioned going for coffee as a way to break the ice after twenty-two years." Kim thought for a moment before needling Jack once more. "Wait a minute. We're in your car, which means that *you* are taking *me* out. Didn't you plan your details ahead of time? What kind of gentleman are you, anyway?"

"Hey, I opened your door for you, didn't I? And because I am truly a gentleman, I am willing to take you to the coffee shop of your choice. How is it my fault that you can't decide where you want to go for coffee?" Jack shot back with a grin. Although he and Kim had met for the first time in over two decades only minutes earlier, already they were cracking on each other just like old times. As a teenager Jack had connected with Kim in a way that he had never connected with anybody else. Despite the years that had passed, he could feel that their special connection was still intact. From the corner of his eye, he gazed at Kim. *You don't know how*

I've missed you, he thought.

"Well, there must be some place where you go for coffee and a bite to eat," Kim said.

"Yes, you are correct. I frequent many of the convenience stores in the area," Jack said sarcastically. "But when I am in the mood to pamper myself, I eat at the truck stop.

"Great! Let's go!"

"To the truck stop?"

"Yes, to the truck stop".

"Well, okay."

"What are you saying, that the truck stop is good enough for you, but you don't think it's good enough for me? Jack Kramer, I ought to smack you in the head!"

"Fine, fine. The truck stop it is," Jack said in pretend submission. "Good God, woman! You don't have to threaten me with violence!"

Their conversation remained light as they drove to the truck stop. Jack pointed out such landmarks as the former locations of a movie theater and a department store, and Kim remarked several times that she couldn't believe how much the streets had changed and how the traffic volume had grown.

When they reached the truck stop, Jack parked in a remote spot well out of the path of the tractor trailers. He and Kim walked across the parking lot side by side, and when they reached the building, Jack took a step ahead to open the door for her. As they stepped inside, Kim remarked, "This is a nice place." Jack quickly turned to see if she was smirking in sarcasm, but she was not. "It's got a cozy, nineteen fifties hometown diner kind of feel to it," she continued. Jack nodded in agreement. He was aware that a number of unfamiliar eyes were following Kim's every move as they made their way to a booth. Kim was either unaware or gracefully pretending not to notice.

Moments later a short, stocky waitress of about fifty approached. She pulled an order pad from her apron pocket and slid a pen from behind her right ear through her graying curls. "Hi. My name is Carol, and I will be your server. What can I get you folks?"

Jack motioned for Kim to order first. "Just coffee for me," she said.

Carol turned toward Jack. "Coffee for me, too," he said, then turned to Kim. "They've got donuts and outstanding pies. Do you want to try some?"

"Oh, no thanks. Maybe some other time," she said.

"So we've got two coffees. I'll be right back," Carol smiled.

"Jack, before I forget, I want to say thanks," Kim said.

"For what?"

"For helping to break my somber mood after my dad passed away. When I talked to you the other night, it was the first time I'd laughed in days."

"Hey, I know it's tough. I lost my father several years ago," Jack said.

"My poor mom, that woman is amazing. She is handling my father's passing well, but I can't imagine how hard it must be for her. When she saw you'd sent flowers, she really leaned on me to call you."

"Well, good for her!" Jack said. "I'm glad you called. It has been way too long."

"Well, actually, I was kind of afraid to call," Kim said. "I mean, it has been a really long time, and I have always felt bad for the way I let us drift apart. It was my fault. I figured you were probably mad at me, and you had every right to be. But I promised my mom I would call you. I tried several times that night, but I kept

getting your stupid answering machine. Then the line was busy.

And then I finally got through to you."

"How did you know I still live in the same place?"

"That part was easy. You're in the phone book."

"Oh. So you never drove past my house?" Jack asked with a

sly grin.

Kim blushed. "Shit! I was afraid you would bust me on that

one! Now you probably think I've been stalking you or something."

"Have you?" Jack asked, enjoying the upper hand for the

moment.

"Ahh, look," Kim began, "that morning I wanted to go for a

ride and spend some time alone. Between trying to come to terms

with my father's death and suddenly finding myself back in this

town, I needed to do some thinking. I felt the need to get back to my

roots, so I went for a ride to see some familiar sights and do some

soul searching. Of course, your house was on the list of places I

wanted to see. I slowed down to take a look, then nearly died when

you came out the front door and looked right at me. I didn't know

what to do. I panicked, and so I drove off." She looked at Jack as he struggled to suppress his laughter. "Oh, why am I bothering to telling you this? Fine! I'm a stalker!" Jack could no longer hold back his laughter. "You aren't going to let me forget this, are you?" Kim asked.

"Hell, no! But I've got to say I'm flattered that you traveled all the way from Maine to stalk me." Kim wadded her napkin into a ball and threw it at Jack. Then she, too, began to laugh, the redness in her face deepening.

Carol returned to their table. "Two coffees. I also brought you some ice water. Can I get you folks anything else?"

"No, this should do it for now, thanks," Jack said. Kim watched Jack's movements and studied his face as he poured sugar from the glass container onto a teaspoon, then dumped it into his coffee. He followed the sugar with cream from a tiny stainless-steel pitcher, then stirred it with his spoon. He glanced at Kim, who was still staring at him. She hadn't yet touched her coffee. "What?" he asked.

"Nothing," she smiled. "I'm just watching." Jack's eyes locked on hers. He leaned forward slightly, gliding his outstretched hands across the table. Kim's fingers met his and interlocked with them. With the meeting of their hands, it was as if a circuit had been connected and current now flowed. They sat speechless, smiling and staring into each other's eyes as their bodies tingled with electricity.

Jack's mind began to whirl in a fury of emotion which had been locked away since nineteen seventy-nine. Although he knew his body was sitting still, in his mind there was the dizzy sensation that he was doing somersaults. From somewhere a distant voice called to him. *Take it easy! You're running blindly into a dark forest without so much as a compass. This was supposed to be a reacquaintance of old friends, remember? Go one small step at a time and be careful. You've waited too long for this moment to fuck it up by being hasty and presumptuous.* But that was just it; twenty-two years was a long time to wait for anything. Twenty-two years' worth of anticipation had led to this moment. Holding back would surely spoil it. So caution be damned, Jack let the flood of feelings gush through his head. "This has got to be a dream," he heard himself say.

"No, this feeling is too good to be a dream," Kim said. After a few more minutes she pulled her hands back. "We've got a lot of catching up to do."

"I know," Jack said. "Tell me, what do you remember?"

"What do I remember? Let's see. I remember that Jack Kramer was a genuine, warm, caring guy with a great sense of humor. He had a great smile, he loved apple cobbler a la mode, and he was absolutely nuts about Christmas. Generally, Jack was a happy person. He was usually the quiet, friendly type who didn't go around with a chip on his shoulder feeling like he had to prove something to the world. He was very intelligent but didn't flaunt it. Jack was one of the few people in this world who could truly be counted on. If he was your friend, he was a true friend. How am I doing so far?"

"Keep going!" Jack said. "You're on a roll. Pretty soon my head won't be able to fit through the door, but I like it! Please continue."

Kim laughed. "Okay, smartass, what do you remember about me?"

For more than two decades Jack had reflected on the happy times he and Kim had shared. But now that he was being called upon to share these memories with her, his mind moved at half speed. "Well, on the day we met, when you came into the gas station, I remember thinking that you were the prettiest girl I'd ever seen."

"Oh, bullshit!" Kim said.

Jack faked a hurt expression. "You doubt my sincerity? I'm crushed!"

"All right, go on," Kim said.

"Okay. Like I said, you were the prettiest girl I'd ever seen. I thought that then, and I still think that now." Suddenly his mind kicked into gear and thoughts began tumbling from his mouth. "But let's see, I remember that the insides of your elbows were your most ticklish spots and that your favorite ice cream flavor was mint chocolate chip. I remember the cute little kink you got in your eyebrow when you were concentrating on your drawings. I remember the ornery look you got in your eyes whenever you set somebody up for a joke, and I remember the way you wiggled when you walked. I remember that you liked animals, the outdoors, and baiting your own fishing hook. But what I remember the most is the way you felt in my arms. I probably shouldn't say this, but I also remember the empty hole that was left in my heart the night you left for Philadelphia, and the way it grew when you didn't come back."

"Oh, Jack," Kim said as she tilted her head. She stroked the back of his hand with her finger tips. "I'm so sorry for that. I never wanted that to happen. If there was one thing about my life that I could go back and change, that would be it."

"Kim, look, I shouldn't have said that. I--"

"No, no. Please, I've felt bad about this for a long time. I owe you an explanation. But unfortunately, looking back on it, I don't have a good one. You see, once I got to Philadelphia I was overwhelmed. There I was hundreds and hundreds of miles from home in a strange city, and for the first time in my life I was alone. Really alone. It was scary. Having to get used to life in the city was bad enough, but I was out of my element in more ways than one. Up to that point I had done cartoons for the school paper and for the local newspaper, but this was the big time, man! Yet, I was there on a scholarship! Me of all people! I was just an ordinary girl from somewhere out west. Jack, I felt like a fraud!

"Since I was sure I had come up short on talent, I told myself I would have to work extra hard to make up for it. So, I threw myself into my school work, and in the process I blocked out everything else. I stayed and worked straight through Thanksgiving, hardly noticing it as it came and went. The same thing happened at Christmas, but by then I was starting to feel that with all my extra work, at least I could compete with those who were more gifted. I know now that I was suffering from an inferiority complex, but at the time I was convinced I had all the reasons in the world to feel inferior.

"By springtime I was starting to feel better about things. I was proving to myself I could do it, and I realized that perhaps I was a little bit more talented than I'd thought. In April that year I was approached by the *Philadelphia Daily News* and offered a position as a cartoonist. Lucky breaks come along only once in a great while, so I had to jump on it. I stayed in Philadelphia through the summer and worked for the paper, then resumed my school work in the fall while keeping my job at the *Daily News*.

"Early on I told myself that if you and I were going to learn to survive without being able to see each other, we would have to make a break. It was kind of like giving up smoking and stopping cold turkey. I knew that if we were going to get through this, we couldn't be crying to each other on the phone every night. As much as I missed you, talking to you frequently would have made it that much worse for both of us.

"So, I tried to put you out of my mind. I buried myself in my work, but somewhere along the way I remember thinking that an awful lot of time had passed since I'd called you. I told myself that you had probably given up on me and moved on. I was heartsick. It was then that I realized how selfish I had been. I wanted to call you, but what could I say?

"I continued to push myself, and after a while some things started happening. I was approached by a local women's shelter to do a couple of drawings that would be made into posters depicting family violence. One of these drawings was later used for a billboard. When that happened, it seemed like the world opened up to me. By the time I graduated from art school I was a freelance artist with about as much work as I could handle.

"I dated once in a while, but not seriously. In nineteen eighty-eight I met a guy named Randy who seemed different. He reminded me a lot of you. We were married in nineteen ninety, and things were good. He worked with computers, and the nineties were a volatile time for that industry. As one company went bankrupt or was gobbled up by another, he had to change jobs frequently. He also did a lot of traveling. That was tough, but we managed. In nineteen ninety-three Stephen was born.

"One day I got a call from Stardom Books. They were looking for an illustrator to work with a handful of children's book authors. The pay wasn't bad, and as long as Randy was willing to come home from work and play Mr. Mom for a few hours I was able to keep doing my freelance work. This worked out well for a while, but as Randy moved up in his field, he started doing more and more traveling, which really put a strain on our marriage.

"In nineteen ninety-six we got a surprise that changed all of this. Randy's family is from Maine, and when his grandfather died, he left us his home. It is a large two-story house just on the outskirts of Bar Harbor. At the time the house was built Bar Harbor was a tiny fishing town. Nowadays it is a tourist attraction. Visitors can take a walk along the water, see lighthouses, or visit Acadia National Park, which is just a few miles away. It was Randy's idea to remodel his grandfather's house and convert it into a bed and breakfast.

"We sold our house near Philadelphia and by the spring of nineteen ninety-seven we were open for business. I was still working for Stardom, but at this point I started to cut back on the freelance work. The summer flew by, and it was the first one we had enjoyed in years. But soon September rolled around, and things slowed down. Within a few more weeks tourist season was over, and soon after that it started to snow. Randy didn't know what to do with himself. He was bored and easily agitated. He stayed grumpy until the following spring.

Tourist season, 'ninety-eight was even busier than the year before. Randy was glad to have something to do, but there was something different about him. He seemed distant. Outwardly he smiled, but through his eyes I knew that deep down he was discontent.

"Soon I could see that we were growing apart. Late in the summer of ninety-nine Randy suddenly left to go visit his parents in Philadelphia. It was weird that he did it on the spur of the moment, but by that time Randy was doing lots of weird things. He phoned a few days later to say that he wouldn't be home for a while, that he'd accepted a job with a computer firm. I should have been upset. Actually, I was relieved. It occurred to me one day that Randy's order of values was different from mine. I always did my best to

juggle my work around family life, but it turned out that Randy
needed his career more than a family. I don't mean to sound bitter;
that's just the way it was.

"Since we separated, I have concentrated on raising Stephen
and running the business by myself. I don't do freelance work per se
anymore, and I am no longer an illustrator for Stardom. Instead, I
am considered an author/illustrator, for I write my own children's
books as well as draw the illustrations."

"Wow!" Jack said. "You've been through some rough times,
but all things considered, you've done well for yourself. Does
Randy keep in touch with Stephen?"

"Well, he calls once in a while, but only when it's convenient
for him. Stephen goes to see him for a week during the summer, but
he spends most of that week with Randy's folks. I know that
Randy's busy and he's back to traveling a lot, but he could do a lot
more than he does."

Jack felt a pang of guilt as he thought of his sons. Just then
Carol appeared and topped off their coffee mugs.

"So, tell me about yourself. How have the last twenty-two
years been for you?" Kim asked.

Jack told Kim of his high points and low points over the last twenty-two years. He told of the passing of his father, the restoration of the Road Runner and its subsequent ten-year hibernation, his marriage to Marsha, and the births of his sons. He also told of his escalating drinking problem, and how it eventually drove his family away. "Marsha convinced me to park the Road Runner in 'ninety or 'ninety-one. By then the car was seeing limited use anyway, and she claimed we couldn't afford to insure it and our everyday cars. But the real reason was that she was afraid I'd get half tanked, and with four hundred horsepower under my right foot I'd end up getting myself killed. She was probably right. Even back then she knew I had a problem.

"Since the time of my 'awakening' I have worked to stay sober. There are still rough spots in the road from time to time, but I haven't had a drink in almost a year now. Bit by bit I'm working to get my life on track. The Road Runner is now back on the road after its long hiatus, and I just bought a 'sixty-eight Dodge Dart to mess around with as I have time.

"Hey, are you hungry yet?" Jack asked suddenly.

"Why, are we going to sit here until I am?" Kim fired back

with a grin.

"That depends on how long it takes you to get hungry. I think I'm ready for some pie. Do you want some?"

Carol overheard Jack and rushed to take their order. "What can I get you?

"I'll have a slice of apple pie with a scoop of vanilla ice cream," Jack said. He turned to Kim. "The coconut custard is fantastic, too!"

"Okay, I'll have a slice of coconut custard, no ice cream," Kim said.

Carol scribbled the order on her pad, then topped off their coffee mugs once more. "Be right up."

Jack and Kim made light talk while they waited for their pie. The dreamy look was back in Kim's eyes, and Jack felt the electric charge return to the air. As he locked his fingers into Kim's he felt his heart thumping so solidly in his chest that he thought it might crack a rib. They talked about nothing in particular as they gazed out the windows, only mildly interested in the large trucks that rumbled into and out of the truck stop. Together they basked in a closeness that neither had experienced since nineteen seventy-nine.

A few minutes later Carol returned with two generous slices of pie. "Here you go," she said as she placed them on the table. She slid the check under Jack's plate and said, "I'll take that when you're ready."

Kim took a bite of her pie. "Mmmmm!"

"See? I told you it was good. You won't find pie like that anywhere around here. That's because the cook is also the guy who pumps the diesel fuel into the trucks. Since he's constantly running back and forth between the kitchen and the fuel pumps, he doesn't always have time to wash his hands. The diesel fuel residue from his hands gets into the food and gives it a unique flavor. Tasty, huh?"

Kim stuck out her tongue at Jack. They talked about nothing in particular as they ate their pie. Afterward, Jack paid the bill and left a hefty tip. "Have you had your meeting yet today?" Kim asked.

"No, not yet. It isn't until seven."

"Good. We've still got some time," she said. They walked toward the door hand in hand. When they got to the car, Jack opened Kim's door for her. "So, where are we off to now?" she asked.

"I don't know. What did you have in mind?"

"Don't you have anything in mind? I thought we went through this already. You're taking me out, remember?"

"Well, I would suggest that we could cruise around and see some of the old places that aren't there anymore, but you say that you've already done that," Jack said sarcastically.

"Cruising is fine. I'd like to ride around for a while in this car and reminisce."

They spent the remainder of the afternoon driving around Colorado Springs. At one point it occurred to Jack that Kim would be leaving in just a few days to return to her life in Maine. Immediately he felt his heart sink. *Put that thought out of your head,* he told himself. *You've waited too long for this day to spoil it now.* Indeed, he had. His reunion with Kim was going better than he had ever imagined, and that was all the more reason not to ruin the mood with this thought. What would be would be. Jack cast a glance in Kim's direction. A happy, contented smile graced her lips. Jack could feel himself falling in love with Kim all over again. But then, he had never stopped loving her.

As the sun sank low and the shadows grew long, Jack guided the Road Runner toward Mrs. Hurley's house. The sun fell from sight in the west and the lower edge of the sky in the east took on an intense shade of blue. Like a blanket slowly being pulled over a glass dome, this brilliant blue hue crept across the sky. Their conversation trailed off to a comfortable silence, and Kim slid closer to Jack. He raised his right arm and placed it on the back of the bench seat, his fingers at her right shoulder. As they drove, the vivid blue sky gradually faded to a deep shade of sapphire. Stars began to pierce the darkening backdrop.

"I forgot how beautiful it is out here," Kim said. "The scenery is awesome! When you live here, you take it for granted, but once you leave for a while you can appreciate it again. This sky is just magnificent!"

By the time Jack and Kim arrived in front of Kim's mother's house the sky had turned cobalt blue and teemed with stars. To the east it was nearly black, and the moon hung suspended in the twilight just above the horizon. Slowly they walked toward the house, stopping half way.

"This day has been incredible," Kim said.

"I couldn't agree more".

A sudden motion in the sky caught their attention. A

glimmering star burst and soared to the right leaving a small tail behind it. Then it was gone. "Whoa, did you see that?" Jack asked.

"Yeah! Don't forget to make a wish," Kim said.

"I already did." Jack turned to face Kim. Gently his hands fell to her waist and he pulled her close. Kim raised her arms and placed them around Jack's neck. Kim's lips were warm, soft and luscious against Jack's. His head began to spin with the sensation that he was in weightless freefall, tumbling and spiraling downward. His heart beat furiously within his chest. When their lips parted, Kim turned her head and placed it against Jack's shoulder. Jack rested his cheek against the back of her head.

"That was nice," Kim said.

"I'll say!" Time lost its meaning as they stood in the moonlight, their bodies pressed together, swaying gently in the darkness. Jack's narrowly open eyes slowly drifted about the yard when he noticed the silhouette in the window. He raised his head slightly for a better look, but the figure vanished.

"What's the matter?" Kim asked.

"I think somebody was spying on us."

Kim laughed. "Was it a big spy or a little spy?"

"It was a little spy."

"I'm sure he's reporting to the big spy now," Kim said. "I should probably get inside and do a little explaining."

Jack had nearly forgotten about his meeting. He glanced at his watch. "Yeah, I need to get going." He took Kim's hand. "Kim, thanks. I had a great time today."

"Me, too! Call me tomorrow." After one more kiss she bounded toward her mother's front door. She smiled and waved, then disappeared into the house.

Chapter Eight

Jack couldn't keep his mind on the meeting. While other group members talked, he reflected on the afternoon he had spent with Kim. More than once he snapped to attention, only to realize that a silly smile was plastered across his face. After the meeting Donald cornered him. "You aren't yourself tonight. Is there anything you need to talk about?" Jack told him about the afternoon. "Be careful, buddy," Donald cautioned. "Be very careful."

Jack hardly slept that night. His blissful insomnia was fueled by exciting thoughts of Kim. *Easy, Jack. Don't get your hopes up. Remember, she's going back to Maine in a few days. You're setting yourself up for a bad fall. The higher you let yourself get, the harder you'll land a week from now,* the pessimist in the back of his mind warned. "Fuck you," Jack responded. Although he knew he might be in for a terrible heartache, he refused to let the fear of getting hurt stand in the way of his feelings now.

At five the next morning he finally gave up on trying to sleep. He rose from his bed, donned a dirty work uniform, and went to the garage. The chilly air sucked his body heat like a swarm of blood thirsty mosquitoes. He checked the kerosene level in his portable torpedo-shaped heater, plugged it in, then set the thermostat to sixty degrees. The heater hummed briefly, then popped and belched a pungent cloud of atomized fuel as it roared to life. He went to the kitchen, set the coffee maker to brew a pot of coffee and retreated to the bathroom.

As he relaxed on the bowl, his mind buzzed in a sleepy, content state. The thought struck him that if somebody would invent a reclining toilet with a headrest, people would spend hours at a time slouched upon it. Add a television and a small refrigerator within arm's reach, most men would never want to leave the bathroom. In amusement Jack envisioned a large room furnished around such a contraption. When fully reclined this new device took on the shape of a dentist's chair. Straight ahead was a thirty-six-inch television screen mounted into the wall. To the left stood a three-foot-high porcelain tank (It takes a hell of a lot of water to flush this baby!) and to the right sat a squatty refrigerator with dimensions similar to the water tank. Neatly stacked atop the refrigerator was a selection of men's magazines and the remote control for the television. Screwed to its side was a toilet paper holder, complete with a virgin roll. He chuckled at the thought of his mind's creation.

Then, from nowhere another thought struck him. He didn't have Kim's mother's telephone number. "I hope it's in the phone book," he said as he finished his business. He rushed to the kitchen and flipped through the thin pages of the telephone directory. His eyes locked on Robert Hurley's listing. Having not called that number in so many years, it had fallen from memory, but as soon as he read the seven-digit sequence it was once more etched into his brain.

Later that morning Jack dialed the number.

"Hello," Mrs. Hurley answered.

"Mrs. Hurley? Good morning. It's Jack. Is Kim there?"

"Good morning to you, too. Hold on while I get her."

Jack sipped his coffee while he held the phone.

"Hello," Kim's cheery voice greeted.

"Hello. How are you this morning?"

"Tired. We went to bed late last night and I had a hard time falling asleep. Even after I did finally get to sleep, I kept waking up. How about you?"

Jack laughed. "Same here. I've been out in the garage

working for the last couple of hours."

"On what? Not the Road Runner, I hope."

"No, I'm working on the Dart I told you about. I'm about an hour away from having the motor out of the car, and I've got the spare motor torn down completely."

"You're not wasting any time, are you?"

"Hey, you know how it is. I'm on a really tight schedule with this hobby," Jack quipped. Kim laughed. "So, what do you have going on today?" he asked.

"I promised Mom that I'd go shopping with her in just a bit, but we should be back by early afternoon. Would you like to come over for a while?"

"Ask him to stay for supper," Jack heard Kim's mother shout.

"Sure!" Jack said. "Say around two or three?"

"Yeah, around two or three will be fine. There is something I need to tell you, but you'll have to wait until then."

"Oh, no," Jack said. "Is it good or bad?"

"It's good. At least I hope you think it's good. But I'm not saying any more. I'll see you sometime around two or three."

"Okay, see you then. Bye," he said.

Later that day when Jack neared the Hurley residence, he saw Kim and Stephen ferrying armloads of grocery bags from the open rear hatch of the Caravan into the house. Jack quickly parked his car and rushed to help.

"Wow! You're strong!" Stephen said as Jack scooped up two full armloads and carried them up the driveway.

"We could have used him at the store, huh?" Kim said to her son as she returned to the van. She turned to Jack. "Hey, there." Jack smiled back as he continued toward the house and, ultimately, the kitchen.

"Oh, hi, Jack!" Mrs. Hurley greeted as he entered the kitchen. She stood atop a chair, stacking canned goods in the top portion of one of the cabinets. "Just put those on the table if you can find room. If not, the floor will do."

The kitchen table was completely filled with grocery bags as were the three remaining chairs. Jack set the bags on the floor next to the table. "You can't possibly eat all of this food yourself. Are you planning to single-handedly end world hunger?" he asked.

Mrs. Hurley laughed. Kim began helping her mother put

away the groceries. "It's been a long time since there was this much food in the house," Mrs. Hurley said. "I don't know where we're going to put it all."

"Stephen, what are you doing?" Kim called.

"I'm watching TV," he answered. "I wish you would hook up my PlayStation!"

Suddenly Kim's face lit up. "Do you know anything about Sony PlayStations?" she asked Jack. "Amazingly, I thought to bring Stephen's along, but neither Mom nor I can figure out how to hook it up to her TV. The poor kid's been going through video withdrawal since we've been here."

"Let me take a look," Jack said. Kim led him to the living room and handed him the PlayStation.

"Are you gonna hook up my PlayStation?" Stephen asked, his eyes bright with hope.

"If I do, are you going to teach me how to play?" Jack asked.

"Yeeaaah! We'll play Hot Shoe!"

"Well, then let me see what I can do." Jack crouched next to the television and made the appropriate connections. "Now what?" he asked Stephen.

"Now I have to put the disk in. The TV has to be set on channel three with the remote." Stephen installed the disk while Jack selected channel three. Instantly, the television began to display a series of warm-up screens. Stephen selected a game, then waited for it to start.

Jack watched as Stephen played the first game. To Jack, the object seemed simple-- blast through the streets of a virtual city in a nondescript gray sedan with a souped up engine and outrun every cop who gave chase. The damage scale in the corner of the screen jumped upward with each collision, and the longer Stephen went, the more aggressive the cops became. After a run of several minutes the damage scale was full and Stephen's car was rendered dead.

"Okay, your turn," Stephen said. He handed Jack the controller, then explained what each of the buttons did.

Soon Jack was navigating the streets in a series of jerky motions. In no time he had collided with enough buildings and parked cars to fill his damage scale, all without ever seeing a cop. "Looks like I need a lot of practice," he said. He handed Stephen the controller, then tousled the boy's hair.

Later, unbeknownst to Jack, Kim and Mrs. Hurley stood in

the wide entrance to the living room watching as Stephen gave him pointers on the game. Mrs. Hurley tapped Kim's elbow and whispered, "Let's get dinner started. We'll leave the men here to bond." Kim nodded, and retreated to the kitchen.

"Looks like they've hit it off already," Mrs. Hurley said once they were out of earshot of the living room.

"Can you believe it?" Kim asked. "Mom, I keep telling myself it's much too soon to get my hopes up, and I keep thinking that this seems too good to be true. But even though Jack and I hadn't seen each other in over twenty years, in a strange way it seems like we were never apart. It's really weird."

"It has been a long time," Mrs. Hurley said, her dark eyes twinkling beneath the ceiling light overhead, "and you have both changed over the last twenty years. There's no escaping that. You've been through some happy times and some rough times, and from what you tell me so has Jack. But when you two were young one of the things I saw in Jack was that he had a good heart, and he thought with his heart.

"That was a long time ago. Over time a man's feelings, likes, and dislikes can change, but a man's heart stays the same, just like the spots on a leopard. If a man was born with no heart, he will

never have a heart. But if he was blessed with a good heart, he will

always have a good heart. In many ways he reminds me of your

father."

"So, you don't think I'm crazy and setting my expectations

way too high?" Kim asked. "I mean, we've only spent one afternoon

together. I *must* be crazy!

"Well, your father and I were married less than three months

after we met. That doesn't sound like a lot of time, and I suppose it

isn't. But for us, the pace just felt right. Like we vowed, your father

and I were married until death did us part." Mrs. Hurley's speech

became difficult as she mentioned the recent passing of her husband.

In an effort to shunt the tears she took a deep breath and continued,

"What I'm saying is to let things go how they will. There is no need

to hurry them along, but there is also no good reason to hold back,

either. Just go with the flow, as you used to say."

Kim smiled at her mother, glassy eyed. "Thanks, Mom."

"Kim, there's one more thing I want to say. Losing your

father is hard on both of us. For me, I know this is just the beginning

of a difficult adjustment period. I have to learn to go on without him. You will go through your own adjustment period. But something occurred to me today while we were shopping. There is a saying that with every door that closes, another one opens. Losing your father is tough, but if that set the stage for you and Jack to get together after all this time, then at least something good will come from our grief. Maybe we can think of it as a final gift from your father."

Kim's mouth fell open as a tear trickled down her cheek. She shook her head. "Mom, you're amazing," she said as she rushed to hug her mother. "There's one more thing I want to ask you. Does Jack's alcoholism bother you? I mean the possibility that he could fall off the wagon?"

"I agree that it's possible. Anything is possible. There are no guarantees in life, but at least he is aware of his problem and he's doing something about it. Speaking of which, we'd better get dinner going if Jack is going to make it to his meeting. I'll get started. You have something to tell Jack, don't you?"

Kim nodded. "I love you, Mom."

"I love you, too."

Kim headed back to the living room. This time she did

nothing to conceal her presence. As Jack fumbled with the buttons on the game controller, his car moved clumsily about the city streets. Within seconds one cop, then a second, arrived and began battering his car until the damage scale rendered it dead. Game over. "From now on when we go out, I'm driving," Kim said.

Jack laughed. "Aw, come on, I'm getting better."

"Mom, it takes lots of practice," Stephen said in Jack's defense.

"Yeah, but if he can't do any better than this with a video game, how can I trust his driving when it's for real? And what about when we're up to our butts in snow? How can I trust his driving then?" Kim asked her son. Stephen grinned, for he knew of his mother's secret and had been instructed to play along.

"I don't know why you're worried about that. You'll be back in Maine before the first snowfall," Jack shot back.

"No, we won't." She said nothing more as she waited for Jack's response.

Her words did not register in Jack's mind for a few seconds. As he handed the game controller to Stephen his head suddenly snapped in her direction. "Huh?"

"You heard me," she grinned. "We're staying here for the winter."

"That's great!" He stood and hugged her. "Is this what you hinted at earlier?"

"Mmm-hmmm," she said.

"This also explains all the food."

"Yup. Mom and I were up late last night talking about things, and we realized that there was no need for Stephen and me to rush back to Maine, other than so he doesn't miss so much school he'd have to repeat the third grade. So, we figured if he was willing to finish the school year here, we'd stay through the winter. We agreed that just being together would make things easier on all of us."

"I knew you were leaving soon, and I've been trying not to think about it. Wow! This is great news!"

"Well, I am going to be leaving on Tuesday to turn in the rental van and fly back to Maine for a couple of days. I've got to go to Stephen's school and get his records and pack up my own van with the things we're going to need. If I leave there Friday morning, I should be back here sometime late Saturday."

"That's a lot of driving for two straight days," Jack said.

"Yeah, I know. But I don't mind. Two days of near solitude will probably do me some good. Maybe I can go over some ideas and start to put together the story for my next kiddie book." Jack didn't respond. Sensing his concern, Kim insisted, "I'll be fine!"

"Mr. Kramer, it's your turn," Stephen said.

"Go take your turn," Kim said with a smile. She kissed her index finger then held it to Jack's lips. "I'm going to go help Mom with dinner."

Jack and Stephen continued playing until Kim called them for dinner. By then Jack still had not mastered many of the tricky moves necessary to escape the law, but by watching Stephen and practicing, he had learned how to powerslide around corners. As with a real car, delicate steering and throttle inputs made all the difference when trying to maintain control of a car that was sliding sideways through a turn.

"Is he getting any better?" Kim asked Stephen as he took his seat at the table.

"He's learning," Stephen said.

"I think there's hope for me," Jack said. He looked down at

the plate of steaming food before him. Succulent fried chicken, a generous helping of creamy mashed potatoes, and a proportionately sized heap of peas adorned his plate. He inhaled deeply through his nose, savoring the aroma of the meal he was about to devour. "This looks and smells terrific," he said, addressing both Mrs. Hurley and Kim.

Mrs. Hurley beamed with pride. "I hope you enjoy it. That chicken is a recipe that's been handed down through several generations of my family."

"I know. I remember," Jack said. "To this day I've never tasted fried chicken anywhere that compares to yours." He picked up a drumstick and took his first bite. "Mmmmm!"

"Oh, you're good!" Kim teased. "But Jack, you don't have to give my mom a snow job about her cooking. I mean, her chicken is okay, and it's nice to pay her a compliment, but come on! You don't have to overdo it."

"Shut up, Kim," Mrs. Hurley snapped in jest. "Jack can compliment my fried chicken any way he likes. Jack, would you like some more? There's plenty. And please, I'd appreciate it if you called me Mom."

Surprised by Mrs. Hurley's request, Jack glanced at Kim. She smiled back at him. "No more chicken just yet," Jack said after he swallowed, "but I will definitely be back for seconds. This chicken is to die for!" He grinned at Kim, who rolled her eyes.

The conversation remained light as the foursome ate dinner. Jack had seconds of the chicken and mashed potatoes. "I don't know why you like those potatoes so much. They're out of a box," Kim said as Jack scooped more onto his plate.

"Oh, they are not!" Mrs. Hurley said. "Jack, don't listen to her. She knows better than that."

Jack laughed, then shoved a heaping spoonful into his mouth.

After they finished eating Mrs. Hurley and Kim cleared the table. Kim then placed four pie plates on the table and Mrs. Hurley returned carrying a fresh homemade apple pie. "I've got a surprise," she said. "I baked it last night, but it's been in the oven warming up while we were eating."

"I thought I smelled something good besides the chicken," Jack commented. "Wow! That looks too good to cut up and eat."

"Are we going to go through this again?" Kim asked.

Mrs. Hurley sliced the pie into eight pieces, then placed one slice on each of the four plates and distributed them about the table.

"This is good, Gramma," Stephen blurted through a mouthful of pie.

"Stephen! Where are your manners?" Kim scolded. Jack began laughing and nearly choked on his mouthful.

"Mr. Kramer, are you all right?" Stephen asked.

"Yes, I think I'll live," Jack replied as he cleared his throat and swallowed. "Stephen, if it's okay with your mom, why don't you drop the Mr. Kramer stuff and just call me Jack?"

Stephen turned to Kim. "Mom, can I?"

"If it's okay with him, it's okay with me," she said.

By the time they finished their pie it was six-twenty. "You've got to be leaving soon, don't you?" Mrs. Hurley asked.

"Yeah, unfortunately," Jack sighed.

"Can we play another game of Hot Shoe?" Stephen asked. "I know you can do better."

"You don't have to," Kim mouthed without uttering a sound.

"Sure, Stephen. I was hoping you'd ask," he said. "But I really do have to leave soon."

"Where are you going?" Stephen asked.

"I have to go to a meeting."

Stephen shrugged. "Oh." With that he hurried to the living room to turn on the television and the PlayStation.

"Don't feel like you have to do this," Kim said. "I appreciate it, and I know he does, but don't feel like you have to keep him entertained."

"I don't mind at all. He's a good kid. Besides, this game is a blast!"

"Can I have a few minutes before you go?" Kim asked as she tugged on his shirt.

"Absolutely," Jack said. As if on cue, Mrs. Hurley left the room. Jack placed his hands tenderly at Kim's waist and she took his shoulders. Softly they kissed.

Before their passion grew too hot Kim pulled away. "You'd better get in there before he gets impatient and comes looking for you. Don't worry. I'll walk you to your car just like the old days."

Jack joined Stephen in the living room just as his game began. A few moments later, while attempting to negotiate traffic, Stephen made an improper approach to a bridge with a steep incline. His car became airborne as intended, but as it soared it slowly rolled to the right. Upon impact it slid on its side, then rolled onto its roof. Instantly his damage scale was filled and it was Jack's turn. Jack found his way to the same bridge but collided with several other obstacles along the way. Therefore, he had accrued much more damage by the time his car took flight from the bridge with a cop close behind. Upon landing his car collided with a light pole, then the police car slammed him from behind. Damage scale maxed. Game over.

"That was fun, Stephen, but I have to get going.," Jack said as he handed the controller back to him.

"Thanks for coming. Bye," Stephen said absently as he began burning rubber on a city street.

Jack found Mrs. Hurley and Kim in the kitchen. "I should get going," he said.

"Okay, let me get our jackets," Kim said.

"Can you come back tomorrow?" Mrs. Hurley asked.

"I suppose I could. Are you sure you don't mind?"

"Of course not. I'm sure Kim would like to see you again before she goes, and I think I could get used to having you around." She kissed Jack's cheek, then continued, "Now you get going. You don't want to be late."

"Here you go," Kim said as she entered the room and tossed Jack his jacket. He slipped into it, then he and Kim walked hand in hand toward his car.

"This sure seems like deja vu," Jack said.

"A lot of things have these last couple of days," Kim said. When they reached the Road Runner, she suddenly wrapped her arms around his midsection and thrust her body against his, knocking him backward against the door. Their lips met and they kissed furiously, flicking their tongues together as they breathed heavily. Kim unzipped Jack's jacket and began exploring his chest through his shirt with her fingers. Jack held her tightly, making large circles on her back with his open palms. After a few minutes she pulled her lips away from his to say, "You'd better get going. You have a meeting to go to, and we'd better not start something we can't finish."

Jack felt a movement in his already inspirited loin. "I can't wait until we can finish," he said, shocked at his own brashness.

"Neither can I, but we both know that now isn't the time," Kim said. Jack began to chuckle. "What's so funny?" Kim asked.

"Once again, here we are, two middle-aged adults acting like we're still teenagers. I think it's great! And speaking of deja vu, I keep waiting for your mother to start flashing the porch light like she used to way back when."

"That wasn't my mother flicking the light. It was my father". Kim looked down, then wiped away a tear. "I'm sorry."

"It's okay," Jack said.

"Dad thought the world of you, but he didn't trust you with his daughter. Nor did he trust his daughter with you. He was a smart man, and I think he realized that there wasn't much he could do about it without taking drastic measures. But by flicking the light and signaling me to come inside I think he felt like he was at least trying."

"Yes, he was a smart man," Jack said.

Kim smiled, her eyes still glistening. "Well, you'd better get going. I heard you and Mom talking. I take it you're coming by for a little while tomorrow night?"

"Yes, but it's going to have to be a quick visit."

"That's okay. I'll see you then." She kissed him once more, then moved toward the house.

The next evening Jack and Stephen played two games of Hot Shoe before dinner. While they ate Kim fretted over the last-minute details of her trip home. "I've got my auto club card and the cellular phone is charged," she told Jack. "I've already called the neighbors, and they've agreed to keep an eye on the place over the winter. I've got the list of stuff Stephen needs, and I have my list. I've also packed a suitcase with the stuff I'll need for the trip. I think I'm set."

Later, as they leaned against the front bumper of Jack's truck, he playfully instructed her, "Call me when you get there, call me when you leave there, and for God's sake, call me when you are back here, I don't care what time it is."

"You're a bigger pain in my ass than my parents ever were!" Kim shot back. They kissed, then Jack left for his meeting.

Chapter Nine

While Kim was gone Jack concentrated on rebuilding the engine for the Dart. Using a basic rebuilding kit from an automotive mail order warehouse, his work progressed quickly. Although she occupied his thoughts while he worked, he was thankful to have something to keep himself busy.

Jack also made it a point to call his sons on Tuesday. He sensed less apprehension in James's voice as he willingly told of the high points of the last few days in school. As usual, Johnny was not at all talkative, but his manner was less caustic, and his words had lost their biting edge. It seemed that the boys were growing accustomed to having to talk him every few days.

On Saturday morning Jack covered the Dart to protect it from paint mist, then throughout the day he sprayed several coats of bright red high temperature enamel on the completed engine. Between coats he performed his household chores.

He had difficulty concentrating at his meeting that night. He offered a few comments but did not speak to any length. As other members of the group spoke, his mind wandered, and he fidgeted with a ball-point pen. Assuming her trip went as planned, Kim would be calling from her mother's house sometime that night. Jack's mind would not be at ease until he knew that she had made it back to Colorado safely.

At eight thirty he arrived home from his meeting. He checked the paint on the engine once more, then flicked on the television and settled into his chair to watch the second half of a Rockford Files rerun. Jim Rockford had been something of a boyhood hero of Jack's. In an era of television super-cops, Rockford was a private investigator of a different breed. Rockford possessed human qualities. He was not above the normal day-to-day annoyances of life, such as receiving an erroneous bank statement or having car trouble, but even in the most trying of situations old Jimbo never lost his smart-assed sense of humor. Furthermore, he was prone to making mistakes; more than once Jack had witnessed him attempting to pick a lock on a door, only to discover that the door had been inadvertently left unlocked. Jack tuned in just as Rockford pulled his pistol from his cookie jar and tucked it into his waist. He dashed out the front door of his mobile home, jumped into his Firebird, and hurried off.

Jack heard a knock at his door. *Great. Probably somebody has broken down,* he thought as he got to his feet. To his surprise, when he swung the door open it was Kim. "You're back!"

Kim smiled and nodded. "I'm back. I'm beat, but I'm finally here, and I'm a few hours ahead of the schedule I set for myself. I figured I'd be here in town sometime around midnight or early tomorrow morning."

Jack stepped back and motioned for her to come inside. Suddenly he was glad he had tidied the house. "You must have dropped the hammer and not let up," he said as he took her coat and draped over the back of his chair.

"Yeah, something like that. Actually, it wasn't too bad. Once I got used to eating and going to the bathroom only during gas stops, I had it made. You know, it seems like a week ago, but when I called you yesterday morning I had the van warming up in the driveway. As soon as I hung up, I left. I drove all the way to western Indiana before I stopped. That was sometime around midnight last night. I found this little shithole motel just off Interstate Eighty."

Jack groaned. The thought of Kim spending a night in one of

the fleabag establishments that peppered the land along the nation's interstates was not a pleasant one. In most of these places the doors to the rooms faced a dimly lit parking lot. Since access to these rooms was by separate outside entrances, visitors did not pass by the lobby desk as they came and went. Neither would an unwanted guest.

Jack thought of Kim lugging her suitcase to her room. Her good looks were sure to garner second and third glances from any virile man and her Maine license plate was a giveaway that she was far from home. Arriving late at night and carrying her own luggage indicated that she was traveling alone and would be sleeping alone. In Jack's mind all of this added up to one word: vulnerable.

Sensing Jack's thoughts, Kim clarified her statement about the motel. "It was well lit and there weren't any winos sleeping in the lobby, but it was still a shithole." Jack smirked. "The funny thing was that I wasn't tired. I could have driven a few more hours, but I decided not to chance it.

"Anyway, at four o'clock this morning I was wide awake, so I took a shower and got an early start. The traffic was light, even around Chicago, so I made good time."

"Made good time?" Jack asked. "Hell, you must have been *flying!* How many tickets did you get along the way?"

"I'm not telling," Kim smiled as she batted her lashes. "Driving across Kansas I knew I was well ahead of schedule. So, I figured I'd drop by and surprise you."

"Well, I'm glad you did," Jack said as he took her into his arms. He gently stroked her golden hair while she nuzzled her cheek against his chest.

"Mmmm. You feel good," Kim said. She tilted her head back, and Jack met her lips with his own. They kissed gently at first, but the intensity of that kiss soon escalated as they began exploring each other's mouth with their tongues.

Their breathing grew deep and rapid as desire laced with adrenaline surged through their bodies. Kim lowered her hands to Jack's waist, and his crept downward to her buttocks. They pulled together tighter as they gyrated against each other. "Oooh, this is nice," Kim said. Jack cupped her left breast and massaged it gently through her sweater. He lowered his head and began kissing her neck, slowly working his way down to the collar of her sweater. Kim sighed. A few minutes later Jack glided his hand up the inside of Kim's sweater and began gently pinching her erect nipple through the satin material of her bra. Meanwhile Kim was stroking the inside of Jack's thigh. Gradually her fingers gravitated toward the bulge in his crotch. "I want to make love to you," she whispered.

Jack suddenly pulled his hand away from her breast and raised his head slightly. "Me, too. But are we ready for this?" he whispered back.

"Huh?" Kim asked.

"Don't get me wrong. I want to make love to you so bad I can't stand it. But I just want to make sure the time is right. I don't want us to rush and take this step before we're ready and make a mistake that will screw up our future."

"Do you feel like you're being rushed?" Kim asked.

"No," Jack said.

Kim smiled. She felt for Jack's fingers through her sweater and guided them back to her breast. "Neither do I." She kissed him deeply.

Jack's head whirled. "Let's go to the bedroom," he heard himself say. Kim nodded. Hand in hand, Jack led her down the hallway past his old bedroom to the larger room he now occupied.

As they stood beside the bed, they fell into each other's arms once more.

For a moment Jack was certain that it was nineteen seventy-nine again, but that feeling quickly passed. In retrospect he could see that during that time their love was ablaze with young lust. In addition to the love and desire they shared there was a newness and curiosity that accompanied their fiery, passionate lovemaking. On the night they lost their virginity they felt like they had conquered the world together.

Now matured, they soon discovered their lovemaking had evolved from the wild, hormone-driven fury of their youth to a slower, longer, deeper, more satisfying burn that they could embrace as adults. Jack and Kim's love felt the same, but the way they made love was different. That night, their lovemaking was fueled by their old love and ignited by the glowing embers of adulthood.

These thoughts ran through Jack's mind as he rolled onto his back in exhaustion much later that night. He pulled Kim close. She placed her head on his shoulder, draped one leg across his, and ran her fingers through the patch of hair at the center of his chest.

"I love you," Jack whispered. He kissed her forehead.

Kim moved her head slightly and looked up at him. "I never stopped loving you." Together they snuggled, basking in the serene afterglow in celebration of their renewed relations.

Hours later the telephone rang. Both Jack and Kim awoke with a jolt. "Christ, what time is it?" Kim asked.

Jack checked the clock. "Two-thirty," he said as he reached for the phone.

"It's probably my mom. Don't tell her I'm here."

"Hello," Jack said into the receiver.

"Hello, Jack? It's Mom Hurley. I'm sorry to wake you up."

"Nah, don't be," Jack said, his voice still groggy.

"I was wondering if you've heard anything from Kim. I figured she would have been here by now, or she would have called if she stopped somewhere for the night. Have you heard from her?"

"Yes," Jack said.

"Tell her I'm still on my way," Kim mouthed as she scurried for her clothes.

"She called me about a half an hour ago and said she was an hour away. She said she didn't want to call you because she was afraid you had gone to bed, and she didn't want to wake you or

Stephen."

"Didn't want to wake me up? I told her I wouldn't sleep until she got here. Well, I guess what's important is that she's okay. So, you think I should look for her in a half hour or so?" Mrs. Hurley asked.

"I would say so. Might want to allow an extra fifteen minutes in case she has to stop for gas," Jack said. With that Jack and Mrs. Hurley bid each other good night and hung up.

"I can't believe we fell asleep," Kim said. "And you! Trying to get in good with my mother while making me look like the thoughtless daughter!" she teased.

"I'd say your mom is capable of coming to her own conclusions," Jack said smugly. "But you really should stop worrying her." Kim stuck her tongue out, then Jack tossed her sock at her.

Once dressed they walked back to the living room. Jack flicked off the television while Kim put on her coat. Before she zipped it Jack pulled her close once more. "Right now, I feel like the luckiest guy in the world," he said.

"You are," Kim said. They both laughed as they hugged

each other. As their lips met Kim pulled back just long enough to say, "No long kisses. I really do have to go." They followed this statement with a long kiss.

"I could stand here and hold you all night," Jack said at length.

"And I'd like to let you, but I've got to go. You don't want my mother calling here again, do you?"

Suddenly Jack laughed.

"What's so funny?" Kim asked.

"Some things never change," Jack said. "Here we are, two adults forty years old, lying to your mother so she won't know we just slept together."

"Yeah, you've got a point," Kim agreed as she, too, laughed. "But I really do need to get going."

"I know," Jack said as he kissed her once more.

"Do you think we can get together tomorrow afternoon?" Kim asked.

"I was hoping we could. Can I call you sometime around noon?"

"Sure. I'll probably be up by ten."

"Okay, I'll call you then," Jack said as he opened the door. "Good night. Love you!" He gave Kim a quick peck on the lips as she moved toward the door.

"Love you, too," she said as she stepped outside.

Jack returned to his bedroom and collapsed into bed. He slept soundly until nine o'clock the next morning.

When he awoke, he stumbled to the kitchen to brew a pot of coffee. He then sought a steamy hot shower. After his shower he poured his first cup of coffee, then plopped himself into his recliner and reflected on the evening he and Kim had shared. By the time his mug was empty, he was wide awake and wearing a dreamy smile.

He returned to the kitchen, poured a second cup of coffee, then went to get dressed. He returned to the kitchen once more, poured a third cup, then called Johnny and James.

James answered the telephone. When Jack asked how school was going, James replied, "I got a detention."

"For what?" Jack asked.

"There's this big fat kid in my class named Matt, and he's a real di-- uh, uh, doofus," James said. "The other day this kid Matt was in the bathroom going, well, you know, number two. So, me and this other kid Dave took paper towels, soaked them in water, and threw them over the door onto him. We took off running out of the bathroom and Matt started yelling at us at the top of his lungs. When we started running down the hallway, Mrs. Snell stopped us and asked why we were running. Then Matt came out of the bathroom and told her. So, me and Dave got detentions."

"You mean Dave and I?" Jack corrected him.

"Yeah, Dave and I. We had to stay after school on Thursday. Now this kid Matt says he's gonna kill us. I hate him. Everybody hates him."

Jack thought for a moment. "James, I think you know that you shouldn't have done that. I'm sure your mother and grandparents have already told you the same thing. I don't think you need to hear it again from me."

"I know, Dad. But he picks on everybody, and he's too big and fat for anybody to beat up. This was just a way to get back at him."

Jack could certainly sympathize with James. He also knew that he could not openly condone pranks such as this, no matter how funny they might be. "James, listen, I understand that Matt is a bully. Although he may be bigger and stronger than everybody else, that doesn't give him the right to pick on other kids. But you throwing paper towels at him isn't going to solve the problem, is it?"

"No, but it made me feel better," James said in stark honesty.

Jack was amused at his answer. "I'm sure it made you feel better at the time, but how do you feel now knowing he's gunning for you?"

"I guess I'm a little worried," James said. "But I think I can outrun him. Fat kids usually can't run too fast."

"James, I know it's hard for you to see this now but believe me when I tell you that everybody gets what they deserve in the long run. He may be a big bully now, but someday someone will cut him down to size. You may have heard the same thing from your mother or grandparents."

"Grandpop says everything will come out of the wash. Does that mean the same thing?"

"I think that's what he means. Someday somebody will put this kid Matt in his place. It might even be you if you keep practicing your karate. By the way, how's that going?"

James told Jack that he and Johnny were doing well with

their lessons and often sparred at home. They had gone to see a competition the previous day, after which Johnny went home with a friend to spend the remainder of the weekend.

"It sounds like you two are doing really well. I'm proud of both of you. Tell your brother I was asking for him."

"Are you going to call again next week?" James asked.

"You bet."

"Okay. I'll talk to you then. Bye, Dad."

"Good-bye, James."

As Jack hung up the telephone, he felt the familiar pang of longing to see Johnny and James, but the thought of actually meeting them face to face made him more than a little nervous. Still, making the telephone calls was getting easier, not just for Jack, but it seemed to be easier for them as well. Having crossed that hurdle, Jack was sure that one day they would all be ready to visit. Perhaps during the next summer, he would fly them to Colorado for a couple of weeks, or maybe he would go to North Carolina. Either way, visiting with his sons was a step that he hoped to take one day soon.

Next Jack dialed Mrs. Hurley's number.

"Hello," Mrs. Hurley answered.

"Mom Hurley? Good morning. It's Jack."

"Oh, good morning, Jack."

"I take it Kim made it there okay last night?"

"Why yes, she pulled in at about three-thirty. Poor lass was exhausted. She looks a whole lot better this morning. She's sitting right here. Would you like to talk to her?"

"Sure," Jack said.

"Hello," Kim's sweet voice filled Jack's ear.

"Good morning, dear. You made it from here to your mom's house okay?" Jack was aware that Kim's mother was still well within earshot, and he could hear Stephen chattering about something nearby.

"Yeah, I got here at about three-thirty. I stopped Friday night in Indiana and slept for a few hours, but otherwise I drove pretty much straight through."

"Did your mother tell you she called here and that she was worried about you?" Jack asked.

"Yes, she told me she called you. And yes, since I didn't call her, I have been named Horrible Daughter of the Year."

"So, did you tell her that you stopped by here for a few hours along the way?"

"Yes, I think I have everything we'll need for the winter," Kim said, ignoring Jack's question.

"Oh, and did you tell Mommy what we did while you were here, and what a bad girl you've been?"

"No, the traffic was pretty light the whole way. I made really good time. Even getting around Chicago was a piece of cake."

"I'm naked," Jack blurted.

Kim erupted in laughter. "I give up! You win."

Jack and Kim spent the next several minutes discussing some of the smaller points of her trip. Jack reaffirmed that he would stop by early that afternoon. Since the weather was nice, at Kim's request he agreed to drive the Road Runner.

When Jack arrived, Kim stepped outside to greet him. The first thing Jack noticed was the pendant that dangled from a thin gold chain which hung about her neck. It contrasted sharply against the Navy-blue background of Kim's plush sweater. The gold charm was in the shape of one half of a heart. Its jagged edge suggested that this once whole heart had been torn in two.

Jack recognized this necklace immediately; it was the one he had placed around her neck at the airport on the night she left for Philadelphia in nineteen seventy-nine. Jack's pendant, the matching half of the heart, still resided in the ashtray of the Road Runner where he had placed it that same night. On more than a few occasions during the ten years the Road Runner sat dormant in his garage he had opened the ash tray and removed the necklace. There he scrutinized his half of the heart as it lay gleaming in his palm beneath the garage light. He read Kim's name, then gently stroked the engraved letters with his thumb as he wished for the things that had not been.

Quickly Jack shifted his eyes from the pendant. He suspected that Kim had decided to wear it to test Jack's response, assuming he even noticed. Rather than acknowledge Kim's necklace now, perhaps later he would think of an excuse to go to his car for a minute. Then he would return to the house wearing his own pendant.

"Hey there, sexy!" Kim whispered as she leaned to kiss him.

"Ooh! Hey there yourself!" Jack said as he slipped his hands around her waist, then pressed his lips against hers.

"It's chilly out here," Kim said, her voice broken by a cold shiver. "Let's go inside."

Hand in hand they entered the house. "Hi, Jack," Mrs. Hurley called from the kitchen.

Just then Stephen darted from the living room toward them, the thumping of his footsteps preceding his appearance in the doorway. "Jack! Will you take me for a ride in the Road Runner?"

"Stephen! Jack just got here. Let him visit for a minute first," Kim said.

"But Mom, you told me I could ask him."

"Yes, I did. But to pounce on him the second he walks through the door is just a little rude, don't you think?"

"I guess so," Stephen said, then turned toward Jack. "So, can I go for a ride?"

"Sure, as long as it's okay with your mom," Jack said.

"Mom, can I go? Pleeease?"

Kim rolled her eyes. "Go get your jacket."

"Yesss!" Stephen ran for his jacket.

"All morning this is all the kid talked about," Kim said to Jack. "You don't mind, do you?"

"Not at all! I think it's really cool that he even has an interest in the car. I'd love to take him for a ride. Is it okay if we stop for a cup of hot chocolate?"

Kim smiled. "Absolutely. Maybe later you and I can go out for a little ride."

Just then Stephen reappeared. "Let's go!"

"Thanks," Kim mouthed to Jack as he turned toward the door.

Stephen ran toward Jack's car then waited anxiously for Jack to catch up and open the passenger's door. Jack helped him with his lap belt, then closed the door and walked around to the driver's side. Once he was belted in he started the engine and jabbed the accelerator a couple of times for Stephen's benefit.

"Wow! This car sounds cool!" Stephen yelled over the snarling exhaust as Jack revved the engine. Jack eased the Road Runner away from the curb. As he accelerated upward through the gears Stephen said, "This sounds like the car in Hot Shoe!"

"How about a cup of hot chocolate?" Jack asked.

"Yeah! That's my favorite," Stephen said. "Mom always makes hot chocolate after I come in from playing in the snow."

Minutes later Jack parked in a far corner of the parking lot at the Sinclair station, then walked side by side with Stephen toward

the building. Inside he prepared a medium cup of hot chocolate for

each of them, carefully adding and stirring in ice cubes until the

wisps of steam had all but stopped rising from the cups. "There. I

think that should do it," Jack said as he handed Stephen his cup.

"Give that a try and see if it needs more ice. Be careful."

Stephen took his cup and slowly brought his lips to the brim.

"It's cold," he said. "But that's okay. It's still good."

"Are you sure?" Tasting his own drink, Jack was convinced

he had overdone it with the ice. "I'm sure there is a microwave

around here. We can warm it up if you want."

"No. It's okay," Stephen said.

Jack paid the cashier, then he and Stephen left the store and

walked toward the car. "There's no picnic table out here, but we're

men. Men don't need a picnic table. We can have a seat right here

on the curb," Jack said, indicating a spot at the edge of the parking

lot beside the car.

"Why don't we drink it in the car?" Stephen asked.

"I don't want to take a chance of spilling hot chocolate inside

the car, and I don't want to take you home with brown stains all over your clothes, either."

Stephen laughed. "Then it would look like I was holding a puppy and it pooped on me."

Jack and Stephen made idle talk on the way back to Mrs. Hurley's house. As they sat stopped at one traffic light Stephen asked, "Is this car fast?"

"Yeah, I guess it's pretty fast," Jack answered casually. Just then the light changed to green. He rolled through the intersection in first gear, then slowly squeezed the accelerator downward. The rear tires nearly broke traction as the car rocketed away from the light, but he modulated the pressure of his foot to prevent them from spinning. Quickly he shifted into second, then continued accelerating. From the corner of his eye he saw Stephen's head snap forward, then rearward as he changed gears. At the top of second gear Jack pressed in the clutch, shifted into neutral briefly, then into fourth gear. They had already exceeded the fifty mile per hour posted speed limit, and he was not eager to receive a ticket.

"Wow! this car's fast!" Stephen commented. "Will it do a burn-out?"

Jack smiled. "Yes, it will if I floor it."

"That wasn't floored?"

"Nope." Jack expected Stephen to ask him to do a burn-out, but he did not. He would have declined anyway, knowing that he had no right to drive recklessly with Stephen in the car. He glanced at Stephen, who sat staring straight ahead, his eyes wide, grinning.

"Why is there a trap door in your hood?" Stephen asked, pointing at the open-Air Grabber scoop.

"That door opens up and lets the engine get more air so it can make more power."

"That's cool!" Moments later Stephen said, "Can I ask you something?"

"Sure."

"Do you want to marry my mom?"

Jack cleared his throat. It was an honest question, but one he had not anticipated-- at least not yet. "Stephen, I don't know. Maybe someday, if things work out for us. I like your mom an awful lot, but I don't know what the future holds for us. What do you think?"

"Well, Mom is happy when you come over. She really likes you, I can tell. I do too."

"And I like you." Unable to think of anything else to say, Jack asked, "Do you want us to get married?"

"Not now, but maybe someday. That might be okay. As long as you stay nice."

Jack patted Stephen's shoulder.

When they arrived back at his grandmother's house, Stephen thanked Jack for the ride then bolted across the yard toward the front door. The heavy wooden door was open, but the storm door was closed. "Mom! That was cool! That Road Runner is so fast!" Stephen shouted as he neared the door.

Jack saw that Kim had begun to unload the van, for the sliding door and liftgate were both open. He rushed to take an armful of boxes from the van, forgetting about his necklace for the moment.

Kim met him at the front door on her way back to the van. "Thanks for giving him a ride. You can take that stuff to the living room." Seeing her half-heart pendant again Jack was instantly reminded that he had forgotten to retrieve his own from the ashtray of the Road Runner. *Damn!* he thought. *I'll have to get it later.*

Jack and Kim continued carrying the contents of the van to

the living room. "I'll sort this stuff tomorrow," she said when they were finished. "But now, let's go for a ride."

"Kim, are you two going out for a bit?" Mrs. Hurley called from the kitchen.

"Yes. Do you need for us to pick up something?"

"I'd appreciate it if you could pick up some corn starch. I need it for the gravy. I thought I had another box, but I must have used it."

"Sure, Mom. Is that it?"

"I think so."

Kim turned toward Jack. "Let's go!"

When they reached Jack's car, he opened the door for her and she sank into the

seat. "Wow! I must've packed on a lot of weight in the last week," she joked as she attempted to buckle the lap belt across her svelte hips and discovered that it was adjusted much too short.

"No, dear, the problem is that your son is built like a bean pole," Jack said.

"So was I at his age."

"Maybe, but you filled out very nicely. Otherwise, you'd

look like Olive Oyl."

Kim laughed. "I suppose that wouldn't be good, would it?"

"Nope," Jack said. He helped her adjust her seatbelt.

As they rolled away from the curb Kim asked, "Is Johnson's Five and Dime still in business?" referring to a small general store that had stood a few blocks away many years earlier. "I used to love going there with Mom."

"I don't know. Let's see," Jack made a U-turn and headed in that direction.

The store still stood in the same spot it had years earlier. Jack brought the Road Runner to a stop in a parking space at the edge of the street in front of the store. The first thing he noticed was that the sign had been updated to read Johnson's Market, and rightfully so. He seriously doubted that anything on their shelves could be had for the paltry price of a nickel or a dime.

The second thing Jack noticed was the row of parking meters that had sprouted from the sidewalk since he had last visited the store. He unbuckled his seatbelt, then thrust his hands deep into his pockets in hopes of finding some loose change. "Great. Two pennies," he stated as he removed the change from his and Stephen's hot chocolates.

"Oh, no," Kim said. "I forgot my purse." She patted her empty pockets, then reached for the ash tray. "You wouldn't have any change in here, would you?" she asked as she pulled it open.

Shit! Jack thought. *Shit! Shit! Shit!*

"What's this?" Kim asked as she lifted the gold chain from the ashtray.

"I saw that you were wearing yours, and I meant to put mine on while Stephen and I were out earlier, but I got sidetracked," Jack said.

Kim held up the necklace, allowing the pendant to dangle. She turned to face Jack, her mouth gaping and eyes misty. "You still have this?"

"Of course, I do! On the night you gave it to me I put it right there so nothing would ever happen to it," he said, pointing at the open ash tray.

"Come here," Kim said. Jack leaned toward her and she placed the chain around his neck just as she had done twenty-two years earlier. Then she locked her lips onto his in a hot, teary kiss.

"We'd better get inside and get the corn starch," she said

moments later as she wiped her eyes dry. "And I just remembered something. We don't need any change for the parking meter. It's Sunday."

Despite the new sign out front and updated higher prices, the inside of Johnson's Market seemed as if it had been frozen in time. The checkered green and white tile flooring and white painted steel racks of household goods had remained unchanged through the years. Jack spied an aging cardboard display with several snap-together balsa wood glider kits. "I haven't seen one of these in years!" he said as he picked up one of the kits. "When I was a kid, sometimes my father would buy me one of these planes. We'd put it together then toss it around out back behind the house." Jack reminisced on those happy times as he stared through the plastic pouch at the disassembled glider inside. "I think Stephen would like this."

Kim found the corn starch, and together they walked to the counter and placed their purchases beside the antique mechanical cash register. The clerk, a college aged young man, entered the prices of the glider and the corn starch into the register using the tall columns of keys. Each column had ten keys, zero through nine.

"Now there's a forgotten skill," Jack said as the clerk's hand flitted about the fifty or so keys.

"Yeah, it took a few days to get used to it. But now that I've gotten the hang of it, I really like this old machine. Definitely a conversation piece," the clerk said.

Outside Jack opened the door for Kim, then took his seat behind the wheel. "Where to?" he asked.

"I don't know. We could go back to your place for a while. I'd like to see this Dart you're working on."

"Do you want to take the corn starch to your mom first?" Jack asked.

"Nah, she needs it for the gravy. That only takes a couple of minutes. I can make that when we get back."

Jack headed toward his house. The clear blue sky of earlier in the day had given way to a puffy light gray cloud cover. As they neared his house white flakes began descending from this grayness. Aimlessly they skittered about the hood of the Road Runner. "I think I'd better put the car away when we get there," Jack said. "I haven't heard a weather forecast. I don't think this will amount to anything, but even if it doesn't, getting the car into the shed will be a problem once the tires and the wooden ramps get wet."

By the time they rolled into his driveway the flakes were falling at a furious rate. The hood, roof, and windshield of Jack's truck were already covered with a thin layer of snow. Jack left the engine idling as he raised the shed door and set the ramps in place. Then he eased the car up the ramps and into the shed. The rear tires spun as they climbed the slightly damp wooden ramps, reaffirming Jack's decision to put the car away before any more snow fell.

On his way from the shed to the house Jack tossed the corn starch and Stephen's glider onto the seat of the truck. Once they were inside Jack led Kim to the garage. "Keep your coat on. It'll be cold out there," he advised. Jack opened the garage door, ushered Kim through, then closed it behind them.

"Ooh, this looks sharp!" she said of the freshly painted six-cylinder engine that hung from its stand.

"I finished assembling it and painted it yesterday," Jack said. He then uncovered the Dart.

"Wow! I like this," Kim said as she stepped closer and peered through the window. "And it's a stick shift!"

"Yup. It ought to be a fun car to bop around in when it's

done."

"I like it." Kim backed away from the car to take in all of its lines and details then nodded again. "That shade of blue looks really good with the black vinyl top, the chrome trim, and the wheels," she said in a shaky voice.

"I think so, too," Jack said as he looked at her. She was starting to shiver. "Let's go back inside."

In the living room Jack removed his coat. "I've got a chill," Kim said as she removed hers and handed it to him. She rubbed her hands together.

"Allow me," Jack said as he tossed their coats onto the sofa. He pressed his own hands together tightly and rubbed his palms against each other vigorously. The friction from his thick, work-hardened skin sliding back and forth quickly generated warmth. Jack then enveloped Kim's chilly hands and fingers with his own.

"Aah, that's better," she said. She looked at Jack, locking her eyes on his. Jack gazed back, peering deep into Kim's eyes. Slowly their lips met, and their arms encircled each other.

They kissed furiously, their fingers exploring each other's bodies. Kim panted as Jack crouched slightly and began kissing her soft neck. He pulled a handful of her golden hair across his face and breathed deeply of its aroma. Finally, his hands settled at her waist. He stood and pulled her close.

"How's that chill?" Jack asked.

"You took care of it," Kim giggled. "But we really should be getting back."

"I know," Jack said as he began kissing her again. They continued kissing for what seemed like hours.

By the time they left the house it was a quarter to five. Jack helped Kim into her coat and slipped into his own. When he opened the front door, he was shocked to discover nearly two inches of fresh snow on the ground. "Kim, look at this," he called.

Kim peered out the open door. "Huh! Looks like you made a good call in putting the Road Runner away when we got here." Moments later, as they rolled down the driveway in Jack's truck, she asked, "Jack, do you really have to go to the meeting tonight?"

Jack thought for a moment then replied flippantly, "I don't suppose missing one night would kill me."

Kim suddenly grew silent, staring straight ahead over the snow-covered hood. Jack could feel an uneasy tension in the air.

"What?" he asked.

"Nothing."

"Must be something. What did I say?"

"It isn't what you said, it's how you said it," Kim said.

"What?"

"Nothing."

"If you don't tell me, how can I apologize? Are you upset
with me because I go to meetings every night?"

"Jack, I understand that you have to go to meetings. I don't
know a lot about alcoholism, but I know it is an ongoing process. I
know you have to go to meetings to remain strong. I know that this
is something you must do, and I would never want to deprive you of
it.

"But Jack, for me the most enjoyable part of the day is the
evening. That is when the work of the day is done, and it is time to
relax. It's family time, time to enjoy the company of the ones you
love. I know this will sound very selfish, but it bothers me to think
that you have to go to your meetings every night forever. Maybe it
is too early in our relationship, our new relationship that is, for me to
be feeling this way. But I can't help how I feel about you. Besides,

if I don't tell you now, one day this might become a serious issue."

Jack thought for a long moment before responding. "When I stopped drinking, I promised myself I would go to a meeting every night. Since I usually drank in the evenings, I didn't want to be sitting around at night thinking of drinking. Another reason was because at first, I knew I would need as much help and support as I could get. I also knew that if I went every night, there was never the chance that I'd lose track of which nights were which, or that I would get lazy and instead of going four times a week I would drop back to three nights, then two nights, and eventually stop altogether.

"But now I'm coming up on my one-year mark. I'm ready to set my sights on living again. And now that we are back together, I feel like I'm being given the chance at a fresh start in life. I know I need to find ways to combine what I need to do to stay sober with what I need to do to start living life again. After all, the whole point to being sober is to get your life back.

"Here's an idea: I'll go to meetings on Monday, Wednesday, and Friday nights, and I'll try to find another group to meet with on Saturday and Sunday mornings. That will leave us Tuesday, Thursday, Saturday, and Sunday nights to spend together. Does that sound like a good compromise?"

"Jack, I don't want you to do this just for me. I'm not asking for you to rearrange your whole life. I just want to spend some time with you."

"And I want to spend time with you. I'm willing to give it a try. But if it doesn't work out, I'll have to go back to my nightly meetings. Deal?"

Kim nodded. "Thanks," she smiled. "I'm sorry for being a bitch. There's just so much going on, and things are moving fast for us. I'm not complaining, just a little bit concerned."

"So, we'll give it some time," Jack said. "Hell, we've waited twenty-two years! No need to be hasty now." His heart, however, said, *Go!*

Jack and Kim pulled up to Mrs. Hurley's house at five o'clock. It was now snowing heavily, and Jack estimated that nearly three inches were on the ground. Kim ran and kicked happily through the fluffy powder on her way to the front door while Jack followed a few steps behind.

When they entered the house, Mrs. Hurley met them at the door. "How about this snow! It sure took the weather people by surprise," she said.

"I didn't think I'd heard anything about snow in the forecast, but then I don't think I've heard a recent forecast," Jack said.

"Even if you had, it wouldn't have mattered. This one snuck up on them. Jack, you're not driving that pretty yellow car of yours in this mess, are you?"

"No, we ran by the house and put it away. We came back in the truck," he said.

"Oh, that's good. I'd hate to see anything happen to it."

While Kim helped her mother with dinner Jack joined Stephen for a game of Hot Shoe. After their meal he assembled the glider. With the falling flakes obscuring much of the light from the floods in Mrs. Hurley's back yard, Jack demonstrated to Stephen how to fly the glider. Soon the cold became unbearable, and they retired to the living room for hot chocolate and a movie.

Chapter Ten

In the weeks that followed, Jack and Kim's relationship settled into an agreeable routine. On the evenings Jack did not attend his meetings he would drive to the Hurley residence after stopping by his own house for a shower. On the nights he attended his meetings Kim would usually go to Jack's house to prepare a meal before he arrived home from work. They would eat supper together, then Jack would leave for his meeting. Most of the time Kim would clean up the dishes, then head back to her mother's house, but sometimes she would wait for Jack to return and surprise him.

Kim still wished that Jack could be home every night, but she knew his meetings were important to his well-being and their future together. She told herself that his meeting schedule would be fine once she grew accustomed to it. In the meantime, she worked to do just that as she arranged her evening activities around his.

Jack was pleased with how the new meeting schedule afforded him time to spend with Kim, but after attending his new Saturday and Sunday morning meetings for several weeks, he remained uncomfortable. Even so, he continued to go. He recalled that he had attended meetings with his original group for months before feeling completely at ease. Given enough time he felt he would probably become comfortable with this group as well.

Donald encouraged Jack to begin moving forward with his life but expressed concern that the changes he was making were drastic and that he was making them too quickly. "I just hope you're not setting yourself up for a fall. Remember, the higher you soar, the harder you land." Still, it was Donald who presented Jack with his One Year pin during a special ceremony two weeks before Thanksgiving. Kim, Mrs. Hurley, and Stephen were all present.

After the first snow of the season Jack left the Road Runner to hibernate in its new home for the winter. He often talked of wanting to install the newly built and painted engine into the Dart, but he continued to spend all of his free time with Kim, Stephen, and Mrs. Hurley. Consequently, the Dart sat untouched, but Jack did not complain. Besides, the balance on his latest Visa statement was considerably higher than he had expected. This further discouraged him from working on the Dart, for there would be additional expenses as his work on the car progressed.

As Thanksgiving neared, the weather forecast called for a

major storm with strong winds and heavy snowfall. Drifting would be a serious problem, the television meteorologist warned. As predicted, the flakes began to fall Wednesday night while Jack sat in his meeting. Kim and Mrs. Hurley had both asked Jack to spend the night at the Hurley residence so that he wouldn't get stranded by the snow alone in his own house for Thanksgiving. "Getting snowed in won't be so bad if we're all stuck here together," Mrs. Hurley had said. "We can still have a nice dinner, no matter what the weather does."

Later that night Kim and Jack unfolded sheets and blankets onto Mrs. Hurley's sofa-bed. Jack stripped to his briefs, then he and Kim slid between the sheets. Kim lay on her side facing away from Jack with her knees bent. Jack assumed an identical position with his chest, stomach, and thighs pressing against Kim's back and buttocks. Jack placed his arm over her side, and she interlocked her fingers with his.

"I've been thinking about something," Kim said.

"What's that?" Jack asked.

"Your sons, Johnny and James."

"What about them?"

"Well, I'd like to meet them. And I'm sure you would like to see them."

Jack could feel his muscles tense.

Kim continued, "You told me how you miss them, and it's so sad that you haven't seen them in well over a year."

"Kim, no, please--" Jack began, but Kim interrupted him.

"Jack, please hear me out before you say anything. I don't quite know how to say this, and I know this might sound like I'm sticking my nose where it doesn't belong, but I want to help you."

"Help me?" Jack asked.

"I want to help you see your sons."

Jack opened his mouth, but Kim cut him short.

"Hold on. I'm not finished." She rolled onto her back to face him. "If Johnny and James come for a few days or even the full week between Christmas and New Year's, they won't have to interrupt their school. I can put my work on hold for as long as they are here, so I can be with them during the day while you're at work. That way you don't have to beg for time off or disrupt your work schedule at all.

"Mom says they are welcome to stay here. And I think

having them here would do her a lot of good because it would help
her keep her mind off Dad. Or, if you think the kids would be more
comfortable at your place, we can all stay there. So, what do you
think?"

"You've put a lot of thought into this, haven't you?"

Kim nodded.

"I know this sounds silly, but frankly, I'm not ready to take
this step yet," Jack said.

"Not ready? What do you mean you're not ready?"

"It took me a long time to work up the courage just to call
them."

"Yeah, I know. That doesn't make sense to me, either, but I
thought you were past that now. Aren't you?"

"No, not completely. You don't understand. You can't
understand." Frustrated, Jack struggled to think of a way to express
his feelings.

"You're right. I'm trying, Jack, but I don't understand.
They're your family, for Christ's sake! Your own children! I can't
believe you don't want to see them, especially during the holidays.
As big a deal as you've always made of Christmas, I can't believe

you don't want to include your sons."

"It's not that I don't want to include them. I can't include them, not yet. Look, you knew me a long time ago, and you know me now. I've told you about some of the things that happened in the meantime. Through the course of my drinking I went through a transition. I became another person, someone who I don't like at all. I blamed my problems on the ones who were the closest to me. I pushed them away and lashed out at them as I crawled deeper into the bottle. That's the monster I became.

"Granted, I'm not a monster anymore. I am now the old me, the real me. I've come to terms with the person I became during my drinking years. I'm not proud of the things I did or the pain I caused, but I've accepted the fact that these things happened.

"Johnny and James have never seen this version of their father. They only know the monster who eventually drove them and their mother away to live in North Carolina. You can't begin to imagine the guilt I feel for that. I won't let that guilt dominate me forever, but I can't ignore it either.

"In each step I take with Johnny and James, whether it was sending them cards on their birthdays, or now in calling them, or when the time comes that we visit--with each step I come to terms with some of that guilt. But taking each step also forces me to face my past, and that takes courage."

Kim shook her head. "Jack, they're your sons! How many steps do you need to take before you're willing to see them?"

"I have to take my steps one at a time, just as I now have to live my life one day at a time. Don't worry, I'll cross that bridge, but I can't do it until I know I'm ready and strong enough." It was the most honest answer Jack could give. "It's also going to take time for them to come around and want to see me. Right now, they don't know how to take me. They don't know what to make of their old man. I've got to prove my worth to them-- earn their respect and trust-- before they will want to see me. I have to prove that my feelings are genuine. Until then, forcing them to see me would be pointless."

Kim shook her head slowly. "How can you be so good to Stephen, but not your own kids?"

"Simple," Jack said. "With Stephen I got a fresh start. I didn't have to explain anything to him, and there was no past to try to overcome. Stephen sees me as who I am now. We get along with each other, and that's that.

"Johnny and James don't see me the same way Stephen does. With them it's not so simple. They remember me as the ogre who was always drunk and intolerant of them and who made their mother cry. There is a lot of bad history that must be worked through if we are to move on as father and sons. If that can ever happen it will take a lot of understanding and forgiveness on their part, a lot of hope, patience, and courage on my part, and a lot of perseverance and strength on everybody's part."

"You're being too hard on yourself."

"Am I? I don't think so. I'm being realistic."

"Everybody makes mistakes. Surely Johnny and James will forgive you."

"Yeah, maybe. I hope you're right, but it's crazy to think that we can all pretend nothing ever happened and be a family living happily ever after."

"I'm not saying that. But I think visiting with your kids will be good for them. It will give them a chance to see firsthand that even when things in life are bad, with work and determination they can become good again. That will be a valuable lesson for them."

"I agree, but not until I'm strong enough to overcome my fear and make it a worthwhile visit. Don't worry, I'm getting there, but it's going to take some more time."

Kim said nothing. She laid on her back looking at the ceiling while Jack laid on his side facing her, staring at an imaginary spot on the carpet several feet away. A chilly, tense silence hung in the room.

After several minutes Jack spoke. "Kim, I hope you don't think this is my choice. I wish it wasn't this way. I really *do* want to see them. I want to talk with them and wrestle with them and go places with them. I want to spend time with them and have fun together. I want to have them back in my life, and I want to be a part of their lives. Between my drinking and the fact that they're now gone I know I've missed out on several years with them. Hell, I've pretty much missed their entire lives so far. And even if we were to see each other as often as we could, with two thousand miles between us I know those times would be few and far between."

"But the longer you wait, the more time you'll miss," Kim said.

"I know that, but I have to be at a point mentally where I can face the past and discuss it openly with them. I have to be able to explain why things turned out the way they did," Jack said.

"Jack, Christmas would be the perfect time to sit them down and tell them what you have to say. Then you'd still have time to spend with them after you've made your amends."

Jack opened his mouth, then paused to reconsider his words. "Kim, please, I'm just not ready yet."

"Well, I can't believe you're so wrapped up in this recovery thing that you're still pushing them away," Kim said. "By the time you finally get around to seeing them, they might be grown up. Then what?"

"Look, I'm hoping to get them out here this summer. By then I'm sure I'll be ready."

"Whatever. I'm just trying to help."

"And I appreciate it."

"I'm going to bed. I'll see you in the morning," Kim said. She pecked Jack's lips as she rose from the bed, then flicked off the light switch as she left the living room.

Jack lay in the darkness, a strange mixture of anger, remorse, and longing brewing in his mind. Eventually he fell into a restless sleep.

Early the next morning, while Stephen and Mrs. Hurley slept, Jack awoke to Kim's delightfully soothing voice calling his name. He was so entranced by its velvet-like smoothness that he pretended to be asleep just so she would keep repeating his name. Finally, she brushed his eyelashes with her finger. Jack flinched. "Ha! I knew you weren't asleep," she said.

"How did you know?"

"After I called your name the first or second time your breathing changed. It became shallower and quieter."

Jack smiled. "I was listening to the sound of your voice. I wondered how long you would call my name before you did something really rotten like pinched my nose shut so I couldn't breathe."

Kim laughed. "I didn't think of that. I'll have to remember that one for next time."

"Aw shit! I should know better than to give you ideas."

Kim paused for a moment, then said, "I missed cuddling with you last night."

"I missed it, too," Jack said. "I didn't sleep very well."

"Me either," Kim said, "but I don't want to talk about it anymore. I don't want to fight. You need to handle this your own way."

Jack did not respond.

Kim tugged at the blankets. "Is there room in this bed for me?"

"Absolutely," Jack said as he moved toward the opposite side of the bed. He pulled the covers down for Kim then draped them over her once she took her place next to him.

"You're warm," Kim said. She wiggled her body against his, and he placed his arm over her.

The room was dimly lit by the faint daylight that shone around the edges of the heavy curtains over the windows. Although he could not make out the hands on the clock, he guessed it was around six in the morning. Outside the wind thrust itself upon the front of the house in strong gusts. "Have you looked outside?" Jack asked.

"Yes. We got quite a bit of snow, and it's still coming down."

"How much do you think we got so far?"

"It's hard to tell. It's blowing around so much, in some places there are only a few inches, but other places look like they have a couple of feet. Makes me glad we don't have to try to go anywhere."

"I was thinking about taking Stephen to the truck stop sometime today if the weather lets up. That is, if you don't mind. I was thinking it would be a men's trip. Just the two of us. I thought he might like seeing some of the big rigs up close and having a piece of pie where the truckers eat."

"I'm sure he'd like that," Kim said. She took Jack's hand and squeezed it. "Thanks for being good to him."

Chapter Eleven

Thanksgiving marked the beginning of the holiday season, which had almost always been a happy time for Jack. As far back as he could remember he and his father had put aside their pain and loneliness and enjoyed the time with each other. This tradition had stuck with Jack, and even now that he was an adult, he made it a point to make the most of the season.

The only exception had been the previous Christmas. Caught in the wake of losing his family while struggling to remain sober, Jack had felt he had nothing to celebrate. Seeing the holiday commercials on television and encountering those filled with holiday cheer only depressed him further, so for the first time in his life he had ignored the approach of last year's Christmas and rejoiced at its passing. Throughout the holiday season he had remained encapsulated in a protective air of indifference.

Now it was difficult for Jack to believe that dark time had been only twelve months earlier, especially in light of the changes in recent months. This year was markedly different because he had nearly all of the things he could have wished for, and far more than he felt he deserved. Although he was not a religious man, Jack still thanked God from time to time for smiling upon him. With Kim back in his life and conversations between him and his boys taking place regularly, this Christmas would be special.

During the two-week period following Thanksgiving, however, a persistent need for a drink began to stir inside him. It was a feeling that never left completely, but one he was able to ignore most of the time. A strong craving seized him one day a week after Thanksgiving, but he triumphed over it. He knew that since he had begun trying to live a normal life again, maintaining sobriety would consume less of his concentration as he focused his attention on other things and other people. It was not that staying sober would become a lesser priority; on the contrary, if he failed to stay sober, he knew he would blow his second chance at happiness. He told himself it was normal for the symptoms of his disease to change with the changes he was making in his life.

Jack continued meeting with his original group on Monday, Wednesday, and Friday evenings. He now believed no matter how long he attended his Saturday and Sunday morning meetings, he would never feel comfortable in that particular mix of people. He considered dropping out of the weekend meetings but refrained for fear that cutting his meeting schedule to just three days a week might jeopardize his strength. Though he did not care for that group, he fed from their strength, and that was reason enough to continue.

Although Kim did not vocalize her displeasure that Jack was still away for the evening nearly half of the time, there was no mistaking the disappointment in her eyes when he left for a meeting. However, it seemed that Jack's aversion to flying Johnny and James to Colorado for the week between Christmas and New Year had ceased to be an issue with her; she hadn't mentioned it since their discussion at Thanksgiving.

With the holiday a little more than two weeks away Jack and Kim set out on a Saturday morning after Jack's meeting to find a Christmas tree. Jack's favorite place was a Christmas tree farm located half an hour east of town. Being a seasoned tree hunter, he took his own bow saw.

When they arrived at the tree farm Jack parked the truck. Before he opened the door, he looked out to the field where row after row of Christmas trees stood waiting. The dark green shapes contrasted against the covering of snow on the ground. He took a deep breath and grinned.

"This is like a sport for you, isn't it?" Kim asked.

"Oh yeah! Let's go!" Jack said as he opened his door and jumped to the ground. Once they passed through the gate they walked past the small building where the people who had already found trees lined up to pay for them. Just beyond this building were two tables where four tree farm attendants wrapped the trees in nylon netting, making them easier for customers to transport. Local folks with their newly cut trees had lined up roughly ten deep at each table.

Jack leaned toward Kim and said, "Most people don't wander out too far. This area closest to the front is usually pretty well picked over. I like to go to the far corner and work my way back. Out there is where the nice trees are."

Kim looked at him, then smiled and shook her head. "You've put way too much thought into this." They plodded through the snow to a remote corner of the field, then began combing the rows as they worked their way back toward the gate. "You know, if we find something, we like out here, it's that much further we're going to have to carry it," she said.

"Oh, I know, but it will be worth it. Trust me on this one. I know what I'm doing."

As they checked tree after tree, they made a game of hiding from each other, then lobbing snow balls when the other one wasn't looking. After twenty minutes or so Kim suddenly darted across two rows of trees, her eyes locked on a tree nearly twenty yards away. Jack followed and saw the tree that had caught Kim's attention. It was much too tall to fit in Mrs. Hurley's living room, but with its full shape and thick endowment of long needles both Kim and Jack knew this was the tree they had come to find. "It's perfect," Kim said. Jack circled the tree, eyeing it from every angle. Only on the northern side was its plush coat of needles thin and patchy, a normal condition due to the lack of direct sunlight that reached that side of the tree as it grew.

"I agree," Jack said. "We'll have to put this side against the wall, but the rest of it is really nice." He stood back a few feet, still examining the tree. "They want everyone to cut the trunk of the tree even with the ground. Once we get it back to your mom's I'll have to cut the trunk about here to fit it into the house," he said, indicating a point roughly even with his knee. "So, is this the one we want?"

"This is the one." Kim reached through the branches and grasped the trunk at its midpoint, steadying the tree for Jack to cut it. Jack kicked the snow away from the foot of the tree on its northern side. There he crouched into position to saw the tree off at its base. His bow saw made quick work of the soft trunk, and within minutes he and Kim were wrestling with the tree to find a comfortable position in which to carry it back to the small shack at the gate.

"I told you this was going to be a pain in the ass," Kim panted as she shifted the top of the tree from her right arm to her left.

"Oh, come on!" Jack said. He was two steps ahead of Kim, the bow saw in his left hand and a few branches near the bottom of the tree clenched in his right hand. "I've got the heavy end."

"It's not heavy, it's awkward," Kim said. A couple of minutes later she asked, "What would you have done if I wasn't here to help you carry this thing?"

"I would have picked a tree closer to the gate," Jack said.

Kim suddenly yanked the tree, nearly tearing it loose from Jack's grip. "Smartass!" she hissed. Jack laughed.

Jack walked with Kim to the end of the line that led to the payment window in the attendant's shack. "We should get a second tree for my place," he said.

"Why? You're hardly ever there except to shower and sleep," Kim said.

"But I love the smell of pine in the house. Even if I don't spend time sitting and staring at the tree, I like to wake up to that smell."

"I'll tell you what," Kim said. "You've got to cut a foot or two from the bottom, right?"

Jack nodded.

"I'll use the branches from the bottom of the tree to make you a wreath that you can hang up at your house. That should give your house the smell you want, and you won't have to be bothered with a tree. You can bring some of your ornaments to Mom's to hang on this tree."

"Okay. That sounds good to me," he said. "I've got a sturdy tree stand. I mounted it to a piece of plywood, so it's rock solid. We can take that to your mom's, too."

Jack paid for the tree, then he and Kim headed toward his house. "All of the Christmas stuff is in the attic," he said. Suddenly he realized he had not been in the attic since Marsha and the boys had left. They had left hastily, and with the three of them piled into her car there was not an overabundance of space for cargo. Still, Jack was sure that Marsha must have gone up to the attic to retrieve some of her belongings.

Jack led Kim to the hallway near his bedroom then grabbed the rope handle that dangled from the folding staircase in the ceiling and pulled it downward. He unfolded the steps, then led Kim up to the attic. Just above the last step was the switch for the attic lights, and Jack flipped it on as he crawled past it. Nothing appeared to be out of place. Most of the items looked as if they had not been touched in years. Perhaps Marsha had decided there was nothing in the attic she needed badly enough to haul to North Carolina.

Kim squeezed past Jack as he knelt on the plywood floor next to the stairs. He could not help admiring her perfectly shaped buttocks as she wiggled past him.

Jack set one box aside and opened the next one. "Here we go. This is the Christmas stuff."

Inside the box Kim spotted an eight-inch-tall stuffed Road Runner doll. "Oh, I remember this!" she said as she reached for the doll.

"You and your mom give it to me," Jack said.

"You're right. I don't remember where we got it, but it must have been sometime right around Christmas, because I think I remember hanging it on your tree."

"You did. And I remember my father doing a double-take when he first saw it, then laughing his ass off. It's been a Christmas ornament ever since."

"Do you mind if we take it to Mom's?" Kim asked.

"Not at all. In fact, why don't we take the whole box? We can sort through it there," Jack said. Kim placed the stuffed Road Runner back in the box then shoved the box to the top of the steps.

Jack took the tree stand and placed it atop the box. "With the plywood attached, getting the tree stand through the opening in the ceiling is tricky," Jack said. "If you go downstairs, I'll hand this stuff down to you." Kim nodded then clambered down the steps. Jack handed her the tree stand followed by the box of ornaments.

They carried the Christmas items to the truck, then drove to Mrs. Hurley's house. Along the way it occurred to Jack that Kim hadn't spoken for some time. Stealing a glance, he saw her brow furrowed as she gazed at the snow-covered landscape and the towering mountains ahead.

At once Kim whirled around to face him. "What are you looking at, mister?" she grinned.

"You. I'm just wondering what you're thinking about."

Kim's grin faded to a smile. "You," she said.

"Me? What about me?" Jack asked.

"Oh, I'm just looking ahead." Kim shifted her gaze to the passing scenery once more. "You know, you, me, us."

"Good stuff?" Jack asked.

"Yeah, of course. It's so weird. We were apart for so long, but now it seems like that never happened. In a lot of ways, it seems like we were together all along. Know what I mean?"

Jack smiled. He knew exactly what she meant. "I want us to be together from now on," he said.

"Me, too." Kim took his hand and interlocked her fingers with his. They drove the rest of the way without a word.

While Jack and Kim were out, Mrs. Hurley had unpacked her own Christmas decorations. "Wow! You two found the perfect tree," she said as Jack and Kim wrestled the tree into place. "Look at those branches. They're so full!"

"You've got Jack to thank for it," Kim said.

"Jack, I have several strings of lights and some extension cords in this box," Mrs. Hurley said as she handed one of the cardboard cartons to Jack. "Would you string them up on the tree?"

While Jack worked with the lights Kim and Mrs. Hurley removed the tree ornaments from the remaining boxes and sorted them. Stephen hovered nearby, anxiously awaiting the chance to begin decorating the tree. He fidgeted and jumped about, prompting Kim to warn him several times to settle down and be patient. When he noticed the box that had come from Jack's house, he pointed to it and asked, "What's in there?"

"Some of Jack's ornaments," Kim said.

When Jack finished putting the tail of the last string of lights in place, Kim said, "Okay, now you can help. Come here and I'll hand you a ball." Stephen rushed to her side. "Now *slowly* take this to the tree," Kim said as she handed him the hook from which a shiny red ball dangled. Stephen carefully made his way to the tree, then slipped the hook over a branch. "Grandmom, will you give me the next one?" he asked as he turned and walked toward her.

"Sure, sweetie," Mrs. Hurley said. She handed Stephen a

silver ball. He returned to the tree and hung it next to the red ball.

"How about if I help you?" Jack asked Stephen. "I'm taller, so I can get the high branches."

"Okay," Stephen said. Soon Kim and Mrs. Hurley joined their effort and within a short while all of Mrs. Hurley's decorations were distributed about the branches of the tree.

Next Jack opened his box of tree ornaments. He removed the stuffed Road Runner and handed it to Stephen. "Do you think there's room on the tree for this?" he asked.

Stephen shot Jack a puzzled look. "This isn't a Christmas decoration," he said.

"Sure, it is. I put it on my tree every year," Jack said. "Your mom gave that to me a long, long time ago. It's been a Christmas ornament ever since."

Stephen remained skeptical, but he carried the stuffed Road Runner to the tree and secured it to a branch anyway. He backed away from the tree and shrugged.

Kim reached into the box and removed a small paper bag. "What's in here?" she asked as she unrolled the top of the bag and reached inside. Slowly she removed two green nylon covered

Styrofoam balls that had been decorated with red felt strips that hung like fringe. Both balls had been adorned with letters of sprinkled glitter glued in place, the first with the name Johnny and the second with the name James.

Jack's eyes became misty at the sight of the balls. "The boys and their mother made those a few years back," he said.

"Let's hang these side by side near the top," Kim said. She placed one of the balls into Jack's hand, then handed him a hook. Together they moved toward the tree and ceremoniously hung the reminders of Jack's sons from two adjacent branches above the Road Runner. "I like them," Kim said.

A few days later, at Jack's request, Stephen sneaked one of Kim's rings from her jewelry box. Jack slipped it onto his pinkie and found it was a snug fit over his second knuckle.

On Wednesday night less than a week before Christmas, Jack left work and headed to his own house to take a quick shower and to wolf down dinner. That morning before leaving for work he had leafed through the previous day's newspaper as he sipped his coffee. In it he spotted an advertisement for a half-price Christmas sale on engagement rings at a jewelry store located in a nearby mall, and that evening he planned to stop there on his way to his meeting and purchase a ring for Kim. If he timed it right, he figured he could dash into and out of the mall before the after-dinner crowd arrived and still make it to his meeting on time.

As he neared his house Jack noticed Kim's Caravan in the driveway. "Shit, not tonight!" But as he turned into the driveway, he told himself that he must act as if it was just another ordinary evening. Surely there was no way to hurry through the shower and dash out of the house without arousing Kim's suspicion. The ring would have to wait.

A sinking feeling came over him as he remembered he had left the newspaper on the kitchen table open to the half page ad where he had spotted a photo of the ring he intended to buy. He couldn't remember if he had circled the picture of the ring. If so, his surprise was as good as blown. But if not, maybe Kim would think nothing of it and put the paper aside as she prepared supper.

"Hey, Babe! I'm home," Jack called as he opened the front door. The aroma of sizzling chicken stir fry tantalized his nostrils, making his mouth water.

"Hey, yourself, Babe! I'm in the kitchen," Kim called back.

As Jack passed through the living room, he spied the newspaper. Kim had folded it neatly and placed it on the seat of his recliner. Jack resisted the temptation to pick it up and search for the ad. Doing so would confirm any suspicion she might have had. Instead, he met her in the kitchen and kissed her. "Dinner smells good."

"Hurry up and get your shower. It'll be ready by the time you're done," Kim said.

Jack left the room and headed for the shower. He wasted no time, but as the soothing hot water massaged his shoulders and streamed down his back his mind raced to come up with an alternate plan. Christmas was the following Tuesday, a mere six days away. He could buy the ring Friday night before his meeting, but with Christmas fast approaching, he thought it best not to risk the availability of the ring he wanted in the size he needed. After all, running a half-price sale was a sure way for a jeweler to move merchandise! Driving to the mall during his lunch hour was out of the question, for an hour was simply not enough time to drive there and back in midday traffic.

As Jack thought of his schedule for the next few days, he

realized there was no time during mall hours when he would not be at work, at his meetings, or with Kim. He decided to skip his meeting that night and go to the mall instead.

After his shower, he rejoined Kim in the kitchen. The meal she had prepared smelled scrumptious, and Jack consumed two generous helpings despite the nervous twinges in his stomach. He and Kim made small talk as they enjoyed their dinner. Afterward, Kim announced, "I'm going to stick around and clean up. There is some stir fry left. I'll put it in a bowl for you to take to work for lunch tomorrow. You'd better get going."

Jack cocked his head slightly as he faced her. "Are you trying to get rid of me?" he joked.

"No, not at all. I wish you didn't have to go, but I don't think I need to tell you that. I wish we could both stay and have some dessert, if you know what I mean," Kim said with a wink.

"Hmmm. Sounds good to me," Jack said as he sidled toward her, draped his arm across the small of her back, and tugged her toward him.

Jack brought his arms together around Kim's middle. He held her in a firm, yet gentle embrace. "I love you. Thanks for coming back into my life and making it so good," he whispered, then kissed the top of her head.

Kim rolled her head back, and their lips met for a long, warm kiss. "I love you, too. You'd better get going," she said at last.

"Yeah, I know. Thanks for dinner." He gave Kim one last kiss then headed for the door.

As Jack drove away, he was still unsure whether or not Kim suspected anything about the ring. He had not had an opportunity to check the newspaper to see if he had circled his ring of choice, but he would be sure to check it as soon as he returned home.

The parking lot at the mall was nearly full. Only a few parking spaces remained at the outer reaches of the expansive plain of asphalt surrounding the building. *Christ, it's going to be a zoo inside,* he thought. A steady string of cars crept up and down the rows of the parking lot nearest to the building, each driver hoping to come upon a car about to back out of its space. Jack considered looking for a parking space among these rows, but he reconsidered and wheeled his truck toward the remote region of the lot.

When he reached the jewelry store, he spotted a copy of the newspaper ad he had seen mounted to a sign board near the edge of the sales floor. *Good. I can just point to what I want.* The sales associate, a pretty young woman with long, curly brunette hair and striking brown eyes turned to him and smiled. "Is there something I can help you with, sir?" she asked. Her name tag identified her as Jessica.

"Yes, I'd like to take a look at an engagement ring," Jack replied.

"Well, sir, we have quite a selection to choose from, and they start at this end of the counter," Jessica said as she waved toward Jack's left. "Is there a particular style of ring you have in mind?"

"Yes. Actually, there is a certain ring I'd like to see," Jack said. "I saw your newspaper ad, and I really like the looks of the half carat marquis."

"Great! Those rings are right this way," Jessica said motioning toward Jack's left once more. She turned and knelt behind a nearby display case. After unlocking it she removed the exact ring Jack had seen in the newspaper ad, then stood and handed it to him.

With trembling fingers Jack took the ring. In the stark white light that shone down from a fixture directly over the counter the diamond sparkled brilliantly, its numerous cuts catching the light and refracting it into tiny prisms all about its surface. *Wow! It's beautiful!* he thought. He pushed the ring onto his pinkie, and it fit tightly over his second knuckle. *Even the size is right!*

He envisioned the ring on Kim's hand, and having now seen it up close, he felt confident the marquis cut would accentuate her slender fingers perfectly. Then he thought of how Kim would react when she saw the ring as he proposed to her. Tears would stream down her smooth cheeks as she laughed and cried, overwhelmed with joy.

Jessica was now rambling about how this ring offered an exceptional value, and that because of its simple style it could be had at such an affordable price, and that the holiday promotion they were running only made a great deal that much better. "But before you make your mind up on that ring perhaps, you'd like to see some of the other rings in our vast inventory. With several different styles of settings and different grades of stones, we have quite a selection to choose from. We carry rings from twelve different designers..."

"I'll take it," Jack said.

Jessica froze in mid-sentence. "Oh, okay."

"I'm sorry. I don't mean to be rude, but there's really no point in looking at other rings. This is the one I want," he said.

Jessica laughed. "If you find that the ring doesn't fit, just bring it back and we'll size it for you at no additional charge. Sizing is included in the purchase price. Now, if you'll step to the other end of the counter, I'll get you a box and your warranty papers and ring you up."

Chapter Twelve

Jack awoke on Christmas morning to the simultaneous bright

flash and click of Kim's camera. The springs of Mrs. Hurley's

folding sofa-bed creaked as he rolled to face the opposite direction.

"Merry Christmas, Babe. Time to get up," Kim nearly shouted.

Jack opened one eye into a narrow slit. Kim had turned on

every light in the room. Even the Christmas tree lights were lit.

"Ugh!" he groaned as he turned his head and burrowed under the

pillow. He was sure that is was still dark outside, for had the sun

begun to rise Kim surely would have opened the drapes as well.

Kim's camera clicked again. Jack was sure he felt the heat

from the flash slap across his skin.

Oh, these shots are going to look just fucking great in the

family photo album, he thought. Lying face down with his head

beneath his pillow, Jack brought both hands to his head and clamped

the pillow tightly over it.

"Merry Christmas, Jack," Mrs. Hurley said as she stood near

the foot of the sofa bed.

Then Stephen bounded onto the bed. "Merry Christmas!

Are you gonna get up now? Mom says when you get up, we can go see what Santa Claus brought! She says Santa knows I'm here. Are you gonna get up now?" He sat by Jack's side in the center of the bed eagerly awaiting Jack's answer.

Pow! Kim's flash fired once more.

Jack looked into Stephen's excited eyes. It was Christmas! Of course, he would get up, but first he would have some fun with Stephen. Jack pushed the pillow aside, yawned, then said, "Stephen, I'm really beat. I need more sleep. You don't mind if we wait another hour or two, do you?"

Stephen paused for a moment before answering. Jack watched as the excitement ebbed from his face. "Can't you get up now, then take a nap later if you need to?" he asked.

"I don't think so," Jack said. "Once I get up, I usually can't fall asleep again. I think I need another couple of hours of sleep now. What time is it?"

"Six o'clock," Stephen said. "Don't you always get up around six?"

"Usually, but I didn't sleep very well last night. I really need some more sleep. Why don't you wake me up around nine?"

"Nine?" Stephen looked at Kim helplessly.

"Yeah, nine would be good," Jack said. He flopped onto his back and tugged the covers up around his neck. "G'night," he said as he closed his eyes.

Jack heard faint whispering, but kept his eyes closed. At once Mrs. Hurley flung the covers from the upper portion of Jack's body while Kim and Stephen began to tickle his bare ribs.

"All right, all right, I'm getting up!" Jack shouted. "Stop! I'm getting up!"

"Good morning, dear. Did you sleep well?" Kim asked in mock sweetness as she bent and kissed Jack's cheek. "I thought you'd change your mind and get up now."

Jack growled playfully. "I can't get up with everybody standing here. I don't have any clothes on," he said.

"I didn't need to know that," Mrs. Hurley said as she turned to leave the room. Stephen followed her into the kitchen.

Kim laughed. "Stop it. I know you're wearing underwear at least," she said.

"I wouldn't bet on it," Jack said. Kim tossed a pillow at his head. Jack flipped back the covers to reveal a pair of green and red sweat pants adorned with cartoon drawings of Santa Claus, Christmas trees, Rudolph, and the other reindeer. "Ha!"

"Okay, very funny, Mr. Kringle. Get your ass up and come get a cup of coffee. The poor kid wants to see what Santa left," Kim said as she, too, headed toward the kitchen.

Mrs. Hurley handed Jack a steaming mug as he sat down at the table. Pow! Kim's flash fired again. Jack winced.

"Can we please go see what Santa brought?" Stephen groaned.

Jack smiled wearily at Stephen, who was seated directly across the table from him, and said, "Sure."

Without another word Stephen sprang from his chair and bolted toward the living room. He bounced over Jack's bed, then landed with a WHUMP as his feet met the floor on the other side.

On the floor between the Christmas tree and the television lay a red wool stocking overflowing with assorted nuts and a folded slip of paper. Behind the sock sat a box with a clear plastic window containing a radio-controlled Dodge Viper GTS Coupe.

"Aw, wow!" Stephen shouted as he reached past the sock and grabbed the package containing the Viper. He tore the box open and swiftly, but carefully, removed its contents.

"Looks like your last-minute impulse buy is a hit," Kim said quietly as she nudged Jack with her elbow. Then she raised her camera and snapped a shot of Stephen as he unpackaged the car.

"Mom! Look! This is cool!" Stephen shouted.

"What kind of car is it?" Kim asked.

"It's a Viper!" He pressed the buttons on the remote controller. "Hey, there's no batteries. Santa forgot the batteries!"

"No, he didn't," Kim said in a quietly so that only Jack and Mrs. Hurley could hear.

"Grandmom, do you have any batteries?" Stephen asked.

"No, dear, I don't think I do. But I'll be going to the grocery store one day this week. If you remind me, I'll pick some up," Mrs. Hurley said.

"Oh, I can't wait that long," Stephen said.

"Stephen, you've got a whole stocking full of stuff there. Why don't you see what else Santa brought you?" Kim said.

Reluctantly Stephen placed the controller on the floor next to his new Viper. "Mom, this isn't a stocking. It's somebody's sock."

"I know, Stephen. Your Christmas stocking is at home in

Maine. Since you didn't have one here Grandmom was nice enough to lend you a wool sock," Kim said. In her haste to prepare for the holiday it was not until late the previous night that she had even thought of a Christmas stocking. The worn red wool sock had been Mrs. Hurley's offering as a last-minute solution.

"But Mom, it's a *sock!* Somebody's foot has been in there," Stephen continued.

"Well, what do you think a stocking is?" Kim asked. "It's nothing but a big sock."

"Yea, but nobody's ever stuck their stinky foot in my Christmas stocking."

"Stephen, that's enough," Kim said. "Now let's see what else Santa brought you."

Stephen begrudgingly scooped the nuts from the top of the Christmas sock. The folded slip of paper fell aside with Stephen paying it no mind. Next, he plucked a hard-plastic CD case from the stocking. "Hot Shoe Two," he read aloud. "Aww, cool!"

"Is there anything else in there?" Kim asked.

"Just more nuts," Stephen said.

"Are you sure? Better dump them out and see," Kim urged.

Stephen held the sock by the toe, then shook it. Out tumbled two lumps of coal, followed by two packs of batteries. "Batteries! Santa didn't forget! Cool!" he shouted.

"Whoa, hold on a minute. What are they?" Kim asked as she pointed at the coal.

"I don't know," Stephen said as he fought to tear the batteries from their plastic packages.

"Stephen, I know what they are. They're coal!" Mrs. Hurley said.

Stephen's hands froze. He shot his grandmother with a puzzled look. "Coal? Why would Santa bring me coal?"

"I don't know," Mrs. Hurley replied. "It looks like he left you a note. Better open it and read it," she said as she pointed to the folded paper lying on the floor near the stocking.

Stephen picked up the paper and unfolded it. Jack moved to his side and coached him as he read the letter aloud. "Dear Stephen, You were pretty good all year, so I brought you some of the things you wanted. I hope you like them. But I remember a few times you gave your mother a hard time. That is why you got the coal. You must remember to do what your mother tells you to do and not give her a hard time. She's the only mother you have, and you don't want

to drive her nuts! I gave you the nuts as a reminder of that point, and

also because I know you like them. I hope you have a Merry

Christmas. But remember, I'm always watching you! Santa knows

all! Love, Santa."

Jack looked up from the letter to see Mrs. Hurley biting her

lower lip to keep from laughing. Kim fired another shot. Pow!

"Stephen, it sounds like Santa means business," Kim said. "I

think he let you off the hook this year, but it sounds like he's going

to be keeping his eye on you for next year."

"But Mom, I have been good."

"I know you have for the most part, but there have been a

few times when you've slipped up. Santa is just reminding you of

that. If you try to be a little more careful, you'll be fine for next

year," she said.

"I'll try, but I'm not perfect. Santa should know that!"

Stephen said.

"Hold that letter up a minute. I think there is something

written on the back," Kim said.

Stephen flipped the piece of paper over. On the back-side

Santa had scrawled more words, and once more Stephen read them aloud. "Check your mother's room." Stephen's brow furrowed, then he ran for Kim's room. Kim, Jack, and Mrs. Hurley followed. "Aw, man! It's a bike! Mom, Santa brought me a bike!"

Kim rounded the corner of her room and clicked off a few more shots as Stephen bounded around his new bicycle.

"You're a nut! Telling that poor kid Santa's watching him, you make Santa sound like a crazed predator!" Mrs. Hurley said to Jack in a low voice as she laughed. "Honestly, I didn't think I'd be able to keep a straight face!"

"The last thing I did before I went to bed was write that note," Jack said. "I guess Santa was getting a bit punchy by then. You had already gone to bed when I discovered half the hardware for the bike was missing. Kim and I were up for a couple more hours going through your husband's stash of old screws, nuts, and bolts just to get that thing together for him."

"Well, to see how excited he is right now, I'd say it was well worth it," Mrs. Hurley said.

While Kim and Mrs. Hurley prepared breakfast Jack observed Stephen as he navigated his new Viper back and forth across the short nap blue carpet. "Don't get too close to the walls,"

he warned. Soon the mingled aromas of sausage, bacon, eggs, and

waffles tantalized Jack's nose. His stomach growled.

A short while later Kim called, "Come and get it, guys!

Breakfast is ready." Stephen took two more laps across the living

room, then motored the Viper toward the Christmas tree and parked

it next to the small heap of brightly wrapped gifts. Jack rose from

his chair, and together he and Stephen walked to the kitchen.

While they consumed their food, Jack sank into thought. He

planned to give Kim her ring sometime that day, but he still had not

decided on the proper place. Once he did, he would have to figure a

way to get her to that place without her suspecting anything.

"Cat got your tongue?" Kim asked, shattering his thoughts.

"No, I'm just feeling sort of groggy this morning. Didn't get

enough sleep last night, and I'm feeling it now." Kim nodded in

understanding.

After breakfast the foursome returned to the living room for

the gift exchange. A few days earlier Kim had rearranged the stack

of gifts, and at the bottom of the pile was a large flat box that Jack

soon discovered was labeled with his name. "We're saving that one for last," Kim said.

They took turns tearing open package after package and exchanging "oohs," "aahs," and "thank-yous." Jack had bought Kim a couple of sweaters, and together they had purchased a CD player with detachable speakers for Stephen and a telephone with caller ID for Mrs. Hurley.

At last, only the large flat package remained. Kim slid it in front of Jack, then took her camera and knelt into position across the room. Jack tore the paper away to reveal a flat corrugated cardboard box with no discernible markings. "There isn't something in here that's going to jump out at me, is there?" Jack asked as he hooked his finger under the flap and prepared to raise the lid.

"Maybe," Kim teased. "Go ahead, dear! Open it!"

Jack tore away the tissue paper to reveal a package of car floor mats. The mats were black and emblazoned on the front of the top mat was a large cartoon Road Runner, and Jack's name in large yellow letters at the bottom. "This is awesome!" Jack said.

Pow! Kim's flash burned his retinas once more.

Jack flipped the top mat up to reveal a nearly identical second mat with Kim's name at the bottom. "Let me guess. Black mats to match the black carpet, and yellow letters to match the color of the car," Jack said. "Where did you have these made?"

"I found an ad in one of your car magazines. They already offered the Road Runner mats. All I had to do was tell them the names to go at the bottom and the color of the letters," Kim said. "Can we take a ride to your house today and put them in the car?" she asked.

"Yeah, we can go this afternoon." Jack smiled, for suddenly the issues of the proper place and how to get Kim there were solved.

Throughout the morning the sun shone brightly, and the temperature rose, melting the previous evening's light snowfall. Jack gathered the torn wrapping paper and stuffed it into a bag. Later he went with Stephen outside to watch him ride his new bike. Meanwhile Kim and Mrs. Hurley straightened the kitchen, then sat at the table for a chat.

After nearly an hour Stephen grew weary. He complained that his chest hurt from breathing the chilly air. Jack put Stephen's bicycle in the garage, then led him through the garage to the house. They spoke briefly to Kim and Mrs. Hurley as they passed by the kitchen on their way to the living room. There Stephen turned on the television and inserted his new Hot Shoe CD into the PlayStation.

"Do you want to play?" Stephen asked Jack.

"Maybe in a little while. I don't know anything about this new game. I'll watch you play first and see if I can learn," Jack said. He leaned back in the recliner and breathed in the scent of pine needles and the fading aroma of breakfast. Even though his boys were nearly two thousand miles away, Jack knew he had much to be thankful for. He pondered this thought as an air of tranquility settled over him. In minutes he drifted off to sleep.

Jack awoke suddenly to find Kim's soft lips against his cheek and her long, blonde hair tickling his nose. "Wake up, Babe," she said. "We still have to go to your house, remember?"

Jack stood, rubbed his eyes, and donned his coat. Kim stood in the foyer holding the package of floor mats. They walked to his truck in silence. Jack opened her door and offered his hand to aid her in climbing into the truck. She tossed the package inside, took Jack's hand, and sprang into her seat. Jack rounded the nose of the truck and vaulted into his own seat.

"This is tough on Mom," Kim said once Jack shut his door.

"What is?"

"Today. Christmas. With Dad being gone and all," Kim said. "For the last couple of weeks, she has been trying hard to get into the spirit, and she has done well. I was afraid that she would become depressed as Christmas got closer, but she didn't. She got through the decorating, shopping, wrapping, and meal planning just fine. But today it has really hit her hard that he's gone."

With a sinking feeling in his chest Jack said, "We don't have to go if you don't want to."

"I know, and thanks. I hope you don't mind, but I suggested that to her already, and she insisted that we go. She said, 'You two need some time to yourselves,'" Kim mocked her mother with a stern tone. Jack chuckled. "Today is really tough for her, but she's doing her best to be strong."

"How about you? How are you handling it?" Jack asked.

"I'm okay, at least for now. I wasn't sure how I'd do, but I think I'll be okay," Kim said. Jack was sure he saw dampness in her eyes, but she quickly blinked it away.

Without another word, Jack buckled his seat belt, started the engine, and pulled away from the curb. They drove toward his house, each enjoying the other's company with a minimum of words.

A few minutes into the ride Kim unbuckled her seatbelt, placed the package of floor mats beneath her feet, and slid to the center of the seat where she could be closer to Jack. She buckled the center lap belt, then leaned against Jack's shoulder.

Jack brought the truck to a stop in his driveway. He opened his door then stepped to the ground. Kim handed him the floor mats then took his hand as she leaped to the ground. Arm in arm they walked toward the shed where the Road Runner lay in wait of spring. Jack thought of taking the Road Runner for a drive, but he quickly reconsidered, for the snow at the edge of the driveway would make the wooden ramps slick. It would be difficult, if not impossible, to put the car away afterward. Should the rear tires spin on the wet wood, the tail of the car could slide to one side or the other, colliding with the wooden frame around the door opening. Jack cringed at the thought.

Kim removed the floor mat with Jack's name from the package and handed it to him. He opened the driver's door and placed the mat on the floor, positioning it so that it would not interfere with either the clutch or accelerator pedal. "I like that!" he said as he stood and admired the mat. "I like that a lot!"

"Here, do my side," Kim said as she handed him the other mat. Jack took the mat with Kim's name, then sat behind the wheel and placed the mat on the passenger's side floor. Kim, who had stepped to the other side of the car, peered through the passenger's side window. With the mat in place Jack unlocked and opened her door from the inside. Kim got in, then scrutinized the appearance and fit of her mat for a moment. "Do you really like them?"

"I love them!" Jack said. "They match the car perfectly!" He leaned toward Kim, and she met him half way. They kissed.

Their embrace lasted for several moments. Frantically Jack searched for the words to summarize his feelings for Kim. He strove to come up with something original and witty, yet profound, but the proper words eluded him. Suddenly he heard himself blurt, "Thank you for coming back into my life. I know I'm the luckiest guy in the world, but you've also made me the happiest guy in the world." *Not exactly what I had in mind, but I guess I could have done worse,* he thought. There was a waver to his tone that he was sure Kim detected. Jack reached into his pocket, produced the box, and flipped open the lid.

"Oh, my God!" Kim gasped as her eyes fell upon the ring.

"Oh, my God! Jack, it's... it's *beautiful!*" At once she thrust her arms around Jack's neck and planted her lips against his. Jack was taken by surprise and nearly dropped the ring box. He placed it on the dashboard, then held Kim tightly. "I love you so much, but I didn't expect this. Not yet. Oh, God, I love you!" Kim rattled on.

After another lengthy kiss Jack said, "Here. Let me see your finger." He removed the ring from its pouch in the padded box and slipped it onto Kim's finger. "How does it fit?"

"Fine," Kim said. She held her hand high so that the diamond sparkled in the sunlight that shone through the rear window of the car. "Oh, Jack, it's gorgeous!" They kissed once more.

"Will you marry me?" Jack asked at length.

"Yes, yes, I will marry you," Kim laughed.

Jack caressed Kim's cheek with his fingers. "I love you so much," he whispered into her ear.

Kim moved her head. Her eyes sparkled as she looked deep into Jack's eyes. "And I love you," she said. "I can't tell you how happy I am to have you back, or how glad I am that you're still the same Jack you always were."

Jack hugged Kim. "I can't believe how good it feels to hold

you like this in the same car after all this time," he said. After a

lengthy embrace, "We should head inside. I want to call Johnny and

James while we're here."

Kim agreed. When they left the shed Jack pulled down the

door. As they walked to the house Kim admired her diamond in the

sunlight. "I'll call Mom before we leave, but I'm not going to say

anything about the ring. In fact, when we get back, I'm going to

wait and see how long it takes her to notice."

Once inside, Jack went to the kitchen to call his sons.

"Hello," Ralph drawled on the other end after the fourth ring.

"Ralph? It's Jack. Merry Christmas!"

"Merry Christmas, Jack," Ralph said in return. "Y'all got a

lot of snow out your way?"

"No, not really. It's been pretty warm here for this time of

year. There is still some in the yard, and we had a dusting last night,

but so far this year the snowfall hasn't been anything like what we'd

expected. How's the weather down south?" Jack asked.

"Weatherman said it was s'posed to hit fifty-five today, but I

don't think it did. Hard to tell with the breeze, but it didn't feel like

no fifty-five to me. I never did look at the thermometer. It was sunny most of the day. Few clouds this afternoon, but other than that it's been pretty nice. Santa Claus had a good night for travel last night. No bitter temperatures, no rain, and no fog." Ralph chuckled. "The boys were outside most of the day, but they're sitting here at the table now. Want to talk to them?"

It had not occurred to Jack that with the time difference they would all be seated at the table for Christmas dinner. "No, no, Ralph, that's okay. I don't want to interrupt your meal. I'll call back later," Jack said.

"Nonsense. Hold on. They're right here," Ralph said. Then he passed the receiver.

"Hello, Dad?" a voice came over the phone.

"Johnny?" Jack asked.

"Merry Christmas, Dad!"

"Merry Christmas to you, too. Was Santa good to you?"

"Dad, there's no such thing," Johnny whispered. "But yes, Santa was good to us," he said at a normal volume for James's benefit. "Thanks for the money. Mom says later this week we can go to the mall and buy some stuff."

"What are you going to get?" Jack asked.

"Probably some CDs and stuff. Maybe a pair of sneakers. I haven't decided yet."

Jack and Johnny talked for several more minutes before Johnny handed the phone to James. "Hi, Dad. Merry Christmas!" James exclaimed into the telephone. "I got a slot car set, and some candy, and some CDs, and an alarm clock, and some pants, and some shirts, and a check! The check was from you. Thanks, Dad!"

"Sounds like you made out pretty well. You must have gotten everything you could have wished for," Jack said.

"No, not everything," James said. "I still need some video games."

"Oh, I see," Jack said. "Maybe you can use the money from the check for your games."

"Yeah, that's what I was thinking. How is Christmas back at home?" James asked.

Jack was stunned that James referred to Jack's house as "home".

"It's fine. Kim and I are going to go back to her mother's house for dinner in a few minutes. We were there earlier, but we came over here for a while this afternoon."

"Is she right there?" James asked.

"Yes," Jack said.

"Can I talk to her?" James asked. It would be the first time either boy had spoken with Kim.

Jack passed the phone to Kim as he shrugged his shoulders. "It's James. He wants to talk to you."

"Hello, James?" Kim asked timidly. "Merry Christmas."

"Merry Christmas," James said. An awkward silence ensued.

"Was there something in particular you wanted to say to me, or did you just want to talk for a little bit?" Kim asked.

"You're being good to my dad, aren't you?" James asked.

Startled, Kim said, "Why, yes, I think so."

"Good. He's a good daddy and he's *my* daddy. Don't be mean to him," James said.

"I think I'm treating him pretty well," Kim said. "Do you want to talk to your dad again?"

"Okay," James said.

"You have yourself a nice Christmas. It's been good talking with you," Kim said.

"Okay. Bye," James said.

Kim passed the receiver back to Jack. "He wants to make

sure I'm being good to you," she whispered.

"James don't worry. Kim is a very nice lady and she treats your old man pretty darned well. Really, she does. I'd like for you and Johnny to meet her sometime. What do you think?"

"We'll see," James said.

"Okay, well I'd better let you get to your supper before the food is all gone. I'll talk to you in a couple of days," Jack said.

"Okay. Bye, Dad. Merry Christmas. I love you," James said.

"I love you, too. Bye," Jack said, then sighed and hung up the phone.

Kim glanced into Jack's misty eyes, then hugged him. "You should see the way your face lights up when you talk to them on the phone! I don't want to bring up a sore subject, but you know, instead of buying me this expensive ring, you could have bought them plane tickets."

"I know what you are saying. And, yes, I feel that the right time is getting closer, but it isn't here yet. When that time arrives, I will do what I need to do. But now was the right time for that ring," Jack said.

"Promise me you'll visit them sometime soon?"

"I promise."

After a lengthy hug, Kim called her mother. She and Jack then drove back in time to help her finish preparing Christmas dinner.

Chapter Thirteen

Mrs. Hurley and Kim had planned Christmas dinner to include both ham and turkey, along with stuffing, cole slaw, macaroni and cheese, mashed potatoes, steamed broccoli with cauliflower, and gelatin salad. They had prepared many of the side dishes in advance so that there would be less work on Christmas day. During the meal Jack stuffed himself until he could eat no more. Collectively the foursome decided to postpone dessert for a while.

After their meal Stephen went to his room to listen to music and set up an obstacle course for his new Viper. Jack, Kim, and Mrs. Hurley remained seated at the table for some idle talk over coffee. Suddenly Mrs. Hurley gasped and pointed at Kim's hand. "Kim, is that what I think it is?"

Kim could not find her voice. Her face beamed as she nodded.

"Oh, Kim! Let me see it in the light," Mrs. Hurley said as she grasped Kim's hand and raised it to eye level. Directly beneath the ceiling light the diamond sparkled as if emitting its own light. "Oh, Kim, this is just gorgeous!" Mrs. Hurley hugged her, then turned to Jack. "Come here, you!" She hugged him, too. "Wow! This is really something!"

"I was beginning to wonder if you would ever notice," Kim said. "I was wearing it and flashing it around the whole time we were eating dinner."

"You were? I can't believe I didn't notice," Mrs. Hurley said. "I guess my mind was someplace else. Tell me, when did this take place?"

"This afternoon at Jack's house," Kim said. "Actually, it was in his shed."

"In his shed?"

"I keep the Road Runner in a special shed next to the house," Jack said. "When I gave her the ring, we were sitting in the car."

"Which was parked in the shed," Kim added.

While they talked, Jack replaced Mrs. Hurley's outdated wall-mounted kitchen telephone with the new Caller ID telephone he and Kim had given her. Eventually the talk dwindled, and Jack fell out of the conversation completely.

While Kim and her mother chatted, Jack wandered lazily into the living room. He sat in the recliner and gazed into the blinking lights of the Christmas tree. His swollen stomach hung painfully like a lump of curing concrete. It felt as if the food had expanded in his stomach to half again its original volume after he had stopped eating. He took a deep breath, then let out a half moan, half sigh as he exhaled.

Jack considered going to the bathroom and making himself vomit, but he was repulsed by the thought of sticking his fingers down his throat then throwing up on his hand. Besides, getting up from the chair would require far more effort than he was willing to expend at that moment. The easiest thing would be to sit still and wait for the agony to pass.

As he sat, Jack's thoughts drifted through the events of the day. Despite his being sick from overeating, it had been some day! Of course, he and Kim were now engaged. But he had also shared this Christmas with Mrs. Hurley and Stephen, who had become very dear to him. But one of the greatest gifts Jack could have hoped for had come to him in the telephone call to his sons. He wished he could be with them, and he again promised himself that one day he would visit them. Though this still seemed like a monstrous step, it was one that seemed more possible with each passing day. It was a step he knew he must take.

As Jack gazed into the blinking lights of the Christmas tree his vision slowly drifted out of focus. The sleep deprivation from the previous night was beginning to take its toll and coupled with his gluttony at the dinner table Jack drifted to the edge of consciousness. The fuzzy, blinking multi-colored lights brought on a soothing feeling which eased the discomfort in his belly. He sat staring trance-like into the quiet incandescence of the tree while his consciousness ebbed away. Soon he fell asleep.

After clearing the dishes, Kim and Mrs. Hurley sat at the table, each with a mug of coffee. "You've had quite a Christmas!" Mrs. Hurley said.

"Yeah, I sure have," Kim said, her cheeks aglow.

"I'm amazed at how Jack and Stephen have taken to each other. So often you hear horror stories about children resenting a parent's new companion."

"I think the reason is because Jack spends time with him. Randy didn't. I just wish Jack would put the same effort into his relationship with his own sons."

"Oh Kim, give him time. He's coming around."

"Mom don't get me wrong. I love Jack, and I want to be with him, but what if it doesn't work out? Then it's not just the two of us, but also Stephen who gets hurt. Is that fair?"

"Stop worrying, will you? If things don't work out, Stephen will adjust. Kids know more than we give them credit for. But I really don't think you have anything to worry about."

"You're probably right. I guess I'm just a little freaked out about getting engaged. I want this, I want it more than anything, but I don't want to be trapped in another bad relationship, either. What if Jack starts drinking again?"

"Well, you've got a legitimate concern, but what if he doesn't? Are you willing to let that concern get in the way of what you and he have? Granted, he could one day have a relapse, but you or I could get hit by a bus on our way to the mailbox, too."

"Mom!"

"My point is, nobody knows what's going to happen. Despite what he's been through, he has worked hard, and he continues to do so." Mrs. Hurley sipped her coffee.

"So, you don't think I should worry about it?"

"Kim, there are no perfect men, and good ones don't come

along often. All I can tell you is trust your heart. Jack's trusting

his."

Chapter Fourteen

Soon the holidays were mere memories. January faded into February, and February into March. During that time Jack and Kim's relationship reached a comfortable plateau. Although they occasionally discussed wedding plans, neither spoke with a sense of urgency. Talk of their wedding was usually of a dreamy and far away quality. They agreed that it would most definitely happen one day, but that day would arrive in its own time.

Often when the conversation turned to the topic of their wedding Kim reminded Jack that she was still not divorced from Randy. Jack saw that the further their relationship progressed, the more this bothered Kim. Although she had mentioned it several times over the months, they had been together, what she had once passed off as a "minor legal detail" had grown to become a more serious issue to her.

Jack knew that before they could be married Kim's divorce would have to be final. With the divorce would come a division of the property she and Randy owned, and in all likelihood, they would have to sell the house in Maine. Kim was certain Randy would object to this, for the house had belonged to his grandfather. Even so, it was Kim who had worked single-handedly to continue building the business and pay all of the house expenses since she and Randy had separated. Unless she and Randy could find an amicable way to divide their worth fairly, Jack feared a court battle was imminent. Jack knew this was Kim's business, and that it was something she would have to handle when she was ready. He chose not to pressure her.

As the winter neared its end Kim worked to complete her latest children's book. She had sent copies of this work to her agent, Marty Shapiro, a former New Yorker who had recently relocated to Boston. Telephone conversations between them now took place a couple of times a week. Several publishers were interested in this book, and soon she learned that most of the publishers expected her to begin promoting her newest book as soon as she signed the contract, months before the book would be printed. Kim dreaded the thought of a promotional tour. She insisted that whatever promoting she agreed to would have to wait until fall.

"Kim, things are starting to happen now!" Marty said during a telephone conversation one Friday afternoon. "You have to be willing to talk to these people and consider what they have to say. You're one lucky lady. Few writers and even fewer illustrators ever get where you are, but you've beaten the odds. This is where you want to be. You're not struggling to get your books published anymore. The publishers are coming to you. You could have them eating out of your hand, but timing is everything in this business. If you turn them off now, they'll go elsewhere. You won't reap the benefits from your years of hard work. Think about it. Call me."

Kim took note of the calculated New York style abruptness in the way her agent ended the call. It was intended to make her dwell on their conversation, and it worked. Over the weekend she began to rethink her stand on waiting until the fall. If there was as much interest in her newest book as her agent indicated, then Kim Hurley, author/illustrator, might just be on the verge of becoming a hot commodity in the field of children's literature. Marty faxed her copies of the proposals from a few of the publishers, and Kim spent most of the weekend poring over them.

On Monday, Kim received her agent's well-timed follow-up call. "Kim, it's Marty. My phone keeps ringing. I've got to tell these guys something, so what's it going to be? Are you going to come see me so we can go over some of these proposals together, or do I have to disappoint them and tell them you're not interested in hearing what they have to say?"

"I think I need to come see you," Kim said.

"Good!"

"Wait a minute. I didn't say I was going to agree totally to any of the proposals you forwarded, but there are a couple that I think we can work with. We need to draw up a couple of counter offers. I will agree to making a few public appearances, but I'll be damned if I'm going to allow myself to get locked into a full-scale tour where I'll have to speak to every PTA group in every little nook of the country. Remember, I still have a child to raise, a business to run, and a life to live."

"That's fine, that's fine," Marty said. "I'm sure we can reach an agreement that will make you and your new publisher happy, whoever that may be. Remember, you're starting at one end of the scale with your demands, and they are starting at the other. You give a little, they give a little, and you start moving toward each other until you meet somewhere in the middle. That's what negotiation is all about, and that's my job."

Later that same day Kim received another telephone call. This time it was Horace Gladding, the neighbor whom Kim had entrusted to watch her home in Maine for the winter. "Kim, there's been a problem you should know about," he said. "I checked on your place this afternoon, and as soon as I opened the door, I knew something was wrong. We've been keeping the heat running at the lowest setting just to keep the furnace working and to make sure the pipes don't freeze, but today the house was cold inside. Then I heard the sound of water running. I think your heater must have quit sometime yesterday after I left. The pipes froze last night and one of them burst."

Kim collapsed into a kitchen chair. She took a deep breath, then asked, "How bad is it?"

"The pipe that broke feeds one of the upstairs bathrooms. It's inside the wall, so I don't know how much of the wall would have to be torn out to get to it. But the ceiling over the dining area is saturated with water, and the carpet in that room is soaked. In fact, one part of the ceiling came down. I think the furniture will be okay, but I can't lie to you; the carpet, ceiling, and maybe some of the plaster on the walls is going to have to be replaced," Horace said.

"Oh, shit!" Kim said under her breath.

"My son and I got the water turned off," Horace said. "He took the nozzle out of your furnace. Some dirt got into the tip, but he cleaned that out and got it restarted. It seems to be running okay now, but we drained the pipes so that if the furnace quits again it won't do any more damage to your plumbing."

"You say the ceiling and carpet in the dining room are destroyed?" Kim asked.

"I'm afraid so. That much I can say for sure. Beyond that, I really don't know. We've got the windows open right now to try to air the place out. I'm thinking we might close it up for the night and open it again tomorrow. If the moisture builds up, you'll have mildew everywhere."

Kim's mind whirled. She knew she must return to Maine immediately. "Can you keep an eye on the place for another couple of days? I can be there by the end of the week," she said.

"Sure, I can do that. I'm sorry to spoil your day, and I hate to see you cut your stay with your mother short," Horace said.

"Oh, there's nothing you can do about that," Kim said. "Horace, thanks. Thanks for everything."

Kim hung up the telephone and sat still for a moment while she gathered her thoughts. She felt short of breath, and although she fought to shrug it off, her chest grew tight. She took a deep breath, held it, then exhaled. After a moment she stood and began stowing away copies of her latest work in progress; Marty would want to see them.

Kim had no way of knowing how long she would be in Maine. Even if the damage to the house was not extensive and the repairs could be made quickly, she reasoned that she would still be there for at least a couple of weeks, perhaps longer. With her current book nearing completion and tourist season approaching, Kim knew she could not afford to lose even two weeks' worth of productivity. Furthermore, she knew she would lose her momentum if she did so. Stopping for two weeks now would likely push her completion date for the book back three or four weeks. With that in mind she packed her drawing supplies, then disconnected the components of her computer.

Kim gathered a load of dirty laundry and carried it to the laundry room. The knot in her chest seemed to tighten and her hands began to tremble. So much had begun to happen, and it was all taking place so quickly. She knew she should consider herself fortunate, for with her career taking off the way it had she now had more control over her destiny than most professionals in her field would ever have. But the excitement over her good fortune was displaced by trepidation. Kim suddenly realized that she was dreading her meeting with Marty. And this small disaster which had taken place at her house fueled further the nervous agitation that now churned in the pit of her stomach. Kim forced herself to keep moving. She started the washing machine and dropped the garments one by one into the water that gushed into the drum inside, then carried her drawing supplies and computer equipment to her van. Her mother should be home from running her errands at any minute, and Kim hoped to be able to discuss with her the situation with the house before Stephen came home from school.

As Kim reached the van with her second armload of belongings, Mrs. Hurley's Crown Victoria bounced into the driveway. "Boy, that took a lot longer than it should have," she said as she stood from her car. "The line at the bank was backed up almost to the door, and only two tellers were open. The line at the post office was almost as bad." Suddenly she noticed the items that

Kim had placed in the van. "What's going on, dear?"

"Mom, I have to go back to Maine," Kim said. She turned and sat on the floor of her van just inside the open sliding cargo door, and her emotions finally overcame her. Streams of tears gushed from her eyes and spilled down her cheeks.

"Oh my, Kim. What happened?" Mrs. Hurley asked as she knelt at her daughter's side.

"I'm sorry, Mom. Everything's getting to me. The publishers, Marty, and now the house," Kim said.

"The house?" Mrs. Hurley asked. She placed her hand on Kim's shoulder.

"Mr. Gladding called. He's my neighbor, the one who is watching the place while Stephen and I are here. He said the furnace quit and the pipes froze and burst. Water poured down the inside of the walls, and he said the dining room has a lot of damage. I have to get it all fixed," Kim blubbered. "I can't believe this!"

"Now, now," Mrs. Hurley said as she hugged her daughter. "I know this is the last thing you need to worry about right now, but I'm sure it will be okay."

"Yeah, but can I get the house fixed, get my book finished,

and get my dealings with Marty and the publishers all out of the way before the school year ends and I have to start booking people?"

Mrs. Hurley fell silent. At length she said, "Kim, you do what you have to. Do what you need to do to get your house in order and come back when you're done. Stephen will be just fine here with me."

"Are you sure you don't mind?" Kim asked as she looked into her mother's eyes.

"Of course not! We'll have a lot of fun," Mrs. Hurley smiled. "And try not to worry. Things have a way of working out for the best. Maybe you need some time to yourself away in Maine to think this publishing thing through."

"Maybe," Kim said. "Mom, thanks." She opened her mouth again as if to say more, but her words escaped her.

"It's okay, it's okay," Mrs. Hurley whispered. "I should be thanking you. If not for you and Stephen, I don't know how I would have survived this winter with your father being gone." Quickly she wiped away a tear of her own as it trickled from the corner of her eye.

At once Mrs. Hurley stood and said, "Let's go inside." Kim

recognized her mother's sudden movement as an attempt to break the melancholy mood and stood to join her. Moments later, as they sat at the kitchen table sipping instant hot chocolate, Kim told her mother of the telephone call from Marty Shapiro and their meeting in Boston, which she had scheduled for the following Tuesday. By now Kim had come up with a plan to drive to her home in Maine, have the necessary emergency repairs made to the furnace and plumbing, and then drive to Boston to meet with Marty. Afterward she would return to her home and address the water damage.

A short while later Kim heard Stephen's school bus pulling away from the curb. Then the front door opened, and Stephen entered the house. "Mom, I'm home," he called.

"We're in the kitchen," Kim called back. "Stephen, come here. There is something I need to talk to you about."

"What's all your stuff doing in the van?" Stephen asked as he rounded the corner of the kitchen doorway.

"Stephen, I have to go home to Maine for a while. There has been trouble with the house, and I need to go back for a couple of weeks, or maybe a month to get it all straightened out," Kim said. She studied Stephen's face to gauge his reaction, half expecting him to object to her leaving.

"Do I have to go?" Stephen asked.

"No, you'll stay here with Grandmom until I get back," Kim said.

"Good! What happened to the house?"

"Mr. Gladding called and said the furnace stopped working. It got really cold inside and the pipes over the dining room froze and burst. The water did some damage to the dining room. Beyond that, I won't know how bad it is until I get there," Kim said.

Stephen shook his head in dismay. "You should sell that house. It's old, and things are just going to keep breaking. Besides, it's too far away. I like it here in Colorado. Here with my friends, and Grandmom, and Jack. There's nobody in Maine."

Kim was taken aback. This was the first time Stephen had ever mentioned wanting to live in Colorado permanently. Hearing him voice this thought brought her a faint sense of relief. "Someday, maybe we will live here for good. We'll have to wait and see what happens. For now, I have to tend to the problems in Maine."

"When are you leaving?" Stephen asked.

"Early tomorrow morning."

"How early? Like before I get up for school?"

"I'll probably leave here right when you get up. I want to see you before I go, but the earlier I get started, the more ground I can cover," Kim said.

Stephen nodded. "Are you going to go see Jack tonight?" he asked.

"Yes. I'm going to pack up my clothes, then go to his house and cook dinner for him. And speaking of clothes, I think the washer stopped. I have to put the clothes from it into the dryer," Kim said.

Except for the load of clothes in the dryer and the garments she planned to wear the following day, Kim packed all of her clothes into two large suitcases. She lugged the suitcases down the hallway, dropped them at the front door, then donned her jacket and shouted, "I'll be back in a little while."

"Okay. Tell Jack not to be a stranger over the next couple of weeks," Mrs. Hurley called back.

"I will." Kim opened the front door and trudged outside with her baggage. She opened the rear liftgate of her Caravan, and one by one she heaved the bags inside.

Kim arrived at Jack's at four-thirty. Having an hour to prepare supper, she selected a package of pork chops from the freezer. Within a day or two she was sure his freezer would be stocked with frozen pizza, burritos, and the like. At least she would see to it that he had one last decent meal before she headed east.

Jack strode through the door at exactly five-thirty. "Hey, babe!" he called.

"Hey yourself!" Kim answered as she took the few steps from the kitchen into the living room.

Jack quickly surveyed her from head to toe. He couldn't help noticing how her jeans clung to the curves of her hips and thighs, or how the dark blue sweater she was wearing accentuated her bust. Wisps of gold danced playfully about her shoulders as she moved her head, but the majority of her long, blonde hair hung about her upper back. Even at her worst Kim was quite attractive, but on some days, it seemed to Jack that her beauty shone like a beacon. This was one of those days.

Kim's form was backlit by the light from the kitchen ceiling fixture, and it almost looked to Jack as if an aura glowed about her. Her lips bore a thin smile, but when Jack looked into her eyes, he found himself unable to turn away. The deeper he peered into her pupils, the deeper they drew him in. Mesmerized, Jack found himself gliding across the room until his lips met Kim's. He had not been aware that she had held some cooking utensil in her hand until he heard it fall to the floor as they eagerly took each other into their arms.

"Wow!" Jack said when their lips finally parted.

"Mmmm. That was nice," Kim said.

"Yeah, I'll say!" They embraced for several minutes, each cherishing the throb of the other's heartbeat.

Finally, Kim asked, "How was your day?"

"I don't know. Seems so unimportant now," Jack said. "How about yours?"

"It wasn't very good. Actually, I got some really bad news today, but I'll tell you about it over dinner," Kim replied. Jack could feel the muscles in her body grow tense as she spoke.

"Are your mom and Stephen okay?" Jack asked.

"Oh, sure. They're fine. It's about the house in Maine. I have to go back for a couple of weeks," Kim said.

"Why? What happened?"

Kim led him to the kitchen where they took their seats at the table. There she relayed what details she knew of the damage to her house as well as the meeting with Marty scheduled for the following week. "I already have the van packed. I want to get on the road early tomorrow morning so I can get back as quickly as possible. If I can get the furnace and plumbing fixed and make the place livable before I go to Boston, when I get back, I can concentrate on having the water damage repaired," she said.

Jack sat silently for a few moments before he spoke. "How about if I go with you?"

"Don't be silly," Kim said. "Even if all the repairs can be done in a couple of weeks, you don't have enough vacation time. And even if you did, doesn't your time off have to be scheduled in advance?"

Jack nodded. "Yeah, you're right."

"Besides, I don't want to bring up a sore subject, but if you plan to spend some time with Johnny and James, you're going to need your vacation time."

Jack nodded once more. He and Kim began eating in silence. Halfway through their meal Jack said, "I don't feel like going to my meeting tonight. What do you say we spend some time together?"

Kim smiled. "I'd like that. I can't stay long because I promised Stephen, I would be home after dinner, but maybe we can find time for some quick dessert," she said with an exaggerated wink. Jack responded by gobbling his remaining food. Kim laughed. "Whoa! Slow down! It won't be any good if you make yourself sick," she said.

Once they finished their meal Jack whisked Kim down the hallway to the bedroom. They kissed as they tore at each other's garments, amassing a heap of mixed clothing on the floor. Kim sank into the bed while gently pulling Jack by his shoulders. Jack kissed the luscious skin at the nape of Kim's neck, then slowly began gliding his fingers and lips along the curves and crevices of her body. Kim moaned in delight. Their actions quickly escalated into a furious, albeit hurried, session of lovemaking.

Afterward Kim went to the bathroom to freshen up while Jack removed a pair of jeans and a gray sweat shirt from the basket of clean clothes on the floor near the foot of the bed. When Kim returned to the bedroom to get dressed, Jack showered, then dressed. By the time he finished Kim had cleared the kitchen table and washed the dishes.

"Do you want to come with me to Mom's for a little while?" Kim asked.

"I will if you want me to," Jack said.

"Why wouldn't I? You know you're welcome there any time," Kim said.

"Oh, I know that. I mean that I know you want to get an early start. If you are planning to go to bed early, I don't want to keep you up," Jack said.

Kim glanced at the clock on the microwave. "It's almost seven now. I'll be up for a couple more hours, at least until nine."

"Okay, I'll follow you there," Jack said.

Jack and Kim spent the remainder of the evening sitting together on the sofa at Mrs. Hurley's house watching television and enjoying each other's company. At a couple of minutes after nine they walked hand in hand to Jack's truck. Jack propped himself against the front bumper and pulled Kim close. "I'm going to miss you."

"I'm going to miss you, too. I keep telling myself that it's only for a couple of weeks, but I don't know how I'm going to get through these next few weeks without you. God, what are we going to do when summer gets here, and I go back for a few months?" Kim asked.

"I don't know, and I don't want to think about it," Jack said. He squeezed her tightly.

"Jack, promise me something."

"What's that?"

"Promise me that you'll go back to your old meeting schedule while I am gone."

"Huh?"

"I want you to promise me that you'll go back to your old meeting schedule," Kim said. "Look, being apart won't be easy on either of us. I'll have several things going on to take up my time and occupy my thoughts, but you're going to have a lot of idle time on your hands. I feel guilty as hell for having to leave, but I'd feel better if I knew you were attending your meetings like you did before. And I don't mean just for the sake of staying sober. It's not that I think you're going to have a relapse as soon as I pull out of the driveway, but I think it will do you good emotionally to spend time with people you are close to. It'll help you cope, and it's a constructive way to spend your time."

"I've thought about that, and I already figured on going back to my original group full time until you get back. I'm also planning to get the motor back in the Dart," Jack said.

"Good. I think working on the car will be good for you."

"Maybe I'll have it running by the time you get back."

"That would be great." Kim placed her head against Jack's shoulder.

As her breasts pressed against his chest, Jack thought of the way they had held each other in the airport two decades earlier. That was immediately before Kim boarded an airplane destined to carry her to a twenty-two-year sojourn in the east. A feeling of uneasiness came over him. He swallowed hard. "Kim, promise me something. Promise me you will be back. And I don't mean in twenty years. Promise me you will be back just as soon as your house is back in shape. Will you promise me?"

Kim looked into Jack's eyes. She paused for a moment before speaking, then smiled. "Considering what happened in nineteen seventy-nine, that's a fair request. Just as soon as the house is back together, I'll be on my way. The three people who mean the most to me in the world are all here. Of course, I'll be back. I promise."

"Thanks," Jack whispered. He and Kim kissed once more beneath the starlit sky.

But as Jack drove home a short while later, he was overcome by a sense of uneasiness. His heart hung heavy in his chest, aching each time it beat.

Chapter Fifteen

Two days later Jack sat in his recliner late at night staring at the television. Earlier that evening he had attended his second meeting in as many days. Normally, after working all day, going to his meeting, then spending a couple of hours watching television, he would have been exhausted. Since Kim had left, however, he'd had a powerful, nervous energy that robbed him of both his ability to sleep and to concentrate. As he sat mesmerized before the picture tube his mind soared to some distant place.

The intrusive ringing of the telephone jolted Jack's mind back to the present. As he stood to answer the phone, he realized that he could not recall where his thoughts had taken him, nor did he know how long he had been gone.

"Hello," Jack said into the receiver. He glanced at the LED display on the microwave. It was eleven-forty.

"Hey, Honey, it's me," Kim said.

"Hey! Where are you?"

"I'm in Maine now. I just got to the house a few minutes ago."

"You sound tired," Jack said.

"I am. Did I wake you up?"

"No, I was sitting here watching TV. So how bad is the house?"

"Pretty bad. It makes me sick to look at it. The ceiling has a huge hole where a big section fell out. The carpet is ruined, and in a couple of places the lower portions of the walls are swollen and stained. There is going to have to be a lot of plaster repair. I just hope the floor is okay once the carpet is pulled up."

"Was all the damage contained to that one room?"

"I think so. I went through the house and didn't see any other damage, but I'll look more closely tomorrow. The furnace is still working after Mr. Gladding's son fixed it, but I want to get somebody out here to give it a once-over. And I have to get the plumbing fixed as soon as possible because right now I have no water."

Jack noticed Kim's voice growing softer as exhaustion overcame her. After two hellish days on the road it was obvious that she needed sleep. Jack suggested that they cut their conversation short.

Kim agreed. "I'm wiped out, and my nerves are frazzled. My stomach has been upset for the last two mornings because I'm so uptight about the house and about my meeting with Marty. I haven't slept worth a damn for the last couple of nights, and the fact that my period is due isn't helping matters."

Jack and Kim exchanged good-byes, then hung up.

They spoke each night that week through Sunday. During that time Kim had the repairs made to her plumbing and furnace. She also secured a renovation contractor to begin repair work on the walls and ceiling in the dining room late in the following week after she returned from Boston.

On Sunday evening Jack and Kim agreed they would speak again on Wednesday evening after her business in Boston was finished. Jack arrived home from work on Wednesday hoping to find the light on his answering machine blinking and a message from Kim telling him that she was home, but the light shone steadily; no message had been recorded. It was five-thirty in Colorado Springs, which meant it was seven-thirty in Bar Harbor, Maine. He was sure Kim had returned from her trip much earlier in the day, but he figured perhaps she had decided to wait and call him once he was home from work. He removed two frozen burritos from the freezer, poked holes in their plastic wrappings, then placed them in the microwave. He then headed for the shower, being sure to leave the bathroom door open so he would hear the telephone when Kim called.

After his shower, Jack returned to the kitchen. Kim still had not called, so he picked up the telephone receiver and dialed her number.

On the fifth ring Kim's voice mail picked took the call. At the beep he said, "Hey, Babe. It's me. It's five-forty-five here, and I'll be here for another forty-five minutes or so. If you can, give me a call. I'd like to talk to you because I miss you, and I want to hear about your trip and your meeting with Marty. I'll talk to you later. I love you." By six-thirty Kim still had not called. Jack began to pace the house nervously. He waited until nearly six-forty, then hurried to his meeting.

Jack did not volunteer to speak that night. Instead, he sat quietly, his mind occupied by thoughts of Kim. Her meeting with Marty had been the previous day. Jack knew she had planned to stay in Boston that night, but even if she had gotten a late start on her drive back to her home in Maine she should have been there long before now. *What if she had car trouble?* he thought. She was certainly levelheaded enough not to panic. She would have simply called for help. She would have also been thoughtful enough to call Jack and her mother so they would not worry about her. *But what if something terrible happened? What if she was in an accident and was unable to call? Worse yet, what if the unthinkable happened? Whom would the authorities notify?*

Jack thought of calling Mrs. Hurley but decided not to. He knew that in all likelihood Kim was fine, and he could see no sense in alarming her mother. He told himself she had probably come home from Boston and collapsed in a tired heap on her sofa or in her bed for a nap. With the house repairs underway and the meeting with her agent behind her, the feeling of relief had probably afforded her the first sound sleep she had gotten in more than a week. No doubt, she needed it.

When the meeting ended Jack rushed home. This time the winking light on his answering machine indicated he had a message. Jack pressed the play button.

"Jack, hi. It's me. Sorry I missed you," Kim began, then

paused. A few moments later she continued, her thoughts seemingly in disarray. "Uh, look, I'm really tired, so I'm going to bed now. I'll try to talk to you tomorrow. Love you."

That's it? Jack thought. He was relieved to learn that Kim had made it home in one piece, but with his worries for her safety now laid to rest, he couldn't help feeling perturbed. What had taken her so long to get home? Was there something else she had wanted to say in her message? And although they had not spoken in days, it seemed to Jack that the tone of her voice sounded indifferent--almost relieved--to wait until the following day to talk to him. Surely, she was tired, but all-day long Jack had been downright giddy at the promise of talking to her that night. Shouldn't she have felt the same way?

Even as these thoughts raced through Jack's head, he felt a pang of guilt. *Stop being so damned needy and insecure!* he thought. *You're overreacting! She went to bed because she's tired. Get over it!*

Still, the brevity of Kim's message ate at Jack. And there was something else about her message that disturbed him, something that he could not easily pinpoint. Jack played Kim's message again, and again. Her voice was soft, slightly muffled, and was nearly devoid of inflection, clear indications of exhaustion. Still, after hearing the message several times, Jack began to feel a melancholy air about her words. He played the message one last time. It was as if halfway through the message she lost track of her thoughts. Suddenly it occurred to him that the presence of something--or someone--could have distracted her. Could it be that she was not alone?

With his heart pounding Jack snatched the telephone receiver from its cradle. He pressed the first few digits of Kim's number. "Get a hold of yourself, man!" he said aloud, challenging his intuition. Slowly he replaced the receiver in its cradle. "Keep your fucking imagination under control. She's home by herself and there's nothing wrong. And if there was, don't you think she'd tell you?"

Jack tried to convince himself that things were just as they should be, but deep down he feared otherwise. He reminded himself once more that Kim had just endured a week's worth of very stressful days, and that she was exhausted. Calling her now would be more an act of selfishness than of concern. She had said that she would speak with him the following day; under the circumstances, was that such an unreasonable request? And considering that it was now nine forty-five in Colorado, it was eleven forty-five in Maine. Surely, she was asleep. "Fuck it." He would have to wait until the following day to speak with Kim.

When he arrived home from work the following evening Jack found the light on his answering machine blinking once more.

"Jack, hi, it's me. I know I told you I would talk to you today, but some things have come up and I won't be around tonight. I'm sorry. The next several days look like they're going to be pretty hectic, too, but I promise I'll talk to you at some point." Kim paused before saying, "Jack, I love you. I love you so much! You've got to know that." She paused again then sighed deeply. In a voice that threatened to crackle into tears, she concluded, "I have to go. Bye."

Jack was stunned. He replayed Kim's latest message several times until a confused anger suddenly burst forth from deep within. "What the fuck!" Jack grabbed his telephone and jabbed the numbers on the keypad in the sequence of Kim's number. Before her telephone rang, he slammed his receiver back into its cradle. *No, this is no good. Take a deep breath first,* he thought to himself. He breathed in, held his breath, then exhaled slowly. He repeated this exercise half a dozen times but felt only slightly relaxed afterward. The throbbing in his temples remained. "Oh, fuck it!" he muttered. He opted to take his shower, then call Kim. Perhaps he would be a little better composed by then.

Jack returned to the kitchen dripping wet. The steaming water did little to ease his mood, but he did feel a little bit more in control of himself. While his rage had passed, his anger still gnawed at him. He picked up his telephone receiver, pressed the redial button, and listened for the series of beeps afterward. As Kim's phone rang, he could feel his quickened pulse thumping solidly in his temples. As he expected, Kim's voice mail took the call.

"Kim, hi. It's me, Jack. I miss talking to you, and quite frankly I've got to say I'm a little confused by all of this. I can't help wondering, is there something I need to know? I really miss you, and I'm dying to know how your meeting went. Give me a call sometime. That is, if you can find the time. Love you. Bye." Jack did his best to suppress his anger, but he couldn't suppress his sarcasm. Still, sarcasm was better than losing his cool.

Jack hung up the phone then immediately picked it back up

and dialed Mrs. Hurley's number. "Hello," Mrs. Hurley answered.

"Mom Hurley? Hi! It's me, Jack," he said in as cheery a voice as he could muster.

"Jack! Well hi! How have you been?" Mrs. Hurley asked.

"I'm doing okay, I suppose. I was just wondering if you've talked with Kim."

"Uh, well, yes I have, but only briefly. She's been very busy, you know. I'm sure she's told you that, hasn't she?"

"Not directly, no," Jack said. "She's left a couple of messages on my answering machine, but I haven't been able to catch her to talk to since last Sunday. That was before she went to Boston. Have you talked to her since she got back?"

Mrs. Hurley hesitated before answering. "Yes, Jack, actually I have."

"Well, is she okay? How did her meeting go? How is the work on the house progressing? I feel like I'm completely in the dark!"

"Her meeting went fine, and the work on the house is progressing, but it's taking a lot of her time. She's pulled a couple of late nights in order to do as much of the work she can," Mrs.

Hurley said.

"Oh! So, she's been there when I've called, but she couldn't be bothered to pick up the phone. That's great! I appreciate that!" Jack said.

"Jack, that's not at all what I meant!" Mrs. Hurley said. "I mean she's been a little preoccupied with what all she's got going on. I'm sure she didn't mean to worry you like this. She was probably waiting until she had enough free time to give all of her attention to you. But I understand that the two of you need to talk."

"Yes, we do!" Jack said. Already he felt guilty for having lashed out at Kim's mother.

"The next time I talk to her I'll have her give you a call right away," Mrs. Hurley said.

Jack thanked her then hung up the phone.

Chapter Sixteen

Jack made no further attempt to reach Kim that week, nor did she leave any more messages on his answering machine. With no sure explanation for Kim's strange behavior, Jack's imagination ran wild. He hypothesized that Randy had entered her life once more. Kim had likely brought this on herself, albeit with the most innocent of intentions.

Jack figured that with the extensive damage to the house, and since it was still jointly owned, Kim had likely contacted her estranged husband. If Randy had any aspirations of patching things up between them, he would have wasted no time in helping her oversee the work as it was being done, especially after learning that she and Jack were now engaged. Of course, he would have insisted on meeting Kim at the house under the pretense of protecting his own interest, but once he was there, he would have subtly acted on cues from his hidden agenda.

Randy would pour on just enough charm to appeal to Kim's soft side. Having been married to her for a number of years, he surely knew how to bypass her defense mechanisms. And as long as

Kim pushed Jack away, he knew he was powerless to stop Randy's advances. Jack found his relationship with Kim suddenly in jeopardy, and he felt helpless. All he could do was to try not to think about it and hope that somehow things turned themselves around.

Looking ahead, Jack saw that he would have to concentrate on living his life as he had before he and Kim had reunited. It seemed now that he had spent that period in a mundane existence. Day after day he had gone to work and attended his meetings, and as time had permitted, he had worked to make the Road Runner operational once more. Having stopped drinking less than a year earlier, these were the constants he had needed to establish in his routine but looking back he saw that during that time he sure didn't do much *living.*

When Kim came back into Jack's life he suddenly felt as if it was springtime and his heart had bloomed. She had showered him with love and charged his soul with vitality. In being with her he soon learned that despite having endured the suffering from the tribulations of a failed marriage, temporary estrangement from his sons, and struggling to learn to live with alcoholism while keeping himself sober, he was still capable of loving her with the same passion he had more than twenty years earlier. Furthermore, Kim had helped him lay to rest a question that had nagged him for two decades: was his longing for her simply the aftermath of a lost first love and a teenager's broken heart, or was his love for her indeed true? At last, that question had been answered.

In the months they had spent together, Jack now realized that Kim had shown him much more than the love that binds two people. His life had become entwined not only with hers, but with Mrs. Hurley's and Stephen's lives as well. They had welcomed him into their lives, and the fondness that grew between them drew them together, soon filling Jack with a sense of belonging, and restoring his sense of purpose.

Sadly, he now realized he had been reduced to his former life of frozen pizza and burritos, nightly meetings, and weekends spent tinkering in the garage. Of course, he and his sons still spoke a couple of times a week. He wondered how he would tell them about Kim, or if he should tell them at all. Suddenly the two thousand miles between Colorado Springs and Charlotte, North Carolina seemed like a million miles.

On Saturday morning Jack awoke at his regular time, put on

his work clothes, then went to the garage to plug in the heater. He left the heater running while he brewed a pot of coffee. When the coffee was ready, he poured a mugful, then returned to the garage to take inventory of the engine and related pieces that still needed to be installed in the Dart. Just then he thought he heard a knock at his door. He raced from the garage through the house toward the front door. There a young man in a courier's uniform stood holding an envelope and a clipboard.

"Are you Mr. Kramer?" he asked, reading Jack's name from a tag on the notebook-sized cardboard envelope.

"Yes, that's me," Jack said.

"Then this is for you," the courier said as he handed the envelope to Jack. He then held out the clipboard and a pen. "Please sign in space number seventeen," he said.

Jack scrawled his name in the space indicated by the courier. "Is this a certified letter?" he asked.

"No, it's an overnight package. The signature is just for verification that the parcel was delivered on time," the courier said. "Thanks, and have a good day, sir."

As the courier backed his truck out of Jack's driveway, Jack noticed that it was Kim's handwriting on the tag attached to the envelope. With his heart pounding and his stomach fluttering, he stepped back from the door. He tore open the envelope and pulled the letter from within.

Dearest Jack:

First, I want to say I'm sorry for the way I've been acting lately. I know this isn't easy on you, and I am truly sorry. Some things have come up, and I've really been a mess. I don't think I can hold myself together long enough to talk to you on the phone just yet. I know I owe it to you to bring you up to date on what all is happening, and soon I will. But I can't yet. I hope you can believe me when I tell you this is for the best. Although you can't know what I mean, I hope you can trust me on this. One day this will all make sense.

The book deal seems to be stalled in negotiations. It looks promising, but it is taking longer than I'd expected, and there have been complications. The repairs to the old house are well underway, and it looks like the place will be ready to open on time for the beginning of tourist season. That's a good thing, because the damage was more extensive than I'd first thought, and the insurance is only picking up part of the tab. I need to get the place open for business as early as possible so I can recoup some of the money I'm spending for repairs. Because of this, I won't be able to return to Colorado before the beginning of the tourist season. Stephen will stay in Colorado until he has finished school, then he and my mom will fly to Maine.

Be sure to tell your sons I was asking about them. I'm not going to harp on you about this, but you really do need to see them. It will be good both for you and for them. I know you're probably thinking that you aren't ready, but Jack, they need you now. This is really important, and it can't wait.

And above all, take care of yourself. I know this isn't easy for you. It isn't easy on me either. One day soon you will understand. Be good to yourself, Jack. You are a good man, and you deserve the best.

Please drop me a line so that I know you're okay. I hope you can

believe me when I tell you I love you with all my heart. Take care.

Love always,

Kim

Stunned, Jack managed to reach his recliner before his knees buckled. He plopped downward onto the edge of the chair, then stared at the page with Kim's signature at the bottom without rereading the words. *Why did she bother to send this letter?* he wondered. Perhaps it was to ease her conscience. Still, why would she be concerned about him if she and Randy were trying to make a go of things once again? Could it be that if things didn't work out with Randy, at least she had the comfort of knowing that Jack was still waiting? It was a plausible explanation, but he gritted his teeth at the thought. It was certainly not Kim's nature to think this way. But then, her actions of late were not characteristic of her, either.

At once Jack flung the paper aside and stomped the floor angrily, only to discover that there was no conviction to his action. He felt that he should be angry, and at that moment he genuinely wanted to be angry. Anger would allow him to vent his frustration and express his pain.

But the anger would not come.

Jack then wished he could cry, but his eyes remained dry. Instead, he sat staring at the floor devoid of expression.

Moments later Jack stood and shook his head much like a dog drying himself after a swim. Realizing he needed to break his sullen mood he returned to the garage with a series of deliberate, purposeful steps. But as he peered at the engine in the Dart it suddenly seemed foreign. He picked up the alternator and placed it on its lower mounting bracket, but when he attempted to slide the long bolt through the alternator and its bracket it would not go. No amount of jiggling would align the bolt holes. Jack soon lost his patience and flung the bolt at the workbench.

"God damn it!" he said as he removed the alternator and placed it on the bench. To continue working on the car in his current state of mind would be futile. Even the simplest of tasks would likely give him fits, and his patience was in short supply. He knew that if he kept working, at the very least he would become aggravated, but he was also likely to break something on the car or injure himself. Instead, he gathered his tools, placed them in a pile on the workbench next to the alternator, then unplugged the heater and turned off the light. He passed through the house to the front door once more, stopping only long enough to pick up Kim's letter from the floor next to his recliner. Then he continued to the shed where he thrust the door open and took his seat in the Road Runner. There he grasped the wheel with both hands as he gazed through the windshield at the rough framed wall ahead. He inhaled, closed his eyes, then sank into the seat as he exhaled.

Thoughts raced through his mind, but a sense of numbness came on stronger than ever, shunting the emotions that accompanied these thoughts. He peered at the ashtray, contemplating whether or not to remove the necklace Kim had given him so many years earlier and hold for a while. He decided not to. Such a powerful reminder of her would only confuse him further now. He had intended to read her letter once more, but he reconsidered that as well, opting instead to fold it and stow it in the ashtray with the necklace.

After closing the ashtray, he sat back once more. His eyes drifted about the interior of the car. The individual round gauges all gazed back at him, their familiarity offering him a small degree of comfort. He gripped the steering wheel with his left hand and the Pistol Grip shifter with his right. Spring would arrive soon, but he yearned to take the car for a drive right then. He refrained, however, for the roads were still partially covered with winter slop. Instead, he started the engine and jabbed the accelerator a couple of times, his ears drinking in the glorious rumble of dual exhaust reverberating inside the shed walls. He pressed his shoulders against the seat to feel the pulses from the engine's choppy idle. He smiled and closed his eyes once more. After a few minutes he shut off the engine.

That evening, as Jack ate his thawed-out pizza slab, he kept an anxious eye on the clock until it was time to leave for his meeting. He had not decided if he would share anything with the group that night; he would wait until the meeting was underway. But whether or not he spoke, he had come to realize the therapeutic value of spending an hour in the company of other alcoholics. He understood these people, and he knew they were the only people who understood him. With or without spoken words, communication still took place between the members of the group. And even if the topic of discussion seemed far removed from alcoholism, Jack knew that nothing in an alcoholic's life was far from alcoholism.

"We will love you until you can love yourself," Molly had told him at his first meeting. On this evening, Jack felt especially needy of the love and companionship that bonded the members of the group.

At six-twenty he put his plate in the sink and slipped into his jacket.

Chapter Seventeen

During the days that followed, Jack tried not to think about

Kim, but he couldn't keep her off his mind. That Thursday night he

left a message on her voice mail. "Kim, it's me, Jack. I got your

letter, but I still don't know what the hell is going on. I'm confused

and I'm hurting. I'm hurting really bad." He paused, took a deep

breath, then continued, "But, I guess if you won't talk to me, there's

not a damn thing I can do to change your mind. They say two can't

be happy if one's not happy. If I don't make you happy, or if there is

someone else who makes you happier, then I guess this is the way

it's got to be. Take care of yourself. I'll try to do the same. Maybe

we'll bump into each other in another twenty years. I'll always love

you." He placed the receiver back in its cradle and began sobbing.

There. It was over. Done. But instead of relief, he felt more

empty than ever. His chest ached so badly that he found it difficult

to breathe. "Oh, God, what the fuck did I just do?" he moaned.

Over the next few weeks Jack spent his leisure time working

on the engine in the Dart and playing Hot Shoe on the PlayStation he

had recently bought, with the video game consuming far more than its share of his available time. Thoughts of drinking occurred far more frequently than they had up to that point; playing Hot Shoe provided an escape from these potentially devastating thoughts as well as his misery over the loss of Kim.

During this time his emotional numbness persisted, and from it grew a new attitude of indifference. It was as if Kim had rammed a liposuction tube far up his ass and sucked his beating heart from his chest. *Floooooop!* He could imagine the sound. All that remained was an empty cavity inside a hollow man. He often found himself muttering, "Fuck it," and "Who gives a shit?" to himself when confronted with minor day-to-day difficulties.

Working on the Dart had become a chore, one from which he derived little pleasure. With the engine in the car, completing the assembly of the remaining pieces should have taken him no more than a full day. Instead, working half-heartedly an hour or so at a time, the project had dragged on for weeks. Making the Road Runner roadworthy had been a labor of love, and his enthusiasm had continued through the engine build-up of the Dart. But now he simply wanted the car to be done. His excitement was gone; his enthusiasm had run out.

By the time he started the Dart for the first time, spring was on the horizon. The snow was melting, with the remains of deep drifts serving as the only reminders of the most recent storm. The mountain air was still quite chilly, but its sharp bite was gone. In its place he could sense the impending warmth that would arrive during the next few months.

With his battery charger connected, Jack trickled about an ounce of gasoline down the throat of the carburetor, slid behind the wheel and turned the key. *Ruh-ruh-ruh-Vroom!* The engine fired almost immediately, ran for a few seconds on the gasoline he had introduced through the carburetor, then began to falter. Suddenly it picked itself up and began to run more smoothly, a sure sign the fuel pump had picked up the gasoline from the tank and was now delivering it to the carburetor.

After allowing the engine to run for twenty minutes he shut it down and adjusted the valves. Finally, he backed the car outside. On any day when his mind was in a normal state he would have been nearly jumping out of his skin with excitement as he prepared to take the trial run in a car with a fresh engine he had built. If the first test drive went without a hitch, he referred to it as a victory ride. On this day, however, he felt little excitement. He held no giddy

anticipation of driving the car. As long as the engine ran well and

the car developed no major problem during his drive, he would be

satisfied.

Jack stabbed the accelerator a couple of times and listened to

the tone of the exhaust. Though it lacked the deep, hearty rumble of

the Road Runner, its exhaust note was healthy in its own right,

hinting that there was ample power on tap. With six header tubes

feeding into one large three-inch diameter pipe, he'd had no doubt

this hopped-up Slant Six would have a distinctive sound.

Jack backed out of the driveway and headed toward town.

The gas gauge showed less than a quarter tank; topping it off with

premium Sinclair fuel was in order.

With a full tank of gas, he began driving aimlessly through

town. After making a couple of turns for no reason other than habit,

Jack found himself driving toward Mrs. Hurley's house. When he

realized where he was headed, his first thought was to change his

course. *This is stupid!* But then he thought, *Oh, what the hell. I'm*

almost there now. Jack continued down the street past Mrs. Hurley's

house. A knot grew in his stomach as he neared the house and his heart sank as he drove by without so much as lifting his foot from the accelerator. "Fuck me," he muttered.

As Jack drove, his thoughts turned to Stephen. How was he doing while his mother was gone? Was he lonely without her? The boy had endured several drastic changes within a short time. Jack wished he could call Stephen and visit with him for a while. Perhaps they could go for a ride in the Road Runner, or maybe they could sit and play Hot Shoe. But he knew that such a visit was not to be. The one time he and Mrs. Hurley had spoken since Kim left it seemed that she was hiding something from him, and that she felt very uncomfortable doing so. Although he loved and missed Mrs. Hurley and Stephen, it was Kim who had pushed him out of her life, and effectively out of their lives as well. In this matter, Mrs. Hurley and Stephen were bystanders, but Jack knew that keeping in touch with them would only complicate the situation.

Jack slowed as he neared his driveway, then wheeled the Dart up to the garage door. He revved the engine a couple of times, listening to the Slant Six crackle through the large diameter exhaust pipe, then flicked off the key.

Jack had planned to have dinner at the truck stop, but first he would call Johnny and James. He went to the kitchen, picked up the telephone, and punched in the number.

"Hello," Ralph Dobson answered.

"Hello, Ralph. It's Jack."

"Well, hey there, Jack! How've you been?" Ralph drawled.

"I'm doing well," Jack replied with a twinge of guilt. Saying that he was doing well was something of a lie, but Jack could see no reason to spill his guts to Ralph. "How about yourself?" he asked.

"Oh, we're doing fine. Jack, the boys tell me that things didn't work out between you and your lady friend. It's none of my business, but I wanted to tell you I'm sorry."

Jack's mouth fell open. Ralph was the last person from whom he would have expected words of sympathy over his troubles with Kim. "Uh, thank you," he said.

"I know you've had your problems over the years, but I also know that over the last year or year and a half you have worked hard to do something about it. I'm glad of that, and I hope it continues. And now that you've been calling the boys regularly for a while now, they've started really looking forward to your calls. They talk about you more in a week now than they did for the whole first year they were here."

Jack was stunned. "I don't know what to say."

"Jack, they would love to see you, and I think it would do you all some good to get together, you and them. A boy needs his father, and any good man needs his sons. And with things between you and your lady friend going to hell, I'm betting you could use the lift."

Jack paused. "I suppose you're right."

"Good. Now, the wife and I were talking the other day, and we had an idea. A friend of ours has some cabins on a lake a little way from here. It's a quiet place with nothing but woods all around, great scenery, and even better fishing. He rents out the cabins to families for a week at a time in the summer, but during the rest of the year folks usually only want to stay there on the weekends. Monday through Friday the cabins mostly go empty. Now the weekends and summer weeks are usually booked up a year in advance, but if you wanted to take the boys up there for a couple of days during the week sometime in the next few months, I can make the arrangements for you. 'Course it means they'll have to miss school, but it'd only be for a couple of days, and their mother says she thinks that'd be okay.

"Now I haven't said anything to the boys about this, and I won't. This is something for you to think over, and if you decide you want to do it, you can ask them, then let me know when you're coming."

Jack was flabbergasted. He couldn't imagine Ralph making such a kind offer. Although he was not keen on being pressured to visit his sons, Ralph was not being pushy. His offer was definitely worth considering.

"You just think it over and let me know," Ralph said.

"I will," Jack said.

"Now I reckon you called here to speak with the boys, but unfortunately neither one's here right now," Ralph said. "Both of them are spending the night at a friend's house."

"Okay, well please tell them I called, and I'll try again tomorrow," Jack said.

"I'll surely do that. They should both be here tomorrow night, being Sunday and a school night. But I'll tell them you called," Ralph said.

Jack pondered Ralph's offer to arrange the use of a cabin as he drove the Dart to the truck stop. He longed to see Johnny and James, but only when the time was right. He still needed time to prepare himself emotionally for the reunion. He told himself that this was as much for the sake of Johnny and James as it was for himself. After all, was it fair to them to plan to get together when he did not feel that he could be with them one hundred percent? And if he was to some degree emotionally incapacitated, would his sons detect it, mistaking it for disinterest? Jack told himself he could not take that chance. Considering his low state of emotional well-being since Kim left, Jack knew he would not likely be in the proper frame of mind anytime soon.

After supper, Jack arrived at his meeting with time to spare. He intended to tell the group of Ralph's offers, then explain his own reservations about getting together with Johnny and James before he felt ready. During the meeting he reconsidered, choosing instead to ruminate over the situation for a day or two before sharing it with the group. After the meeting he led Donald outside to show him the Dart.

"So now what?" Donald asked.

"So now that it's running, I'm going to sell it," Jack said.

"Oh, I knew you were planning to sell once it was done. I mean, what's your next project?"

"I really don't have anything in mind at this point. Right now, I need to get the money out of this car. Afterward maybe I'll do a few things to the Road Runner, but right now I don't have another project to take the place of this car. Why do you ask?"

"No reason. I was just curious," Donald said. "I'll keep my eyes open and if I see anything, I think you would be interested in, I'll let you know."

Jack thanked Donald, then started the Dart and headed for home. With the car now finished he considered storing it in the shed until he sold it, thereby returning the Road Runner to its rightful place in the garage. Then he remembered that the exhaust header on the Dart offered little ground clearance. Surely it would collide with the shed floor if he attempted to drive the car up the short ramp and into the shed. No, the Road Runner would have to remain in the shed until he sold the Dart.

Once home, Jack parked the Dart in the garage, then headed toward the living room for another session of Hot Shoe. As each game gave way to the next, Jack could feel his eyelids growing heavier. He observed his virtual motoring skills gradually

deteriorating. Despite his physical exhaustion, his mind buzzed with

thoughts of his boys and of Ralph's offer. He envisioned a cabin

nestled in the woods at the edge of a quiet lake. *What better place to*

spend quality time with Johnny and James and really get to know

each other? he thought. Suddenly, waiting for the perfect moment

seemed absurd! *Why have I wasted so much time? How could I*

have been so foolish?

"A good man needs his sons," Ralph had said. Jack

considered Ralph's offer once more. The present was as perfect a

time as any. The right time was now!

Chapter Eighteen

Having decided to go to North Carolina as soon as possible,

the following two weeks were extremely busy for Jack. His boss

approved his vacation for the first full week of April and Ralph

agreed to make the cabin arrangements for Sunday night through

Tuesday night that week. Jack placed an ad for the Dart in the *Auto*

Buyer, and within two days he sold it for three thousand dollars.

With the Dart gone, Jack moved the Road Runner back into

the garage. There was no question he would drive it to North

Carolina. Seeing his sons for the first time in a year and a half--and

for the first time ever through sober eyes and with a sober mind--was

a huge step for Jack. Undoubtedly the boys had grown and changed

during that time, as had Jack. Perhaps having the Road Runner there

would be something of an emotional crutch, but to Jack it seemed

only fitting since that car had seen him through every other

significant event in his life.

In addition, Marsha had talked Jack into parking the car in

the garage and dropping the insurance and registration before the

boys were born. To them, the car was nothing more than a yellow hulk of which their father was extremely protective. It was a stationary object that occupied one room of their house like an overgrown piece of furniture. What a charge they would get out of hearing it run for the first time, not to mention experiencing their first ride in a true muscle car!

There was also something symbolic about the car. Having sat dormant for so many years, the car had experienced a rebirth of sorts when Jack had finally decided to put it back on the road. But the years the Road Runner had spent sitting in the garage were the same dark years during which Jack sank deeper and deeper into his alcoholic dependency, the same years that his marriage to Marsha had unraveled, and the same years the boys had watched their father drink himself to sleep night after night as he drove a wedge through the center of their family. During the time he prepared the car to go back on the road it passed through a metamorphosis. At the same time Jack went through a metamorphosis of his own as he continued his day by day fight to remain sober. Having gone through their rebirth together it only seemed appropriate that he drive the Road Runner to North Carolina.

As Jack prepared for his trip, he played Hot Shoe less, but

thought about Kim more. He did his best to put thoughts of her out of his head, but they kept sneaking back in. Did she miss him too? Kim had said she had a good reason for breaking off her contact with Jack and leaving him hanging. He believed Randy was that reason, and that out of selfishness she did not want to risk losing Jack if she and Randy were unable to rekindle whatever flame had once burned for them. But still Jack wondered, what if he was wrong?

Reuniting with his sons was an enormous step for Jack. Emotions would surely run high, and there was nobody he would have liked more to share that with than Kim. He wished she could be there to take the trip with him.

On Saturday night a week before he was to leave, Jack sat at the kitchen table poring over his road atlas. This had become a nightly ritual, his last activity of the day before retiring. The uncertainties of his situation with Kim still weighed heavily on his mind. Although the idea had probably been lurking in the back of Jack's mind for some time, on this night it occurred to him that Bar Harbor, Maine was slightly less than two days' driving time from Charlotte, North Carolina. Because Kim refused to talk to him, much less give him the answers he needed, why not drive to Maine and get the answers for himself?

If he left Colorado early the following Saturday morning, Jack figured he could be in Charlotte by late Sunday afternoon. He could pick up Johnny and James, and they could reach the cabin by nightfall. If they stayed through Tuesday night, he could drop them off at home on Wednesday morning, then head north. By Thursday night he would be in Bar Harbor. On Friday he would make one final attempt to talk to Kim, this time in person. Then he would have Saturday and Sunday to drive back to Colorado.

Jack knew that showing up on Kim's doorstep would be risky, but he could think of no other way to get her to talk to him. She might slam the door in his face. Even so, he hoped at the very least to learn why she had pushed him away.

The following day Jack sorted through his fishing gear. He chose a variety of lures, bobbers, sinkers, two extra spools of heavy fishing line, and a couple of canisters of plain barbed hooks, then placed them in a tackle box. He selected the rod that had been his favorite. The reel still operated smoothly, so he pulled the two halves of the mast apart and placed them and the tackle box on the floor next to the Road Runner.

Jack then began picking through his remaining rods hoping to find two that would be suitable for Johnny and James. Then he reconsidered. Johnny and James were at the age when they should have their own rods and reels. With that thought, Jack drove to the mall where he found two sporting goods stores, one with a sizable selection of fishing gear.

Jack picked through the inexpensive freshwater rods, finally deciding on a model with a smooth rolling reel and enough flexibility to whip a lure far into the lake. At forty-nine ninety-five it wasn't cheap, but he felt this model would serve his sons well. Jack selected two identical rods and took them to the cashier.

"Hi. How are you today, sir?" the tall, thin man behind the counter asked.

"I'm doing okay," Jack said as he handed the clerk his Visa card.

The clerk scanned the bar codes on the boxes, then swiped the card through the card reader. A perplexed look came across his face as he leaned toward Jack and said, "Sir, I'm sorry, but your card has been declined."

Jack felt his face grow hot. He knew he was near the credit

limit on his Visa card, but he did not think he had reached it yet. In embarrassment he rifled through his wallet. There he found sixty-two dollars. "Can you put one on the card and let me pay cash for the other one?" he asked.

"I can try," the cashier said. This time the transaction for only one rod was approved. "Okay, sir, please sign this slip and I'll ring your other one up as a cash payment."

Jack drove home angry with himself for allowing the balance on his card to spiral out of control. Though Kim's engagement ring accounted for the majority of the balance, he chastised himself. While sitting at a traffic light he pulled his wallet from his back pocket, removed the Visa card, and shoved it into his shirt pocket. When he emptied his pockets that evening, he would put the card into his top dresser drawer where it would remain until he paid off the balance.

Suddenly it occurred to him that with no Visa card to use in the event of an emergency, he would have to carry a large sum of cash during his trip east. With further dismay he realized that the cash he would have to carry was the money he had taken in exchange for the Dart--the same money he had planned to put toward his Visa balance. He had no intention of blowing the entire three thousand dollars on his trip, but if he encountered trouble along the way he might be glad he had brought it.

Friday night Jack attended his meeting as usual. Afterward Donald took him aside. "Tomorrow's the beginning of your journey, huh? Nervous?" he asked.

"A little," Jack admitted. "I just don't know what to expect. I have lots of hopes, but I don't know how it's going to go," he said.

Donald nodded. "You should be nervous," he said. "Tell me again, how many nights will the three of you be in the cabin?"

"Three. Sunday night through Tuesday night," Jack said without thinking.

"Wait, I thought you said you weren't coming back until the following Sunday night. That's only two days to get there, but..." Donald paused while he counted the days, "...*five* days to get home. Why in the world would it take you five days to get home?" He searched Jack's eyes. "That doesn't add up."

"No, I don't suppose it does," Jack said, looking away.

"Well, are you going to tell me where you are going, or are you going to make me guess?" Donald asked.

"Maybe I'll do some sightseeing," Jack said.

"Oh, come on! Don't try to bullshit me! I think we both know where you're going," Donald said.

"Fine. I'm going to Maine. I'm going there to talk to Kim and find out what the hell happened," Jack said.

"You might not want to know what happened."

"You're right, I may not want to know, but I *have* to know. Whatever it is, I have to know."

"I know you're not obligated to spill your guts to me, but why didn't you tell me about your plans to go to Maine?" Donald asked, obviously hurt.

"Because I knew you would be against me going. I just knew you would try to talk me out of it," Jack said.

Donald affixed his eyes on an imaginary spot on the wall, then stared at the spot as he spoke. "Jack, I know I couldn't talk you out of this one if I tried. But I'm not so sure I would try even if I thought you would listen to me." Donald sighed, then shifted his gaze to Jack. "There's nothing like being in love," he said with a sad smile. "Love is powerful! People don't usually think of it that way, but it is. It's far more powerful than hate. When you're in love, you can do 'most anything. No mountain is too high, no river too wide, no ocean too deep. Love can empower you to do things like nothing else can.

"But for many people, when they fear losing love, they will stop at nothing to get it back. In this sense love is very dangerous. It can make you do some really stupid and irrational shit. Take for instance the guy who comes home and finds his wife in bed with another man. His first instinct might be to grab his gun and blow them both away. Why is that? Is it hate? Hell no! That's love! If the guy didn't love his wife, would the sight of her boffing somebody else make him flip his lid like that? Of course not!

"So, Jack, keep that in mind. I'm not saying that's what I think is happening in your case, but you don't know what you're going to find there in Maine."

Jack nodded.

"Contrary to what you think, I agree with you. I think you need to go to Maine. You need to know where you stand. But Jack, don't do anything rash. No matter what you find, no matter what happens, try to be prepared for it. And for God's sake, if you need to talk, call me. I don't care what time, day or night."

After two long days on the road Jack neared Charlotte on Sunday afternoon. He removed the sheet of paper on which he had scrawled the directions from the interstate

to Marsha's parents' place. Minutes later Jack wound his way through a suburb of Charlotte. He found their street, and then their house with no trouble. He guided the Road Runner to the curb behind Ralph's pickup truck then shut off the key. *Here goes,* he thought as he stepped from the car and started across the lawn.

"Dad's here! Dad's here!" came a muffled scream of delight from within the house. Seconds later the screen door burst open and James dashed toward Jack as if propelled by a rocket. Jack squatted and opened his arms toward him. In his excitement James failed to slow before colliding with Jack and bowling him down. While Jack lay on his back in the front yard hugging James, Johnny dashed from the front door and dove on top of them. Jack held them both tightly as tears streamed from the corners of his eyes. "Boy am I glad to see you guys!" he said.

"Me too!" James said.

"We've missed you," Johnny said.

"I've missed both of you, too," Jack said as he squeezed

them tighter. "I can't believe how big you two have gotten. And how heavy!"

As the Kramer trio got to their feet Jack spotted Ralph watching from the porch. "Hi, Jack. I'm glad you made it," he called in his deep southern drawl.

"So am I," Jack said as he wiped his eyes dry. "So am I."

"I've got you a cabin reserved. It's a nice one with electricity, so you'll have a stove and a refrigerator," Ralph said. "Kitchen's furnished with pots, pans, plates, and utensils."

"Where exactly is this place?" Jack asked.

"Oh, I thought I told you. It's on a quiet, secluded part of Lake Norman, not too far off Seventy-Seven," Ralph said, referring to the interstate which ran due north from Charlotte.

"So, it's not far?" Jack asked.

"No, no, not far at all. Heck, you could get lost finding the place and still make it there in under an hour."

"Is there a store nearby?"

"There is, but it's just a little mom-n-pop kind of place just down the road a piece. In fact, that's where you'll sign in for the cabin. They've got some stuff there, but they're kind of pricey. But sometimes folks forget to pack things, or they find they need something they never thought to bring. When that happens I s'pose they don't mind paying the high price too much," Ralph chuckled.

Both men fell silent for a moment. It was Jack who spoke first. "I guess we should get going. If you say there's a refrigerator and a stove, then when we hit the grocery store maybe we'll get some eggs, bacon, milk, and stuff like that since we'll be able to keep it cold."

"Actually, I think we've got that pretty much covered for you," Ralph said. "We didn't know what time you would make it here, so the boys and their grandmother and I fetched you a couple bags of groceries and packed you a cooler with some things we know the boys like to eat."

"Ralph, you didn't have to do that! You've done so much with making the arrangements for the cabin and all."

Ralph stared awkwardly at his toes. "Ah, it's nothing. We just want you all to have a good time up there in them woods."

Jack and Ralph loaded the grocery bags and cooler into the trunk. With the trunk now full there was still ample room on the back seat for the boys' clothes.

"Marsha will be right back," Ralph said. "She ran out to get the boys new sleeping bags." He turned and headed into the house.

"Dad, is this the yellow car from in the garage at home in Colorado?" James asked.

"Yes, it is," Jack said.

"Told you," Johnny said.

"But I didn't think that car ran," James said.

"It didn't for a long, long time, but a while back I started working on it and got it running again. I drove it here so you guys could see it and so we could all ride in it together."

A puzzled expression spread across James's face. "Did you start working on it because we weren't there anymore?"

"With you guys not around I needed something to keep me busy. So, in that sense, yes, that's why I started working on it," Jack said.

"Are you lonely there all by yourself?" James asked. Johnny jabbed James's shoulder with his elbow. "Ow!" James yelped.

"Johnny, it's okay," Jack said. "Yes, I get very lonely sometimes, but it is a big help being able to talk to you guys on the phone." Not wanting to put a damper on their mood he continued,

"But I'm not lonely now because we're all finally together! Now, why don't you run and get your stuff? Then, as soon as your mom gets back, we can go!"

Johnny and James raced toward the house. "I'm sitting up front!" Johnny called.

"No! I wanna sit up front!" James said.

Jack smiled and shook his head. Their bickering might grate his nerves over the next couple of days, but for the moment he welcomed it. Until now he had not realized how much he missed the arguments which stemmed from their incessant rivalry. Without a doubt he would find it necessary to mediate spats between them, but for the moment he was content to stand back and watch his sons treating each other like brothers. For the first time he relished the competition that was so typical of them.

Jack was jarred from his thoughts as a new dark green Pontiac Grand Am slowed and turned into the driveway. He heard the click of the trunk release, then the driver's door opened, and Marsha stepped from the car.

"Hey! I see you made it," Marsha said. "Did you have any trouble finding the place?"

"None at all. Actually, the whole trip went pretty well," Jack said as he moved toward her. "Nice car."

Marsha wrinkled her nose. "I had to get a new car, Jack. The other one was falling apart. It got to the point that I was spending more to keep it going than I'm spending now on payments. I really needed a new car," she said.

"Whoa! You don't have to justify anything. That wasn't meant as an attack, it was a compliment. I don't doubt that you needed a new car. In fact, I'm surprised the other one lasted as long as it did."

Marsha sighed. "I'm sorry. I know you didn't mean it that way. It's just that this whole thing feels so weird!"

"Yeah, I know it does. I think it probably feels weird for all of us," Jack said.

Weird, indeed! he thought. Talking with Marsha felt surreal, bringing a rubbery feeling into his heart. Her movements, the tone of her voice, the way she looked at him--all of those things were familiar to him. But for all that familiarity there was now just as much about Marsha that seemed strangely foreign. There was no one aspect of her persona that he could readily identify as having changed, but so much about her seemed different just the same. Jack wondered how it could be possible that they had been together for so many years yet feel so strange together now.

It was obvious to Jack that Marsha, too, felt uncomfortable. Although any shared feelings had died, there was still history between them. History could not be erased. Furthermore, Johnny and James were proof of that history, and perhaps the only two positive remnants of their marriage. In a moment of uncertainty Jack clumsily raised his wooden arms to hug Marsha, not out of love, but in celebration of their history.

Instead of falling into his arms, Marsha stepped back. "Jack, please," she said.

"I'm sorry. I didn't mean anything..."

"It's better that we don't."

Jack nodded. An awkward silence ensued.

"I see you're driving the Road Runner again," Marsha said at last.

"Yup. I figured, what the hell. Now that I'm sober, I'm less likely to do something stupid in the car and get myself killed," Jack quipped. But upon seeing the anger that suddenly flashed in

Marsha's eyes, he immediately regretted his choice of words.

"Oh, so you drove it all the way here just so you could flaunt it in my face. That's good, Jack! That's really good!"

"No, that's not at all why I drove it here," Jack said. "It has nothing to do with thumbing my nose at you. Think about it. This car was parked long before Johnny was born. Neither one of the boys has ever seen it move! They've never ridden in this car, or any other muscle car for that matter. I want them to experience that. I want them to hear and feel the sounds and vibrations of a big, powerful engine and large exhaust pipes. Besides, this car is a part of me. It's part of who I am! And if they're going to get to know me, they should get to know this car!"

Marsha raised her eyebrows as she stared at the Road Runner. "And that's a big part of you I never understood," she said sadly. She bowed her head as she stepped past Jack to the rear of her car and raised the trunk lid. Without a word she handed the sleeping bags to Jack, who placed them on the back seat of the Road Runner.

Just then the boys returned, each with a gym bag bulging with clothes. Johnny also brought a jacket; James did not. "James, where is your coat?" Marsha called to him as he and Johnny raced toward Jack and the Road Runner.

"Oops! I forgot it," he said as he handed his bag to Jack, then darted back toward the house.

"That thing's got seatbelts, doesn't it?" Marsha asked Jack.

"Yes, it has seatbelts!" The manner of Marsha's nagging was still quite familiar.

James and Ralph passed through the front door together, James carrying his jacket. Jack addressed the boys. "On the way to the cabin, Johnny, you ride up front, and James, you ride in the back. On the way home, James, you ride up front, and Johnny, you ride in the back."

"Yes!" Johnny hissed. James groaned but did not object further. Jack buckled the boys into their seats and thanked Ralph.

"Aren't you forgetting something?" Ralph asked. He handed Jack a folded slip of paper with the directions to the cabin.

"Thanks," Jack said once more, then bounded into the driver's seat of the Road Runner and started the engine. Both boys expressed delight as it rumbled to life.

In no time they reached the entrance ramp for Interstate Seventy-Seven North. Jack started up the ramp in second gear.

"Hold on!" he said as he mashed the accelerator. The yellow beast responded by raising its front end slightly as it rocked backward, settling on its rear tires. A loud, low pitched moan emanated from the open-Air Grabber scoop; the volume and pitch of the moan quickly escalated with engine speed as the Road Runner soared up the ramp, nearly reaching the posted speed limit in second gear. Jack quickly shifted into third gear as the speedometer needle continued to swing clockwise. At the end of the ramp Jack merged into the light traffic on the interstate, shifted to fourth gear, then slowed the car back to a more reasonable speed.

Jack glanced at Johnny, who was sitting bolt upright in his seat and wearing a silly grin. He stared straight ahead, his eyes open so wide that Jack feared his eyeballs might fall out.

"Eighty-five miles per hour! Yes!" James yelled from the rear seat.

Oh shit! I'm sure their mother will hear about this! Jack thought. It had not occurred to him that James could easily see the speedometer from where he sat. "Oh, James, come on. This car is pretty fast, but it's not *that* fast!" Jack said.

"Yes, it is, too, Dad," James said. "You were busy watching

the road, but I could see. You were doin' eighty-five!"

Jack knew it was pointless to argue with James. He was sure they had bested the eighty-five mark and were fast approaching ninety before he had backed off, but he had not counted on James seeing the speedometer and making an issue of it. "Well, James, if you say so. I didn't think this car would go that fast, but if you say it did, I believe you."

"It did, Dad! It really did!" James said. But don't worry. I won't tell Mom or Grandmom or Grandpop."

"Me either," Johnny said, still grinning.

Jack chuckled to himself. "Okay, then it will be our little secret. It will be a *men's* secret, just like this is a *men's* trip."

Soon they reached their exit, then threaded their way along the rural roads per Ralph's directions.

"I like this car, Dad," James said.

"You do, huh?" Jack smiled.

"Yeah, me too," Johnny said.

"How old is this car?" James asked.

"It was built in nineteen seventy, so it's more than thirty years old," Jack said.

"Are all old cars fast?" James asked.

"Oh, no. But in the late nineteen sixties and early nineteen seventies there were many fast cars built. These high-performance cars are called muscle cars today.

"Dad, did you race this car?" James asked.

"Sure. Everybody I hung around with raced their cars."

"Did you win?" James asked.

"I won some, and I lost some. Nobody wins all the time. But I can say that I won more than I lost," Jack said. He stole another glance at Johnny, who was still grinning, now staring at the open-Air Grabber scoop.

After several miles of twisting, curving two lane roads that snaked through the tall pines they reached the tiny store where Ralph had said to sign in and pick up the key for the cabin. Johnny and James waited in the car while Jack went inside. When he returned, they headed up the well-maintained dirt road that ran behind the store. Jack crept along the road, idling in first gear to keep stones from being flung against the sides of the car behind the wheels. The boys waited patiently as Jack inched along, and eventually their cabin came into sight. Jack pulled just past it, then backed into the clearing at the front of the structure.

As they stepped from the car Jack saw that behind the cabin a steep embankment led to the edge of the water. The afternoon sun hung low in the sky on the west side of the lake. Its gentle rays flitted about the shimmering ripples of the water's surface.

Jack and the boys wasted no time in lugging their gear into the cabin. Both Johnny and James brimmed with excitement. "Dad, can we go down to the lake?" Johnny asked.

"We will in a few minutes. I want to check everything here in the cabin first," Jack said. He opened the refrigerator and touched one of the steel racks inside. It was cold, indicating that the unit was working. Next, he turned all four knobs of the stove. Within seconds the four spiral shaped burners began to glow orange. Satisfied, he turned off the burners and checked the cabinets and drawers one by one, happy to discover that they were well stocked with cooking and eating utensils, plates, cups, pots, and pans. "Not bad," he said to himself.

Jack now turned his attention to the boys. "I've got something for you guys." From a plastic bag he produced the two fishing rods. He twisted the halves of each mast together, then handed each of the boys a rod. "I think you're going to need these."

"Oh, wow, Dad! Cool! Can we go to the lake now? Let's go fishing! Come on, Dad! Let's go!" Johnny and James shouted, their words spilling over each other's.

"Now hold on a minute. Do you guys know how to use these? Do you know about casting, tying on hooks and lures, and all that stuff?" Jack asked.

"Sure. Grandpop taught us. He has a couple of old fishing rods he lets us use when we want to go fishing," Johnny said.

"I see. Well, now you have your own rods," Jack said. "Let's go catch some fish!"

The trio took their fishing gear and clambered down the bank to the edge of the lake. There a wooden dock jutted into the water, affording a nearly perfect spot from which to fish. For the next hour they cast their lures into the late day sun. Jack and James each felt a few strikes, but neither landed a fish. Johnny reeled in a tiny bass, but at a paltry four inches, it was too small to keep.

Jack and the boys returned to the cabin prizeless, but not disappointed. "I'll tell you what. I'll go through the groceries and figure out something quick for dinner. Then, after dinner, we can walk to the store and get some fresh bait. Tomorrow we'll be sure to catch plenty of fish. How's that for a plan?" Jack asked. The boys agreed.

In the cooler Jack found a one-pound package of hamburger. He divided it into four large patties, then placed two patties in each of the two frying pans from the cabinet next to the stove. While the meat sizzled atop the stove, he stowed the perishables into the refrigerator and took inventory of the items in the grocery bags.

One quarter pound patty between two slices of bread satisfied Jack's hunger. The boys each consumed a patty, then split the fourth one. Afterward they headed toward the store on foot.

"What are we going to do when we get back?" Johnny asked.

"I want to watch TV," James said.

"There is no TV, stupid!" Johnny said.

"Shut up, butt face!" James said.

"Hey, that's enough!" Jack said. Johnny and James immediately fell silent. Neither spoke until they reached the store.

Once inside the store, the boys' volleying of insults and Jack's intervention were forgotten. Johnny and James dashed toward the games and toys, pointing, joking, and laughing as they scoured the racks. Suddenly Jack thought of the dream he'd had months earlier in which the boys had acted in exactly the same manner as they giggled their way through a rack of naughty greeting cards. Jack's heart swelled as he realized that no longer was, he standing outside their lives. This time, as they laughed and clowned their way through the store, he was not an onlooker, but an integral part of their activity. This was the culmination of the months of telephone calls, conversations with the boys, and his own soul searching. Their warming up to him was his reward, and what a reward it was!

Jack took two large plastic cups of earthworms to the counter and placed them next to the cash register. "Dad, can we get a toy?" he heard Johnny call from a few aisles away.

"You can each get one," Jack said. Moments later both boys appeared, each with a rubber band powered, propeller driven balsa wood airplane kit. Jack smiled. "They had those things when I was a kid. Go ahead and set them on the counter." He thought of the glider he and Stephen had flown months earlier in Mrs. Hurley's back yard.

Just then the store attendant, a heavyset middle-aged woman

named Millie, appeared from the back room. "How are you folks tonight?" she asked. "Did you get all settled in?"

"We're doing well, and yes, we're settled in. Now we're going to enjoy a couple of days of quiet fishing," Jack said.

"Well, I wish y'all the best of luck. Some folks say the fish aren't biting, but other folks seem to do just fine," Millie said.

Jack paid her for their purchases, then he and the boys headed back to the cabin. Idle conversation fueled their walk. Jack's exhaustion from his two full days on the road caught him by surprise. Upon entering the cabin, he secured the door then flopped across his bed "just for a minute," he told the boys. He immediately fell into a deep slumber.

The next morning Jack awoke to find both Johnny and James up and dressed. Outside the sun was bright; daybreak had long since passed. "Good morning, Dad!" James nearly shouted upon seeing Jack move.

"'Morning. What time is it?"

"Nine-thirty," James said. "You must have been really tired."

"Have you guys eaten anything yet?"

"We found some Oreo cookies, so we ate some of them," Johnny said.

"Cookies for breakfast. That's good," Jack said sarcastically to himself as he stood from his bunk. Slowly he made his way across the floor to the kitchen counter. There he filled a metal pan with water and placed it atop the stove. While the cold water drew heat from the burner beneath it Jack shoveled a heaping spoonful of instant coffee into a mug. On the table he spied the open package of Oreos, which by now was half gone. *Oh, what the hell.* He took four cookies, popped them into his mouth one at a time, and chewed slowly while he waited for his coffee water to become hot enough. Also, on the table were the tattered remains of the two balsa wood planes. He remembered from his childhood that they did not take kindly to colliding with stationary objects or hard landings. *At least the planes kept them busy for a while.*

After a few cups of coffee and another handful of cookies Jack was awake and chipper. He and the boys took their fishing gear to the dock once more. One by one they cast their lines into the water. Almost instantly James's bobber disappeared beneath the surface of the water, then reappeared and began hopping about. "Dad! I got a fish! I got a fish!" he screamed as he stomped his feet in excitement.

"Reel him in!" Jack said.

James cranked the reel frantically, but as the bobber neared the dock the line went dead. As he reeled in the last few feet, the bobber, sinker, and bare hook rose from the water. "He got away, and he took my bait! Stupid fish!"

"Don't worry. He's still out there," Jack said. "Get another piece of bait on your hook and go back after him."

James did just that. By early afternoon they had all felt nibbles and had their bait stolen numerous times, but none had reeled in a fish. The threesome sat quietly on the wooden dock, their feet dangling above the water, as the sun passed directly overhead. Sensing his sons' mounting boredom and disappointment Jack stood and said, "Let's go get some lunch." Johnny and James quickly reeled in their lines, placed their rods across the wooden planks, then sprang to their feet and joined Jack as he headed for the cabin.

Using paper towels as plates they ate bologna and cheese sandwiches while they talked about the boys' school, friends, and Karate. As Jack listened to Johnny and James tell story after story it occurred to him that these were perhaps the most delicious bologna sandwiches he had ever tasted.

The afternoon went much like the morning had, with each of the three exchanging bait for an occasional nibble, but none landing a fish. Jack experimented with some of his various lures to no avail. The fish simply were not interested.

By four-thirty even Jack had become disgusted. "I'm going to go get dinner started," he said. "You two can stay here if you want. I'll come back and get you when it's ready." Johnny and James both nodded without looking up.

"What are we having?" James asked as Jack took his first step onto land.

"I haven't decided yet. What do you want?" Jack asked.

"Hamburgers!" James said.

"Johnny, is that all right with you? We just had hamburgers last night," Jack said.

"Yeah, that's fine. I like hamburgers. Do we have any onion soup mix? Mom always mixes that into the hamburgers. Makes them really good," Johnny said.

"I'll check," Jack said as he turned and scrambled up the bank. Despite a full day of restlessness, aggravation, and disappointment the boys had both been incredibly well behaved. Only once or twice had either taken a verbal jab at the other. It seemed to Jack that they wanted this visit to be a success as much as he did.

Jack decided that the dock would be a splendid place to eat supper that evening. The setting sun cast its soft rays across the lake, which glistened as they played among the ripples caused by the gentle breeze. This aura of natural beauty was further enhanced by the tranquil sounds of birds chirping and the rustle of leaves high in the trees. He gathered cups, condiments, a loaf of bread, and a two-liter bottle of Coke into a bag, then carried the bag and the plate with the burgers to the dock.

As he neared the dock, he heard the muffled sounds of his sons' voices. Only when he got closer did he hear Johnny say, "I don't think Dad will want to. He came here to fish."

"Don't think Dad will want to what?" Jack asked, startling the boys.

"Aw, nothing. We were just talking," Johnny said.

"Is there something you guys want to do?" Jack asked.

Johnny and James looked at each other for a moment. It was

Johnny who spoke first. "Well, we know you came here to fish. And we like to fish, too," he said.

"But..." Jack prompted.

"But I--we were wondering if maybe tomorrow we could do something different," James said.

"Like what? What do you guys have in mind?" Jack asked.

"I don't know. Maybe we could go for a hike or something in the morning, then maybe we could go to the mall and see a movie in the afternoon," Johnny said.

"Yeah, and we can get ice cream at the food court!" James said.

Jack shook his head. "Look, I didn't come here to fish. I came here to see you guys, and it's important that we make the most of the time we have together. Who knows when we'll have this chance again? If you guys want to do something else, we can. This isn't *my* trip. It's *our* trip. Of course, we can go hiking tomorrow morning, then we can see a movie, and even get some ice cream if that's what you want to do."

Johnny and James looked at each other again then cheered.

The next morning, they walked the length of the dirt road,

which extended a quarter mile past the last cabin in their small rustic community. Afterward they piled into the Road Runner and headed toward town. Johnny guided Jack directly to the mall without making one wrong turn. There they ate lunch, caught a matinee, then devoured ice cream cones. It was mid-afternoon when they returned to the cabin. To Jack's astonishment James asked, "Dad, can we go fishing again?"

Within an hour Jack and James had each caught a bass large enough to keep. During that time Johnny, who had removed his bobber, reeled in several catfish, but only one was large enough to keep. Jack cleaned the three fish at the dock while Johnny and James watched. Back in the cabin, the aroma of frying fish filled the air.

After dinner Jack washed the dishes and packed all of the unused food and condiments, then joined the boys in a card game. At nine o'clock he said, "You two need to brush your teeth and get to bed. We've had a big day today and we have to get an early start tomorrow." The boys complied with surprisingly little objection.

As Jack tucked Johnny into bed, Johnny said, "Dad, will you promise me you'll be careful on your way home?"

"You bet. I promise," Jack said. He kissed Johnny's forehead, then moved toward James.

"I love you, Dad," James said as he squeezed Jack's neck in his arms.

"I love you too, son," Jack said. He kissed James's forehead, then bade both boys good-night.

"Good night," Johnny and James said together.

Jack went to the kitchen for a glass of water. He waited a few minutes, then checked on the boys. They were both sound asleep. *They must have been exhausted,* he thought. The soft light from the fixture which hung above the table in the main room filtered through the doorway where Jack stood and illuminated the boys' room with a shadowy grayness. As his eyes strained to discern the outlines of the two slumbering heaps of stuffed nylon before him, Jack felt his heart swell with the love and pride that only a parent can know. "Good night, guys. Sleep tight," he whispered.

Later that night Jack sat at the table and opened his road atlas. His stomach was nauseous with anxiety as he reviewed the course he had mapped out for the following day. If he timed it right, Jack figured he could reach Washington, DC early in the afternoon, then continue past Baltimore ahead of the evening rush hour. He would continue north around the tip of the Chesapeake Bay, pass through Delaware, and into Pennsylvania. If all went according to plan, he would spend the night in Philadelphia.

It occurred to him what a strange coincidence it was that he would spend the night before he arrived in Maine in the town to which he had lost Kim so many years earlier. He hoped this time Philadelphia would hold better luck for him.

Just then Johnny came into the room. "What's the matter?" Jack asked.

"I can't sleep." Johnny sat in the chair across from Jack.

"What's on your mind?"

"I don't know. Everything just seems so different."

"How? In a good way or a bad way?"

"I don't know."

Jack decided not to press him.

Looking at the atlas, Johnny asked, "What are you doing?"

"After I drop you guys off, I'm not going straight home. I'm going to Maine to talk with Kim."

"Can't you just call her?"

"No, I'm afraid it's more complicated than that. I have to see her in person."

"Oh." Johnny fidgeted with a pencil that was lying on the table. "Dad, have you ever thought about getting back together with Mom?"

"Yeah, Johnny, I have. In the beginning, right after you guys left, I wanted that more than anything. But your mom and I aren't the same people we used to be. We used to love each other. Both you and your brother were born out of that love. But we grew apart. We just can't be together anymore."

"Is that because of... you know...."

"My drinking?"

Johnny nodded, then shifted his gaze from Jack to the pencil in his hand.

"Yes, I'm afraid so. See, when people drink a lot over a long time it messes up their thinking. They see things all wrong, they say things all wrong, and they hurt the people they love most."

"That's why Mom used to cry every night when we lived in Colorado."

"I knew she cried sometimes, but I didn't know it was every

night."

"Yeah, usually after James and I went to bed, before you got home. She tried to hide it from us, but we knew. And sometimes when you and Mom would fight, James and I would cry under our covers. Mostly him, though. I didn't cry that much."

"James, I-- I'm sorry. I really don't know what to say. I'm so sorry!" Jack bowed his head and shielded his eyes. Johnny darted around the table and hugged him. Together they wept.

As they dried their eyes Johnny said, "Mom told us to be on good behavior while we were with you. Have you been on good behavior too?"

"Are you asking if I've tried to be extra nice? I haven't gone out of my way to be overly nice, if that's what you mean. Why?"

"Well, things are so different. You haven't yelled at us once. I'm trying to figure out if it's because you're on good behavior too or if it's because you stopped drinking."

Jack held Johnny's shoulders and looked into his eyes. "The person you're seeing right now is who I really am. This is me without the booze. Look, you know I'm an alcoholic. The truth is, I was an alcoholic before you and your brother were born, and even before your mom and I got married. I didn't realize it way back then, and even when your mom pointed it out to me, I wouldn't admit it. But actually, I was a monster."

"You weren't *that* bad."

"Yes, Johnny, I was. But I couldn't see it until I stopped drinking. By then it was too late. I'd already broken up our family. So, to answer your question, I was on bad behavior all those years before. I'm on normal behavior now, if that makes sense."

Johnny went back to his chair. "Okay. I thought you were always on normal behavior when we lived in Colorado, and I thought you were on good behavior whenever we talked on the phone, just like now. But if it was all bad behavior before and *this* is normal behavior, then you're not just pretending to be nice?"

"Johnny, I'm not pretending one bit. I only hope that one day you can forgive me for the pain I've caused you."

Johnny left his chair to hug Jack once more. "I forgive you, Dad. I forgive you."

Chapter Nineteen

When the alarm sounded at four-thirty the next morning, Jack sprang from his bed. It was not that he felt well rested or refreshed; on the contrary, he was exhausted after a night of shallow cat naps interspersed with senseless dreams. He tried to recall what he had dreamed, but the memories of his dreams had become ensnared in the fuzzy boundary between slumber and wakefulness.

A sense of urgency weighed on his mind. By five-thirty he and the boys were idling down the unpaved road, leaving the cabin behind in the first glimmer of daylight. Both boys fell asleep once more before they reached the main road.

Jack parked the Road Runner at the curb in front of Marsha's parents' house shortly after six o'clock. "Come on, guys. We're there," he said into the empty stillness after shutting off the ignition and silencing the pipes. Both boys stirred, then unbuckled their seatbelts. Jack went to the other side of the car to help his groggy sons. "Don't worry about your stuff. You two only need to worry about finding your beds." With an arm around each boy Jack walked them to the front door, then knelt and hugged them both. "I love you guys," he said.

"I love you, too," Johnny and James both said in sleepy voices. Johnny opened the door and stepped inside. James rubbed his tired eyes, then waved to Jack. "Bye, Dad," he said with a weary smile as he followed Johnny inside.

"Take care, son," Jack said.

Jack returned to the car to gather the boys' belongings. Ralph joined him moments later. "So, did y'all have a good time?" he asked.

"Had a great time," Jack said. He handed the boys' sleeping bags to Ralph, then scooped their remaining baggage from the rear seat and carried it to the house. The two men then removed the cooler, food, and the boys' fishing rods from the trunk.

"Well, I guess that'll do it," Ralph said.

"I suppose so," Jack nodded. "Ralph, I want to thank you for all of this. I could see that the last couple of days meant a lot to the boys, but it meant a lot to me, too. Thank you."

"Ah! It was nothing. I'm glad the three of you had a good time. I know they needed to see you, and I expect you needed to see them just as bad," Ralph said. "Now you be careful on the road and have a safe trip."

Jack shook Ralph's hand, then sank into the driver's seat. He cranked the four-forty to life, then pulled away from the curb.

At one-thirty he reached the Interstate 495 beltway around Washington, DC and headed east around the city. In Alexandria, Virginia he exited the interstate, for the gas gauge indicated an eighth of a tank and his hunger pangs reminded him that he, too, needed refueling. He found a gas station a couple of blocks from the exit ramp. While filling the gas tank he popped open the trunk and exchanged his windbreaker for a quilted flannel shirt. Not only would the padded shirt be more comfortable for driving, but its breast pocket would be more convenient for keeping gas and food money than his wallet. When he finished refueling, he paid the attendant with a crisp one-hundred-dollar bill from the wad in his left front pocket, then shoved the change into his shirt pocket. His next stop was at a McDonald's, where he devoured a Big Mac, a cheeseburger, and a large Coke. In short order he was back on the interstate.

Jack switched on the radio and rolled the tuner knob until he found a classic rock station. Boston's *Peace of Mind* was near its end, which was followed by Aerosmith's *Sweet Emotion.* Driving the Road Runner in the mid-afternoon sun while listening to songs of his youth transported him backward to the happiest time of his life, back to a time before the complexities and troubles he had found in adulthood. *Sweet Emotion* was followed by Peter Frampton's *Do You Feel Like I Do,* which was in turn followed by a cluster of commercials.

Memories of the old days he had shared with Kim led to thoughts of his current plight. As he looked ahead to the second mission of his trip he was gripped with apprehension. The further north he got, the greater his feeling of dread for what he might find in Bar Harbor. For an instant he considered taking Interstate Seventy west from Baltimore and heading home, but that would never do. He needed answers from Kim, and this was the only way he knew to get them. Whether or not he would go to Maine was not the question. How he would deal with whatever he discovered there was the pertinent question now.

As Jack neared Baltimore the radio signal grew weak and heavy with static. Traffic also became much heavier, both of which prompted him to turn off the radio. Soon the heavy flow of traffic swept him toward the Fort McHenry Tunnel much like a fast-moving brook whisking away a child's ball.

When he reached the toll booth north of the tunnel, he was thankful for having put the smaller bills in his shirt pocket. He would appreciate his foresight again forty miles later when he reached the toll booth at the Susquehanna River Bridge and once more at the toll booth just north of the Delaware state line.

At the Delaware tolls several long lines of vehicles crept forward. Through his open window he detected the unmistakable petroleum stench of hypoid gear lubricant. "Ooh boy! Somebody's got trouble brewing!" he said to himself. When his turn came, he handed the toll collector a five-dollar bill, took his change, then resumed his seventy mile per hour speed without another thought.

Traffic was heavy but moved at a brisk pace for the next four miles. Suddenly it slowed to a crawl. Jack sighed. At a quarter past five he was approaching Wilmington at the height of rush hour. As he negotiated the bumper to bumper sea of cars, he stole a quick glance at his atlas. Interstate Ninety-Five ran directly through Wilmington, while the Interstate 495 bypass ran to the east around the city and converged with Interstate Ninety-Five near the

Pennsylvania state line. He opted for the bypass. Despite the rush hour traffic on Interstate Ninety-Five, he was surprised to find very little traffic on the bypass and was comfortable cruising at seventy MPH. Then he heard a faint grinding sound from the rear of the car. The sound turned to a low roar as he crossed the Christina River bridge. *Philadelphia is only another thirty or forty miles,* he thought, but with a sinking feeling he realized that the ailing Road Runner probably wouldn't make it that far.

Just then the driver of the car to Jack's right began honking his horn and pointing at the Road Runner's rear tire. Jack waved to the other driver in acknowledgment, then flicked on his turn signal and pulled to the shoulder. As the car grated to a stop the pungent odor of gear oil was stronger than ever, and as he stepped from the car, smoke was rolling from the right rear wheel well. "Oh fuck!" He dropped to his knees and peered beneath the bumper. Gear lubricant from the rear axle dripped from the right rear brake drum. The slimy, smelly stuff coated the inside of the wheel well and tire, and droplets clung to the trunk floor pan behind the wheel.

Nauseated both by what he saw and by the suffocating smell of burning gear oil, Jack sat on the guardrail behind the car. It was obvious that he shouldn't drive the car any further, but in this age of

computers and cellular phones, until now Jack had maintained that

he needed neither. Besides, who would he call in Delaware anyway?

He spotted a motorist call box some distance away, but he figured

that calling for help would only land him a hefty towing bill.

Furthermore, the driver of the tow truck would either want to deposit

the Road Runner in his towing yard where it would accrue a hefty

storage fee, or he might suggest a repair facility which could

probably make the needed repairs sometime the following week. He

had no time for this. With the smoke clearing he took the wheel and

limped the injured Road Runner along the shoulder.

After a mile of creeping he came to the next exit, which was

marked Edgemoor. He guided the Road Runner around the

cloverleaf past some dingy warehouse buildings to the stop sign at

the base of the ramp. He turned right at the stop sign and proceeded

to the traffic light a few hundred feet away. For no reason other than

because the light was red Jack decided to turn right. This was a

rather seedy part of town. *Hell, the whole damned city might be a*

shithole, he thought.

By now the axle bearing was grating so badly that he could

feel the rumbling in the floor of the car. He needed to find a place to stay, then to see how much damage had been done. It was Wednesday. If the damage was not extensive, and if he could find the parts and a shop equipped to press a new axle bearing onto the axle shaft, there was still a slim chance he could reach Maine late the following night.

Beyond an abandoned gas station on the left, the sign for the Holly Oak Motel caught his eye. He signaled, then made a left into the parking lot. He guessed the single-story L-shaped structure to have been built sometime during the 1950s, but its tidy outward appearance suggested that the rooms were both well maintained and clean. Moreover, the place exuded a warm, homey feeling to which Jack was particularly receptive at that moment.

Jack brought the Road Runner to a halt in a parking space. The car was immediately enveloped in its own foul odor, for the thick stench of hypoid gear lube hung like a vile fog. He stepped from the car and headed toward the office, passing between two large potted rose bushes as he strode through the office doorway. Already new buds had begun to appear on the thorny green stalks like a batch of fresh blemishes on a teenager's cheeks.

"Good afternoon, sir. How can I help you?" the short, stout woman behind the desk asked. Her voice was raspy, her speech slow and deliberate. She wore her gray hair in a bun and the large lenses of her glasses hung on either side of her beak-like nose while gaudy gold earrings dangled from her lobes. Despite her initial grandmotherly appearance, Jack noted that the piercing eyes behind those porthole windows looked as if they could burn through a man's flesh. While she appeared as sweet as cotton candy, he thought she might become nasty if crossed.

"I'd like a room for the night," Jack said.

"Okay. All of our rooms have two double beds, heat, and air conditioning. No pets are allowed. All rooms are fifty-nine dollars a night paid in advance. We do not accept checks. Cash or credit card only. Check-out is at ten sharp," the woman said in a few well-rehearsed sentences. "Would you like smoking or non-smoking?"

"Non-smoking, please," Jack said as he peeled the top bill from the wad in his front pocket.

The woman took Jack's bill, held it toward the light and examined it for authenticity, then handed Jack his change and a key on a fob with the number seven and the words Holly Oak Motel emblazoned on it. "Before you go, I need you to read and sign this. Our rules are simple. They protect you, the other guests, and us. My name is Teresa. If you have any trouble or questions, I'm in the office from six in the morning until eight at night."

"That's a long day." Jack said as he skimmed over the rules.

"I can't find dependable help!" Teresa said.

"Do you know of any auto parts stores nearby?" Jack asked as he signed the bottom of the form and handed it back to Teresa.

"Go up this side street three blocks. Make a right. Go two blocks and look to your left. Are you having car trouble?" Teresa asked.

"Yes."

Teresa gazed over Jack's shoulder to the parking lot outside. "Is that your car? The yellow one?"

"Yes, it is," Jack said.

"Wow! That's pretty. Honey, you don't want to leave that pretty car out front where it can be seen. Not in this neighborhood! I'll tell you what. There is an alleyway that runs behind the building. Why don't you park it there? Go ahead and make whatever repairs you need to make, and nobody will bother it. All I ask is that you clean up your mess and don't disturb the other guests. You'll see two junkers back there. They belong to my nephew. If you put your car near his two, you'll be out of the fire lane."

Jack thanked Teresa, then drove the car into the alley behind the building. Fortunately, it was paved. He spotted the cars Teresa had mentioned--a green Dodge Shadow ES that had been clobbered in the left front and a partially dismantled white Plymouth Sundance, presumably for parts. Jack parked a comfortable distance from the other two cars. He took his duffel bag from the trunk, then walked to the front of the building to find room seven.

Once inside, Jack guessed the room to have been last renovated sometime in the seventies. The dark, wood paneled walls seemed to suck the light from the room, reminding him of a dark, dingy bar room. The low nap carpet was of a busy design with interlocking squares and rectangles of blue, green, yellow, and brown. The plaid green and brown bed spread had obviously been chosen to match the carpet. Adjacent to the bed stood a lone wooden desk chair, its brown cushion barely worn after its many years of service. *No wonder!* he thought. *That thing looks uncomfortable as hell!* With a shrug of his shoulders he plopped his duffel bag on the bed, then exited through the back door. The car sat roughly fifteen yards away.

Jack popped the trunk open once more and removed his toolbox. Next, he kicked about the weeds at the edge of the property in hopes of finding something suitable on which to set the rear of the Road Runner once he removed the wheels. Behind the white Sundance Jack spotted four cinder blocks. He picked up two of them and carried them back to his car.

Overhead, heavy storm clouds invaded the clear blue sky and a chilly breeze began to blow. Jack knew he must work quickly to beat both the rain and nightfall. From the trunk he removed and assembled the pieces of the bumper jack, then wrapped the hook with a rag to prevent it from marring the chrome bumper. He raised the left rear corner of the car, removed the wheel, then lowered the jack until the axle housing rested on one cinder block. He did likewise with the right side, then returned the bumper jack to the trunk.

Next, he pulled the right-side brake drum from the axle and inspected it and the brakes. As he suspected the brake linings were saturated with gear lubricant and all the hardware was coated with the smelly goop, but aside from the contaminated linings, none of the brake components was damaged. Next, he removed the nuts securing the axle shaft and bearing into the housing. After a few raps with a hammer he jarred the bearing loose, then slid the axle shaft from the housing. The axle bearing disintegrated in his hand, but upon further inspection he discovered that the shaft and inside of the housing had escaped damage. He then disassembled the left side. The axle seal on that side showed signs of wear, but the bearing and all the other pieces checked out fine. "One axle bearing, a couple of seals, and a set of brake shoes," he muttered.

Suddenly he was pelted by the first few rain drops of an early evening shower. He slammed the trunk closed, then stuffed a rag into each end of the open axle housing. He shoved both axle shafts and brake drums under the car, then gathered his tools into the toolbox and lugged it to his room. By now the sky had taken on a dark purple hue tinted with green and the rain was falling in torrents.

Once inside his room he nudged the door closed with his elbow and set the toolbox on the floor. He flicked on the bathroom light, then turned on the water in the sink and tore the wrapper from the tiny bar of floral scented soap. Jack scrubbed his hands but was not surprised that the mild soap would not cut the petroleum film. Next, he unscrewed the cap from the small vial of matching shampoo and poured a generous puddle into his open palm. The shampoo worked only slightly better, but after several scrubbings alternating between soap and shampoo he realized that despite their oily feel, his hands were as clean as they were going to get. "Won't have to worry about chapped skin." He shut off the water, then dried his hands with one of the two bath towels which hung from the metal rack above the toilet.

Jack left the bathroom and took the television remote control from its plastic pouch on the side of the ancient Zenith television. He pressed the power button, then sat on the bed. Rolling up and down through the channels, he found they were all were static and snow. *The storm must have knocked the cable out.* In dismay he clicked off the television and leaned back against the wall.

This is great! Just fucking great! On the tight schedule he was running there was no time for lengthy delays, yet now he found himself stuck in a motel room in a strange town a couple thousand miles from home--a town where he had not even planned to stop. Outside, the Road Runner sat on blocks in a downpour. Jack could not recall the last time the car had seen rain such as this.

I have to get to Maine! No matter what, I have to know what the hell is going on! Jack considered having the car towed to a repair shop, then renting a car for the Maine leg of his trip, but quickly decided against that. How would he know who to trust with the car? If the repair was not done properly, he probably wouldn't make it back to Colorado before trouble arose again. In addition, how could he be sure his Road Runner would not be joy-ridden and abused at the hands of some thrill-seeking stranger before he could return for it? And what if the car was not ready when he returned to Delaware? For that matter, there would be no time to return to Delaware on his way from Maine back to Colorado.

Furthermore, in a time of need he would be thankful to have his old friend close at hand. Should his talk with Kim not go well or, worse yet, should Randy be there, he would seek refuge behind that simulated woodgrain steering wheel. The throbbing exhaust would ease his anxiety, and the familiar round gauges would smile up at him in a way that would reassure him and soothe his pain. And if he needed to scream, by mashing the accelerator the howling tires and bellowing exhaust would scream for him. Such a knowing and understanding companion could never be found in a rented Ford Taurus!

The rumbling in Jack's stomach reminded him that his usual suppertime had passed. The flood lights mounted high atop the sign pole out front cast bright rays which fanned across the parking lot. In this light Jack could see sheets of rain being swept across the front of the motel by strong gusts of wind. Even if he knew for sure that there was a diner or fast food restaurant nearby, walking there in this heavy rain was unthinkable.

A laminated card at the end of the dresser listed area attractions, restaurants, and the like. Restaurants offering delivery were marked with asterisks. At random Jack selected Tony's Pizza Palace.

"Tony's," a young male voice answered after the eighth ring.

"Do you deliver to the Holly Oak Motel?" Jack asked.

"Yeah, we go there," the youth replied. In the background Jack could hear muffled voices, the ringing of a cash register, and the bustling sounds of a busy pizza shop.

"I'd like to order a large pizza," Jack said. He knew he would not consume a large pizza in one sitting, but there was still breakfast and possibly lunch the following day to consider, and with no mode of transportation other than his sneakers, Jack thought he might be glad to have half a pizza sitting around. Pizza was a staple that would keep for at least a day in nothing more than its cardboard box, and what tastier a breakfast was there than cold pizza and hot coffee?

"One large pizza. You want anything on that?"

"I'll take a little pepperoni. Oh, and do you have Coca-Cola?"

"Only by the six-pack," the young man said.

"Fine. I'll take that, too."

"Okay, so we've got a large pepperoni pizza and a six-pack of Coke, and that's going to the Holly Oak Motel. What's your room number?"

"Seven."

"Room seven. We'll be there in about half an hour. Thank you for your order."

"Thanks," Jack said, then hung up the telephone. He sprawled across the bed on his back and closed his eyes. The soothing sound of the rain driving against the roof filled the room.

Gradually he felt his tension ebb away as he sank into a state of relaxation.

The knock at the door startled him. As he scrambled to answer he glanced at the clock. What seemed like five minutes of rest had actually been a forty-five-minute nap. He swung the door open, then took his pizza and Coca-Cola from the delivery driver.

"That's sixteen-fifty," the driver said. Jack handed him a twenty, told him to keep the change, then thanked him and closed and locked the door.

The aroma of fresh hot pizza teased Jack's nostrils and renewed his hunger. He flipped open the box, took the first slice, and raised it high to break the cheese strings that stretched like thin yellow rubber bands between the edges of his first slice and the adjacent slices. His mouth watered as he blew on the tip of the slice a few times to cool it, then he shoved it deep into his mouth and tore off a huge bite. Jack chewed slowly at first, savoring the cheesy flavor and ignoring the droplets of grease that dribbled down his chin. He chewed his second and third bites much more quickly, and soon the first slice was gone. Not until after he had begun eating did Jack realize how hungry he was. Within minutes he devoured three more slices and downed two cans of Coke.

With a full gut and the sense of satisfaction it afforded, Jack's eyelids began to grow heavy. He moved the pizza box and the four remaining cans of Coke to the dresser, undressed himself, and slithered beneath the covers. "I'd better get all the sleep I can now. I don't know what time I'll get on the road tomorrow, and I might end up driving all night to get to Maine," he said to himself. He immediately fell into a deep, dreamless slumber.

Chapter Twenty

Jack awoke suddenly, his stomach ablaze. It seemed that several hours had passed since he had gone to bed, but the clock told otherwise-- it was eight forty-seven. He had been asleep for barely an hour.

Jack sat upright on the edge of the bed. The fire in the pit of his stomach had begun to climb his esophagus, burning its way upward through his chest, its flames licking at the back of his throat. He swallowed repeatedly, but the burning persisted. He considered making himself vomit but subjecting his already irritated stomach to the rigors of puking was unthinkable. Instead Jack took a can of Coke from the dresser, guzzled half its content, then belched. He tipped his head back and consumed the remainder of the Coke, then belched a few more times. The last burp brought up a mouthful of bile. He dashed into the bathroom and spat into the toilet. Still, the fire inside raged out of control.

Jack tore through his duffel bag looking for antacid tablets but found none. At this hour the motel office would be closed, but he thought he remembered passing a store of sorts a block or two before he reached the motel. "God, I hope they're open," he said as

he slipped into his trousers. Outside the rain had nearly stopped.

Jack was thankful for that much, but in consideration of the

remaining drizzle he chose his nylon windbreaker over the quilted

flannel shirt he had worn throughout the day.

Jack walked briskly toward the Interstate 495 exchange.

There was something creepy about this neighborhood. He had

sensed it earlier, but now a strong feeling of uneasiness came over

him. His eyes darted about the shadows as the aftermath of Tony's

pepperoni pizza charred his gut.

As Jack neared the store, he was relieved to find the place

well lit. Above the door hung a large illuminated sign which read

Lu-Lu's Market. Light from within the store shone through

windows cluttered with faded posters and signs touting store

specials. To Jack, Lu-Lu's Market seemed like an oasis in this

desert of misfortune. Inside, display racks containing bread, snacks,

household items, and the like were arranged in tidy rows on the worn

green and black speckled tile floor. The place reminded him of

Johnson's Market. The clerk was a thin young girl of about sixteen

with frizzy black hair gathered in a ponytail. She glanced at Jack as he entered the market, then looked away in disinterest.

Jack took three rolls of antacid tablets from the rack below the counter. At the end of one of the aisles, two metal shelves filled with snack cakes caught his eye. *Hmmm. Tony's pizza topped with pepperoni and a sprinkle of Drano for breakfast? Not a chance in Hell!* he thought. He selected two coffee cakes, then took his purchases to the counter. At the far end of the counter he spied a short rack of local street maps. Realizing such a map might help in his quest for parts and supplies to fix the Road Runner, he took a map and placed it on the counter with his other items.

Jack stood patiently at the counter waiting for the clerk to acknowledge him. It was then that he noticed the small television behind the counter. Although the volume was set low, the girl appeared totally engrossed in her program. He cleared his throat to get her attention. She ignored him for a few more seconds, then shot him a contemptuous look. "Is that all?" Her voice was barely audible, but laden with attitude.

"That'll do it," he said, ignoring her tone.

The clerk stood and slowly shuffled her way to the counter. She scanned each of his purchases, then stated the total, "Eight forty-five."

Jack reached for his shirt pocket, then remembered that he had left the shirt-- and his smaller bills-- in the motel room. He checked his wallet. It contained two dollars, not enough even for the antacid tablets.

"Can you break a hundred?" Jack asked. The clerk nodded. Jack shoved his hand into his left pocket, fidgeted with the wad of bills, and produced a single one-hundred-dollar bill. "Here you go."

The girl stared at the noticeable bulge in Jack's pocket for a moment, then took the bill and held it up to examine it under the light just as Teresa had earlier in the day. Satisfied that it was not counterfeit she rang up the sale and counted back his change. Jack stuffed these smaller bills into his right pocket with the intention of moving them to his shirt pocket later. The clerk then reached below the counter-- Jack assumed for a bag. Instead, she picked up a cellular phone and dialed a number, then turned away from him. Disgusted, Jack scooped his items from the counter, jammed them into his jacket pockets, then left the store.

Outside he tore open one of the rolls of antacid tablets. He popped three tablets into his mouth, chewed, then swallowed. The chalky paste clung to the back of his throat like drywall spackle. He popped two more tablets into his mouth and allowed them to dissolve. He swallowed repeatedly, washing the mud down his esophagus. Relief came quickly. Finally, he stepped from the curb and began moving across the vacant parking lot toward the shadows at its fringe.

"Yo, whitey!" a deep voice called from behind. Jack whirled about to see three figures emerge from the darkness behind Lu-Lu's and move quickly in his direction. "Yo, we need to talk to you, man!"

Jack's heart leapt into his throat. He snapped his head forward and began walking at a hurried pace. *They're just fucking with you,* he told himself. *Ignore them and maybe they'll go away!* But the scuffling of feet behind him told him otherwise. Glancing over his shoulder Jack saw the trio of black men sprinting toward him. Immediately he broke into a run.

"Yo, whitey! Where you goin'? We want to talk to you!"

As Jack bolted past the abandoned gas station next door his pursuers overtook him. One thrust him into the chain link fence that surrounded the property. Jack's coffee cakes and map were scattered. Hands grappled with his arms and shoulders, then Jack found himself face to face with the spokesman, his back against the fence, and his upper arms in the clutches of the other two men who stood at each side.

"Why you gotta be like this, man?" the leader asked. "I said we want to talk with you. What you runnin' for?" he grinned. Even in the dim light Jack caught the glimmer of snow-white teeth between thick parted lips.

Jack's throat was blocked so tightly he felt as if he had swallowed his fist. Unable to utter a word he shook his head. *Don't act scared. These fuckers can smell fear!*

"Now you know what this is about, so just hand it over," the spokesman said. "Don't make us get shitty!"

"But... but I don't have much money," Jack squeaked, immediately furious with himself for sounding like a sissy. "Let me get my wallet and I'll show you."

The spokesman nodded to the man at Jack's right, who in turn released Jack's arm. Jack removed his wallet. He struggled to gain control of his trembling fingers as he opened his wallet to show the speaker. The speaker snatched the wallet from Jack, then removed the two one-dollar bills. "Two dollars. This muhfugga's got two muhfuggin' dollars!" he said as he shoved the bills into his pocket. With his fingers he explored the cavities of the wallet. Jack's driver's license and a few scraps of paper on which he had scribbled notes fell to the ground. "No credit cards, neither."

Then the leader shot Jack an icy grin. "I suppose you think we just a bunch of dumb ass street niggas. Well, lucky for you, we ain't! If we were, we'd take your shitty two bucks and pop a cap in your head just for the fuck of it. See what I'm sayin'? They'd find yo' cracker ass in a Dumpster here on the dark side of town! But we're smarter than that. Smarter, and informed!"

The leader moved toward Jack. Jack felt the fingers around his upper arms tense as the leader reached for the bulge in Jack's pocket. As if by reflex Jack raised his foot and kicked with all his strength. His shoulders sprang backward against the fence as his foot collided with the leader's breast bone. The leader staggered backward, lost his balance, and fell from the curb. At that instant the man to Jack's right brought his fist through a wide arc and thrust it deep into Jack's midriff. Jack doubled over as his air escaped him in a sharp huff.

Jack coughed and gasped for breath. The men at his sides clasped his arms tighter now. Suddenly Jack felt a hard object pressing against his scalp just above his forehead. Slowly he lifted his head. His suspicion was confirmed as he found himself peering up the barrel of a small pistol held in the leader's clutch.

"You're a dumb muhfugga!" the leader-turned-gunman barked.

Jack looked downward. His pulse throbbed in his temples and his mouth went dry. *Don't shoot! For the love of God, please don't shoot!*

"Look at me, whitey!" the leader commanded. Without moving his head Jack rolled his eyes upward, meeting the leader's gaze. "The next dumb thing you do will be the last dumb thing you do. See what I'm sayin'?" He took a step toward Jack, thrust his fingers into Jack's pocket, and plucked the bundle of bills from Jack's possession. "See? That didn't hurt a bit!" He grinned as he shoved the wad into his own pocket.

"Aw shit! Cops!" the man to Jack's left shouted suddenly. At once Jack's captors released their hold on him and fled into the night. As the police cruiser rolled by, Jack saw the officer gaze in his direction. He thought to flag him down, but instead he leaned against the fence unable to move.

As the cruiser disappeared from his sight he was overcome by the feeling of extreme vulnerability. He had been violated. Now alone in the presence of the haunting shadows, fear gripped his heart. *Christ, what if they come back?* He told himself that they wouldn't, for they had gotten what they were after. Still, irrational thoughts pervaded his mind. *If they come back, they'll kill me for sure!* He scoured the sidewalk and roadway while keeping a lookout for anybody who might be approaching. He located his wallet, driver's license, map, and coffee cakes all quite easily, then hurried back to the motel while keeping a watch over his shoulder to be sure he was not being followed.

Once in his room Jack slammed the door and secured both locks. He checked the window to be sure it was locked, then ruffled the drapes so that they completely covered the glass and sealed out any spying eyes. Last, Jack opened the back door a few inches-- just far enough to peek at the Road Runner with one eye. In the darkness he could barely make out the shape of the car, but it did not appear that anybody was tampering with it. Satisfied that it was secure, at least for the time being, he closed and locked the door.

Jack's pulse thudded in his temples as the robbery played over and over in his mind. The phone call the clerk had made as Jack left the store had certainly been to tip off the Assault Trio that some unsuspecting guy with a fat wad of cash in his pocket was leaving the store at that moment, traveling alone and on foot. Hadn't the gunman remarked about being informed? Furthermore, Jack's purchase of a street map made it obvious that he was unfamiliar with the area, making him even more a vulnerable target. "That bitch! That fucking little bitch!"

Still, what had just happened seemed surreal. This was the sort of stuff that happened in movies, not in real life, not to him. As Jack's mind whirled, a thought struck him: Even if he got the Road Runner fixed early the following day, how would he complete his trip with nearly all of his money gone?

Jack picked up the telephone receiver to dial 9-1-1, then reconsidered and hung up. "What's the point? The money is gone!" He knew there was no way to trace the money, and even if he could positively identify his assailants, there was virtually no chance of recovering his money. Furthermore, dealing with the police would only further complicate his already difficult situation and delay his

trip. "Oh, fuck it!" he shouted as he kicked the bed.

By now, thoughts of drinking had begun to stir in Jack's

mind. His demons reminded him that a cold, savory beer would

placate his nerves, soothe his mind, and help him make it all better.

He stood and shook his head as if to quell the demons. Then he

removed his jeans and slid beneath the covers. That night he left the

light on.

Chapter Twenty-One

Jack awoke at seven-thirty the next morning soaked with sweat and feeling like he had lost a boxing match. He was exhausted, every muscle in his body ached, and his head pounded. His sleep had been comprised of a string of short naps during which senseless dreams played through his head like movie clips. Reminding himself of his current plight he showered, then gathered and counted all of his remaining money. "Two hundred and thirteen dollars. Fuck! That's not even enough to get home! And I still have to fix the car and get to Maine!" Jack lowered his forehead into his palms. "What the hell am I going to do?" Money or no money, Jack knew that a broken car was doing him no good. His first priority had to be to get the Road Runner fixed. Perhaps in the meantime he would think of a solution to his money crisis.

Jack pulled the axle shaft with the damaged bearing from beneath the Road Runner, then walked to the auto parts store per Teresa's directions. The sign above the door of the large block building read Big John's Auto Parts in bold letters. Along the bottom of the sign in smaller font were the words, Foreign and

Domestic, Machine Shop Services. He crossed the street and entered the store.

Jack found the showroom area cramped, but well organized and tidy. He strode to the counter which was manned by two fellows of around his age, each wearing a gray work shirt. One was engaged in a telephone conversation while the other, who wore metal rimmed glasses with thick lenses, was punching numbers from a price quote sheet into a calculator. "Give me just a second," he said. Jack noticed the name Dave embroidered on a patch above the parts man's shirt pocket.

"Take your time," Jack said.

A few moments later the man scrawled a number at the bottom of the quote sheet, then turned his full attention to Jack. "Yes, sir. What can I help you with?"

"I've got a problem," Jack said as he placed the axle shaft on the counter.

"So, I see," Dave said as he examined the bearing. "Old Chrysler product?"

"Yup. 'Seventy Road Runner," Jack said with more than a hint of pride.

"I haven't seen one of these bearings since I can't remember when. Not that we ever did that many. They were pretty durable. But you obviously need one." Dave turned and began keying information into his computer. "Seventy Road Runner you say?"

Jack nodded, then gave the particulars of the car, such as the original engine size, transmission, and rear axle type. "I also need the axle seals and a set of brake shoes."

After moving and clicking the mouse a few times Dave said, "Okay, I've got the inner seals and brake shoes here. The outer seal is at the warehouse, and they are also showing one of the axle bearings. You need the new bearing pressed onto the axle shaft too, right?"

"Yes. How long do you think all of this will take?" Jack went on to explain that he was stranded at the Holly Oak Motel, but that he was supposed to be in Maine that evening.

"I don't know that we can have you in Maine by nightfall, but I can definitely have this axle shaft back to you so you can be on the road by then. Our machine shop's not too busy today, and it won't take them long to press a bearing. If you want to pay for everything now, I'll have one of the delivery drivers drop off the axle shaft to you as soon as it's ready."

"That would be great!" Jack said. While Dave filled out the machine shop repair order Jack perused the aisles for hand cleaner, a small tub of wheel bearing grease, three quarts of hypoid gear lubricant, and a tube of gasket sealer.

Dave rang up Jack's purchases and the machine shop charge. "Your total is one thirty-eight eighty-six. Will that be cash or charge?"

"Cash," Jack replied. He opened his wallet and counted out seven twenty-dollar bills. Only two twenties remained with the tens, fives, and ones. *That's only a couple of tankfuls of gas!* Jack pushed this thought and his panic aside, then handed Dave the money. "I'm in room number seven, but I'll be checking out soon. Tell your driver to look for me out back. That's where the car is. And if for some reason I'm not there, just leave the axle under the car."

"Okay. I'm shooting for early afternoon to get this thing back to you." Dave counted Jack's change. "Good luck on your trip."

Jack thanked him and left the store. He carried the other items he had purchased in plastic bags that swayed at his sides. As he walked, he pondered his money situation. With no credit cards and not even a checkbook in his possession, he knew he had no access to cash via traditional channels. He considered calling his bank, but only a few dollars remained in his savings account and his checking account was equally slim. He thought of the items he had brought on his trip, but there was nothing valuable enough to pawn for the cash he needed. Of course, there was the Road Runner. Selling it was unthinkable, but he knew there were companies that offered loans against car titles. Still, with the title tucked away at home in Colorado, obtaining such a loan wasn't an option. Under a dismal gray sky and with no easy path to quick money in sight he plodded back toward the motel.

Jack spotted a sign which read Ronnie's Tavern half a block away. Somehow, he had missed Ronnie's when walking to Big John's, but now the place had his full attention. He felt himself being drawn toward the brick structure with neon Budweiser, Heineken, and Miller Genuine Draft signs in the front windows. He stopped, resisting his urge, but unable to break his gaze from those neon signs. Strong feelings of unrest and anxiety welled inside, the first symptoms of a bad craving. "Once I get the brake shoes on, I'll call around and see if I can find a meeting," Jack said aloud. Although he didn't know if he really would, saying it gave him a small feeling of control, enough that he could break his gaze. He looked down at the sidewalk and moved quickly, not looking up until he was past Ronnie's. *Yeah, I'm going to find a meeting.* At least for now he could keep the beer demons at bay.

When he reached the motel, Jack began installing the new rear brakes on the Road Runner. The travel time he was losing worried him, but he tried not to dwell on it while he worked. *If I get the car back together this afternoon, then drive straight through, I can be there early tomorrow morning,* he thought.

By nine-thirty Jack could go no further in his reassembly without the axle shaft. He gathered his tools, then went to his room to wash his hands and pack his clothes. He would easily make the ten o'clock check-out deadline.

Teresa greeted Jack as he entered the office. "I saw you working out there. Did you get your car all fixed up?" she asked.

"No, I'm waiting for Big John's to deliver my axle shaft. They've got to press on a new bearing, and then I'll finish it up," Jack said. "I'll be on my way this afternoon." He held out his room key, but Teresa shook her head.

"No, you hold onto that until you're done. Check-out is at ten, but under the circumstances I'll make an exception. You'll need to wash up when you're done, and you'll probably want to watch TV while you're waiting. Don't worry about it. Stay in your room until you're ready to leave, then come check out."

Jack tucked the key in his pocket, then winced at a sharp pain in his bruised abdomen.

"Are you okay?" Teresa asked.

"I had a little problem last night," Jack said.

"You didn't hurt yourself working on your car, did you?"

"No." He told her of his encounter with the neighborhood thugs after he left Lu-Lu's Market.

"Oh, that place is bad news. Rumor has it that it's a drug money laundering operation, and I don't doubt it."

As Jack walked back to his room, he tried to shake the craving that was building. It would be a difficult day, but he told himself he had weathered worse. Inside, he flopped across his bed and pondered his money situation further. He could think of only one solution-- he would have to call on somebody and ask that person to wire him a few hundred bucks.

His first thought was to call Donald, for he was the closest friend Jack had these days. But Jack knew that Donald didn't have much money. His military pension covered his bills with little to spare. Although he was sure Donald would help him, Jack feared that he would do so at the risk of becoming delinquent on some of his own bills. Furthermore, upon learning of Jack's predicament, Donald would give him a lengthy dissertation about how alcoholics who find themselves in precarious situations need to draw from the pooled strength of other alcoholics. Those alcoholics who tread alone on slippery surfaces are likely to slip. "I'll send you the money, but first I want you to promise me you'll make some calls and find a meeting, and then I want you to promise me you'll go to that meeting," he could imagine Donald saying. It was sound advice, but Jack had no patience to listen to somebody a couple of thousand miles away tell him what he should do.

Jack also considered calling his boss, Russell Wilkins, but then remembered that it was against company policy for employees to lend money to each other. Such activity was especially frowned upon if it took place between a supervisor and a subordinate. Jack could not afford to lose his job, and he knew Russell would not jeopardize his.

For a moment Jack thought of calling Ralph. Surely, he would understand Jack's plight, but only recently had they reached speaking terms. It was much too soon to test the strength of their association.

That left Jack with only one possibility, Mrs. Hurley. He dreaded the thought of asking her. With his situation involving Kim, simply talking with Mrs. Hurley would be awkward, even more so if he called and asked her to wire him a substantial sum of money. For that matter, how would he explain why he was in Delaware?

Jack sighed in disgust, then sat up and turned on the television, hardly noticing that the cable service had been restored. He wondered what Kim was doing at that moment. Was she curled up beneath an afghan with Randy, staring into the cozy flames that flickered between the logs in their fireplace? He tried not to think about it as he scrolled through the channels.

Concluding that there was nothing worth watching, Jack clicked off the television and tossed the remote onto the bed. He grabbed the telephone receiver and dialed Mrs. Hurley's number.

On the second ring Stephen answered, "Hello."

"Hello, Stephen? It's Jack. How are you doing?"

"Fine. How are you?"

"I'm okay." Jack thought for a moment. "Today's Thursday. What are you doing home from school?"

"Teachers' in-service day. That's when the kids don't have to go to school, but the teachers do. They have meetings and stuff. How come you're not at work?" Stephen asked.

"I guess you could say I have off today, too," Jack said.

"Can you come over? We can play Hot Shoe!"

"No, I'm not home right now. I'm someplace far away from home."

"Are you with Mommy?"

Jack was used to Stephen firing question after question, but this one took him by surprise. "No, I'm not with your mom."

"Oh," Stephen sighed. "She hasn't been feeling good. She's been sick in bed a lot. Not getting sick in her bed--that's gross. Just being sick and lying in her bed. Know what I mean?"

"I think so," Jack said, trying to hide his alarm. "Is your grandmother around?"

"Yeah. Want me to get her?"

"Would you please?"

"Grandmom!" Stephen shouted, forgetting to move the telephone receiver away from his mouth first. Jack cringed as he yanked his receiver from his ear. "Grandmom! Phone! It's Jack!"

Finally, Mrs. Hurley came to the phone. "Hello, Jack."

"Hello. How are you doing?"

"Oh, we're getting by okay. And you?"

"I'm okay," Jack lied for the sake of getting the pleasantries out of the way. He would amend this statement soon enough. "What's this I hear Kim's been feeling under the weather? Is everything okay with her?"

Mrs. Hurley hesitated for a moment. "Stephen, why don't you run along? Jack and I have to have some grown-up talk," Jack overheard Mrs. Hurley say to Stephen. He also overheard Stephen groan as he left the room.

"Jack, I take it Kim has not been in touch with you."

"No. Not at all. Not since she got back from meeting with her agent in Boston."

"Oh boy!" Mrs. Hurley said. "She told me she was going to

call you. I thought she did. She will kill me if I tell you this, but you need to know. Oh, boy!"

"Look, if this has to do with Randy--it's okay. I mean it's not okay; I'll be really upset. But I'll understand. Sort of," Jack's voice trailed off.

"Oh no, no, Jack! This has nothing to do with Randy. He and Kim barely speak. But it's got everything to do with you." She paused for a moment, then said, "Jack, Kim's pregnant!"

"Pregnant?" Jack asked, allowing the word to sink in.

"Yes, she's pregnant."

Jack's body went numb. "Pregnant," he said once more. A flood of unintelligible emotion gushed through his mind. Just as he was sure his knees would fail him, he turned and collapsed onto the edge of the bed. *Kim is pregnant! My God! We're going to have a baby!* Jack thought his chest would burst with excitement. Several seconds passed while he tried to get a handle on his thoughts.

"Jack, are you there?" Mrs. Hurley asked.

"Yeah, I'm here. I'm just kind of blown away by all of this," he said.

"Jack, I'm sorry. I shouldn't have been the one to tell you this."

"No, I'm glad you did. But I'm confused. All this time I thought she and Randy might have ironed out their differences, and I thought that was probably the reason why she broke off contact with me. But you say that's not the case. And she's carrying *our* baby! What's wrong? Why did she push me away like this? Why won't she even talk to me?"

"Jack, the reasons are complicated. I don't think it's my place to--"

"I'm listening," Jack said.

Mrs. Hurley took a deep breath. "Jack, this has been no ordinary pregnancy. There have been some complications. You and Kim aren't spring chickens anymore, and the doctor thinks it's due mostly to her age. He says the baby seems healthy so far, but it is still early in the pregnancy. You know Kim isn't one to sit still, but the doctor says she is in grave danger of losing the baby if she tries to go about her normal daily activities. He wants to see her on complete bed rest, but being by herself, of course that's impossible. But she has slowed down a lot, and when she is up, she rests frequently.

"Of course, this means that the repairs to her house have fallen way behind schedule, and since she is unable to do any of the work herself the cost has been much higher than she had initially thought."

"What about her book deal?" Jack asked.

"That's pretty much on hold, too. She can't do much in the way of promoting it because she won't be able to do any traveling until after the baby is born. Even then she will have to work her schedule around caring for an infant. Once the publishers heard that it seemed everything went cold. Of course, she's disappointed, but this might be a blessing in disguise. Her doctor wants her to avoid as much stress as possible," Mrs. Hurley said.

Holy shit! Jack thought. He had never dreamed that Kim was in such a predicament. Suddenly he felt foolish for believing that she would do something so vain, so *wrong* as stringing him along from a couple thousand miles away while secretly renewing her involvement with her estranged husband. How stupid he had been! Kim was far more honorable than that. She would never do such a thing! Jack felt his face flush.

"I had no idea she was going through all of this," Jack said.

"But why didn't she tell me? My God, this baby is my responsibility just as much as it is hers! She doesn't have to do this alone. She *shouldn't* be doing this alone! If she had only told me I would have gone there immediately! I could look after her and the house repairs!"

"I know you would have, Jack. You're a good man," Mrs. Hurley said. "And Kim knows you would have, too. But she didn't want you to turn your life upside down."

"And you think she hasn't done that already by shutting me out like this? I don't mean to sound selfish considering what she's dealing with right now, but I need her. She and I should be handling this together," Jack said.

"Jack, she didn't want it to be like this. She needs you now more than ever, but she is afraid. Afraid for you," Mrs. Hurley said.

"I'm not following you. What do you mean 'afraid for me?'"

Mrs. Hurley paused, choosing her words carefully. "Jack, you've been through an awful lot, and you've worked hard to put yourself back on track. I don't have any idea what it's like to go through what you did, but I know it hasn't been easy. When you got your One Year pin Kim and I were both very proud of you, but we both knew your struggle would be on-going. Kim was afraid if she piled all of this on you it might be more than you could handle. She thought it would be better for you if your life went back to the way it was before she came home to Colorado. But I suppose she couldn't bear to tell you for fear that she would lose you.

"Jack, please don't be angry with her. She loves you. She's proud of you, and she didn't want to do anything that would jeopardize the hard work you've done or the progress you've made."

"Oh Christ! Is that what this is all about? Do you two think I'm so weak I can't handle the truth? Well I'm not!"

"Jack--"

Jack took a deep breath. "I'm sorry. But let me explain something. Alcohol is my weakness. Sure, I want to drink when things are going rough, but I also want to drink when things are going just fine. I want to drink during bad times, and I want to drink during good times. Some days are tougher than others, but I deal with them a day at a time. That's how life is for an alcoholic.

"Once you've been sober for a while your life becomes more precious than ever and you don't take it for granted. Becoming sober is like a rebirth. Afterward life seems more colorful and vivid.

It's this new appreciation for life that makes you want to stay sober.

"You can't hide things from a recovering alcoholic in hopes that he stays sober. Alcoholics want to drink regardless. But by hiding things from an alcoholic in recovery you're cutting him off from a part of his life--part of what he needs to know and feel in order to keep wanting to stay sober. I know Kim's intention was good, but honesty is always best, even when dealing with a recovering drunk."

Mrs. Hurley hesitated before responding. "Jack, I never knew. I never thought about it that way. But I'm not the one you should be telling this to. You need to explain this to Kim."

"And I will just as soon as I get to Maine," Jack said.

"Jack, I'm not so sure that's a good idea. I don't think it would be good for Kim or the baby if you showed up on her doorstep unannounced. Let me talk to Kim first. I'll tell her what you said, and I'll have her give you a call. Will you be home tonight?"

"Actually--" Jack began, then stopped.

"What?" Mrs. Hurley asked.

"Nothing, nothing. That will be fine. Thank you."

"You take care of yourself, Jack."

"Send Kim my love."

"I will. Good-bye."

Jack hung up the telephone and rested his forehead in his palms. Stephen knew he was not at home, but he had decided not to mention it to Mrs. Hurley. It would have only complicated matters. Furthermore, he had elected not to ask her to send money. He doubted that she would have anyway without speaking to Kim first.

Jack's thoughts shifted to Kim. He envisioned her lying still in bed, caring for their unborn child per her doctor's orders. *Bed rest. Complete bed rest. If you try to do much more than that I'm afraid you'll lose this baby!* All the while she was forced to stand on the sidelines and watch as the other areas of her life--her book deal, the bed and breakfast, and her relationship with Jack--crumbled about her feet.

But what of her feelings for Jack? Were they really so strong, and was she so selfless that she was willing to shoulder the responsibility of her pregnancy alone? Jack disagreed with her decision to hide her pregnancy from him, but he understood why she had. Her intention was certainly noble. Even so, she had made numerous personal sacrifices in order to spare him from being saddled with the responsibility that was rightfully his. Had she done all of this for him, so that he might maintain his sobriety? Was this whole horrible separation brought about by such a simple and honorable objective on Kim's part?

Jack's face grew hot as he thought of how foolish he had been to think she and Randy had rekindled their fire, and that Kim had hoped to keep Jack on hold in case she needed a safety net. A woman like Kim needed no safety net, nor would she compromise her standards.

Jack sprang from the bed, exited the motel room through the rear door, and took his seat in the Road Runner. He opened the ashtray, removed the necklace, and gazed at the pendant. He placed the chain around his neck and tucked it into his shirt. Next, he unfolded the letter Kim had sent him and read it once more.

Dearest Jack:

First, I want to say I'm sorry for the way I've been acting lately. I know I've got to be putting you through hell, and I am truly sorry. Some things have come up, and I've really been a mess. I don't think I can hold myself together long enough to talk to you on the phone just yet. I know I owe it to you to bring you up to date on what all is happening, and soon I will. But I can't yet. I hope you can believe me when I tell you this is for the best. Although you can't know what I mean, I hope you can trust me on this. One day this will all make sense.

The book deal seems to be stalled in negotiations. It looks promising, but it is taking longer than I'd expected, and there have been complications. The repairs to the old house are well underway, and it looks like the place will be ready to open on time for the beginning of tourist season. That's a good thing, because the damage was more extensive than I'd first thought, and the insurance is only picking up part of the tab. I need to get the place open for business as early as possible so I can recoup some of the money I'm spending for repairs. Because of this, I won't be able to return to Colorado before the beginning of the tourist season. Stephen will stay in Colorado until he has finished school, then he and my mom will fly to Maine.

Be sure to tell your sons I was asking about them. I'm not going to harp on you about this, but you really do need to see them. It will be good both for you and for them. I know you're probably thinking that you aren't ready, but Jack, they need you now. This is really important, and it can't wait.

And above all, take care of yourself. I know this isn't easy for you. It isn't easy on me either. One day soon you will understand. Be good to yourself, Jack. You are a good man and you deserve the best.

Please drop me a line so that I know you're okay. I hope you can believe me when I tell you I love you with all my heart. Take care.

Love always,

Kim

Suddenly Kim's letter made sense. Tears welled in Jack's eyes as he realized that her words had indeed been from the heart.

At first, he thought to call her, but then figured she probably would not answer. "Oh, God! I've got to get to Maine!" His voice trembled. The thought of Kim enduring her troubled pregnancy alone two thousand miles from home was more than he could bear. "I have to go. I have to get there!" But with the rear of the Road Runner still supported by cinder blocks and without the cash to keep its gas tank fed he was stymied.

Jack returned to his room to call Big John's and check the status of his axle. He pulled the receipt from his pocket, then dialed the number.

"Big John's. Dave speaking."

"Hi, Dave. This is Jack. You know, the guy who dropped off the axle shaft this morning. I don't mean to be a pest, but I was wondering how it's coming."

"Buddy, I'm afraid I've got some bad news," Dave said. "When we got the bearing from the warehouse the box had been opened. In addition to the actual bearing there is a lock ring that is supposed to come with it. That ring gets pressed onto the axle after the bearing and holds the bearing in place. That ring was missing. We can't reuse your original lock ring because it has to be destroyed to get the old bearing off. The only way to get the lock ring is with the bearing. We've located another bearing, but it's coming out of Dallas. The soonest I can get it here is tomorrow afternoon."

"Oh shit!" Jack said. He knew the lock ring that Dave was talking about. But if the Road Runner remained disabled until Friday night, going to Maine would be out of the question. "Can you reuse what's left of the old lock ring and tack weld it to the axle shaft to hold it in place?" He knew it was a bad idea, but if it enabled him to complete the Maine leg of his trip it was a chance he was willing to take.

"I'm not saying it wouldn't work, but that axle shaft is some pretty hard steel. If we weld on it the heat will draw some of the hardness out of it. That could cause the axle to shear completely, and you would lose that wheel. I'd hate to see that happen to you, and quite honestly, I don't want that liability hanging over my head," Dave said.

"That's okay. I understand. It was just a thought," Jack said. "Well, if the part won't be here until tomorrow, then I guess there's nothing we can do about it until then."

"'Fraid not," Dave said. "Sorry for the delay in your trip, but

I can promise you the minute this thing comes through the door we'll get it pressed on your axle and get it back to you."

Jack thanked Dave, then hung up the telephone. "Fuck!" he shouted. He left the room and took a seat in the Road Runner once more. *How did things get so fucked up?* he wondered.

Thoughts of Ronnie's Tavern flashed through his mind. He stood from the car. "I need to call AA and find a meeting. Then maybe I can begin to think my way out of this mess," he muttered as he headed to his room. Only then did he discover there was no phone book in the room. Jack considered calling information but decided to ask Teresa instead. Certainly, she'd had guests ask her about meetings from time to time. She might even have copies of the local meeting schedule.

When Jack strode through the office doorway Teresa smiled. "Did you get your car fixed up yet?" she asked.

"No. There is one part I still need, and it won't be here until tomorrow," Jack said.

Teresa shook her head. "You're having a run of bad luck, aren't you?"

Oh, if you only knew! Jack thought. "Yeah," he said. He

decided not to ask her about local meetings or a meeting schedule.

"There is no phone book in my room. Do you have one?"

"Oh honey, I'm sorry about that. People keep swiping them, and I keep replacing them. I knew the one from your room was gone, and I meant to put another one in there," she said as she walked to a file cabinet in the back corner of the room. From the top drawer she procured a Wilmington area telephone book. "Here you go," she said as she walked back and handed it to him.

"Thanks," Jack said.

"You know, there's an old gas station across the way. It's been closed for years, but there are still a few old junkers sitting around the place. I wonder if you could use the parts from any of those cars to fix yours," Teresa said.

"Who owns the place, and who owns the cars?" Jack asked.

"It's a funny thing. New Castle County bought the property about a year ago. They were going to build a police station there, which this area really needs. But then there were a number of budget cuts, and so far the police station is on hold. The first thing they are going to do is tow the cars away, and then tear down the building. But they haven't done anything yet."

Jack thanked Teresa, then returned to his room. He thumbed through the telephone book, then called the local chapter of Alcoholics Anonymous. The only meeting within walking distance would be at a church a dozen blocks away at seven that evening. "I'll be there," he said.

He laid on his back and closed his eyes. Thoughts of Kim, their unborn baby, and his cash crisis whirled through his head. Suddenly Jack had an idea. He sat up, flipped the yellow pages open to used car dealers, then unfolded his street map. If he could find a used car dealer nearby, perhaps he could make a couple of minor repairs to one or two of the cars on the lot and earn some quick cash. Unfortunately, the nearest used car dealer was half a mile away, too far to lug his toolbox. He didn't bother calling.

With nothing but time at his disposal, he decided to check the cars Teresa had mentioned. By now the sky had cleared and the sun shone brightly overhead.

A vacant lot separated the motel from the gas station. Much of it was covered with crumbling blacktop that had once been a parking lot. Tall weeds had sprouted through the crack-riddled pavement. At the center of the lot was the foundation of a building that had once stood on the site. It had long been demolished; its block perimeter was all that remained.

Jack balanced himself as he walked upon the tops of the blocks that had once been part of the back wall. When he reached the far corner, he looked toward the sidewalk in front of the gas station to the exact spot where he had been held up at gunpoint. In the daylight everything looked different. Although the place still exuded an air of depression, there was nothing scary or intimidating about it. For an instant he questioned whether the robbery had happened at all.

His gaze shifted to the decrepit, forgotten jalopies quarantined by the fence. There was a 'sixty-six Plymouth Valiant, a 'sixty-eight Pontiac Bonneville, an early 'seventies Chevy Malibu, and what Jack thought to be a 'sixty-three Ford Galaxy all parked beside the building. Their flat tires, dusty windshields, and light surface rust stood as testament that these cars had sat idle for years, and possibly decades. Behind the building sitting in the tall weeds among scattered oil drums, partial engines, fenders, and other debris were a battered Lincoln Continental, the gutted carcass of an early 'seventies Mustang, and a rusty 'sixty-seven Dodge Coronet four-door. Absent from the Coronet were its fenders, hood, grille, and

front bumper.

As he looked over these decaying hulks his mind shifted the

scene backward in time--back to when the gas station was a thriving

business, the now rotting cars were current, and this shitty

neighborhood was still a decent community. This gas station could

have been any one of a thousand scattered across the country. It sure

reminded him of his old Sinclair station.

He looked back at the cannibalized Coronet once more and

smiled. On the surface there were few similarities between this car

and his, but he knew they shared nearly identical underpinnings. If

the right-side axle bearing in the Coronet was good, he could use

that axle shaft in his Road Runner.

Jack dashed back to the motel and gathered the bumper jack

from the Road Runner and the tools he would need. When he

returned to the gas station, he spotted an area where the dirt had

eroded and a gap of nearly a foot existed between the ground and the

bottom of the chain link fence that surrounded the property. He

shoved the tools under the fence, then scaled the fence and dropped

to the ground inside.

Within minutes he raised the right rear corner of the car and removed the wheel. He broke the rust bond between the brake drum and the axle flange with a few well-placed hammer blows, then cast the drum aside. After a few more minutes' work, he pulled the axle shaft from the car and inspected the bearing. It was remarkably clean, showed no damage, and very little wear. "Score!" he said to himself. He placed the wheel under the car, then lowered the car onto it. Finally, he gathered his tools, the jack, and the axle shaft, and hurried back to the motel.

Once there he cleaned the old grease from the bearing and packed it with fresh grease. He installed the pirated axle shaft, checked the bearing free play by hand, and filled the axle with gear lubricant. In short order he lowered the Road Runner onto its wheels once more.

Chapter Twenty-Two

Jack stowed his tools in the trunk of the car, then went to his room to scrub his hands. Afterward, he planned to take the car for a short test drive, then do his best to earn some gas money from one or two of the closest used car proprietors. He would also stop by Big John's to cancel his order for the axle bearing and collect his refund. If things went well, there was still a chance he could check out of the motel and be on the road to Maine by nightfall.

As Jack dried his hands, he was startled by the ringing telephone. "Hello," he answered.

"Jack? Hi, it's me."

Jack gasped. *Holy shit!* "Kim! How are you? I mean, how's the baby? Uh, I mean, I know there isn't one yet...."

Kim laughed while Jack took a breath and regained his composure.

"Kim, I talked to your mother today, and she told me everything," Jack said at last.

"I know, and she just called me and told me what you said. And I'm sorry, Jack. I'm so sorry. I've put you through hell, when all I was trying to do was protect you."

"Kim, listen. I understand."

"Oh, Jack, I never meant to leave you hanging, but I didn't want to burden you with this, either."

"But it's *not* a burden! Kim, this is our *baby* we're talking about!"

"I knew you would say that, and I knew if I told you sooner, you would be on the first plane here. You would turn your life upside down, then swear it wasn't a burden," Kim said. "You've made so much progress in your recovery, and I didn't want to see you jeopardize that. But now I see that in hiding this from you I might have done more harm than good."

"Things have definitely not been easy, but the worst part has been not knowing what happened. Of course, when you don't know something, your imagination does a good job of filling in the blanks," Jack said.

"I know it does. Mom mentioned that you thought Randy had come back. That sounded absurd to me at first, but I didn't have to think too hard to see how you came to that conclusion. Oh, Jack! I never meant to make things so rough on you. I've been wrapped up in this pregnancy, trying to follow the doctor's instructions, and the house repairs.... I think about you constantly, and I worry about you, but I thought I was handling things the best way I could. I never realized what I was putting you through."

"It's okay. I understand now. You made the best decision you could. But now that we're finally talking, you don't know what a relief this is!" Jack grinned as he sat on the bed. "First things first, I want to hear about this pregnancy!"

Kim explained that while the baby seemed to be developing normally, the doctors had determined that due to a hormonal imbalance, she was extremely susceptible to miscarrying. "Full bed rest is what the doctors have ordered," she concluded. "What have you been up to?"

Jack told Kim of his recent activities-- selling the Dart, maxing out his credit card, and his visit with his sons. "After I left North Carolina I set out to find you. I needed answers. The not knowing was tearing me up! I hope you understand."

"I do, I understand completely. So that explains why you are in Delaware," Kim said.

"Yeah, and speaking of which, how did you know where to

find me?"

"Remember the Caller ID phone we got my mom for Christmas? She gave me the number you called from. I was afraid you would be gone from that motel by the time I called you, and I would miss you. How long before you leave there?"

Jack then told her of his situation with the failed axle bearing, his mugging, the ordered bearing, and the axle shaft he had taken from the long-forgotten Coronet. "My car is up and running again, but I don't even have enough gas money to get there and back to Colorado."

"Can't you get your money back for the part you ordered?" Kim asked.

"Well, yeah, but that's still not going to get me home."

"Don't worry about getting home. Can you make it here?"

Jack considered his remaining cash and that which would be refunded to him. "I'm sure I can."

"Good. I'm dying to see you...." Kim stopped short.

"But?"

"There is something I need to tell you first. It might upset you, but I hope you understand."

"What's that?"

"There's more to why I didn't tell you about this pregnancy--at least not right away. It wasn't only to protect you, but to protect our baby and me too. I know this will sound selfish, and it seems foolish now, especially with all you've done since I left. Jack, I hope you don't hate me for it."

"Hate you? I could never hate you! Whatever it is, go ahead and tell me."

Kim swallowed. "The whole time we've been together I've worried that someday you would have a relapse. I figured something bad would happen and it would send you over the edge. I didn't know when it would happen, but I always expected it, and that's not fair to you. You're stronger than I ever imagined. You've proved it."

"You're giving me too much credit. I haven't slipped, but that doesn't mean I never will. Like Donald says, 'I haven't drank yet today.'"

"I think you're not giving yourself enough credit. Seeing what I've put you through and the mess you're in now, and still you've stayed strong. On top of that, you finally visited Johnny and

James. I'm shocked about that."

"Well, yeah, but that was something I'd planned to do all along. It was just a matter of how and when."

"But you did it. It was a big step. Don't minimize it. I know it was important to you and your sons, but with this pregnancy it means a lot to me, too. Honestly, I was afraid you would put it off until it was too late." Kim cleared her throat. "You know, when I first found out I was pregnant I thought, 'If his history of drinking is so bad he can't show his love to the kids he already has, how can I be sure he won't do the same to this one?' I know it sounds harsh, but that's what I thought, and it really bothered me. I know the situation between you and your sons is your business, but I was afraid that someday things might end up the same way with our child."

"So that's it? You were going to break off the relationship just like that? Over something that, in reality, would never happen? You weren't even going to give me a chance?"

"No, Jack! I wasn't going to break it off. I couldn't! I thought I made that clear in my letter. I love you, and this is *our* child. Yours *and* mine. Don't you see? I need you! This baby needs you!"

"Then why push me away?"

"Because I didn't want to dump all of this on you at once. I thought if I waited until things settled down here it would give me a chance to pull myself together and it would give you more time to build up your own strength. I was afraid that if I hit you with all of this early on, it would be too much."

"And you thought you'd send me crawling back into my bottle?"

"Well, maybe. If that happened, it would be terrible for you. But it would also be terrible for our baby and for me. Since the aftermath of your drinking is what stood between you and your sons, don't you think I'd do everything I could to keep history from repeating itself? If I overloaded you and you started drinking again, where would that leave us? I didn't want this baby and me to become your second alienated family."

"Aw, Christ!"

"Jack, please! I didn't mean to put it that way. Look, I know I made a mistake. I handled this whole thing wrong. You didn't deserve this. I don't know what it's like to have to fight terrible urges day by day, but I underestimated you, and I'm sorry."

Jack snatched a pillow and threw it at the wall. *God damn it!* he thought. The beer demons swarmed.

In the next instant Jack saw himself out for an evening stroll with Kim. In her arms she cradled a sleeping infant bundled in a pink blanket. The sidewalk eventually led them to Ronnie's. When they reached the place, Jack kept his eyes to the ground, resisting the urge to look at the building or its signs. But as hard as he tried not to look, he couldn't help himself. The neon Miller, Budweiser, and Heineken signs beckoned him. He hesitated, as if acting out a one-sided stand-off against the warm, glowing colors set to lure him in. Then Jack spotted the Coors sign in the lower corner of the window. "They have Coors. That's my flavor!" Unable to resist, he felt himself being drawn toward the door.

"Jack, what are you doing?" Kim asked. "Jack don't do it! Please don't!" Jack saw his hand reach for the handle on the door. As he pulled it open Kim cried, "Jack, where does this leave us?" Then their baby wailed.

Jack sat trembling on the bed. *That's just how easy it would be to slip up, to throw it all away.* It could happen before he knew it.

Kim could see it. Why couldn't he?

"Jack?"

"I'm here." Jack held the receiver to his ear with his shoulder and wiped his sweaty palms on his jeans.

"Are you okay?" Kim asked.

"Yeah, I'm fine."

"I love you."

"I love you, too."

"Can you forgive me?"

Jack sighed. "Yes, of course I do! Look, I don't like how you handled things, but I understand why you did it. But please promise me you'll never shut me out again. I don't care what the situation is or how bad things seem. We're a team. And soon we'll have a child to raise."

"I promise, Jack. I promise," Kim sniffled. "So, are you still coming to Maine?"

"Of course, I am!" Jack clutched his pendant through his shirt. "Our hearts can't be whole unless we're together. Remember?"

"I remember. Jack, I can't wait to see you, but please be

careful."

"I will. You know, I love you no matter what."

"I know you do. You don't have to tell me. I know. And I love you no matter what, even though it seems I have a strange way of showing it."

Once they hung up, Jack gathered his belongings and put them in the trunk. He then went to the office, gave Teresa his key, paid her for his telephone call to Mrs. Hurley, then thanked her for her generosity.

Next, Jack drove to Big John's Auto Parts. Dave returned all but a small portion of the price of the axle bearing, citing the overnight shipping charge as non-refundable. Jack thanked him, and he wished Jack a safe and uneventful drive to Maine.

From there Jack headed to Interstate 495. By now the beer demons had settled. As the sun hung low in the western sky to his left, he headed north, accelerating briskly through all four gears. The exhaust growled as he merged with traffic on the busy interstate.

Jack pulled the half heart pendant from within his shirt and studied it. He kissed it, then grinned as he let it dangle against his chest. While guiding the Road Runner up the crowded highway he thought of Kim and how they would soon bask in each other's love once more. Driving to Maine, he was heading toward making their hearts whole again. Nothing could have felt more right.

Other titles from Higher Ground Books & Media:

Wise Up to Rise Up by Rebecca Benston

A Path to Shalom by Steen Burke

Overcomer by Forrest Henslee

Miracles: I Love Them by Forest Godin

32 Days with Christ's Passion by Mark Etter

Knowing Affliction and Doing Recovery by John Baldasare

Out of Darkness by Stephen Bowman

The Magic Egg by Linda Phillipson

The Tin Can Gang by Chuck David

Whobert the Owl by Mya C. Benston

Add these titles to your collection today!

http://highergroundbooksandmedia.com

www.ingramcontent.com/pod-product-compliance
Lightning Source LLC
Chambersburg PA
CBHW051518250626
47156CB00001B/143